THE TURN OF THE SCREW

&

IN THE CAGE

Henry James

The Turn of the Screw

& In the Cage

Introduction by Hortense Calisher

Notes by James Danly

THE MODERN LIBRARY

NEW YORK

Grateful acknowledgment is made to the following for permission to
reprint previously published material:
Doubleday, a division of Random House, Inc.: Excerpt from the introduction by
Morton Dauwen Zabel to *In the Cage & Other Tales.* Copyright © 1958 by Morton
Zabel. Reprinted by permission of Doubleday, a division of Random House, Inc.
Harvard University Press: Two letters from *The Letters of Henry James,*
Volume 4, edited by Leon Edel, found on pages 87–88 and 149–52 (Cambridge,
Mass.: Harvard University Press, 1984). Copyright © 1984 by Leon Edel,
editorial. Copyright © 1984 by Alexander R. James, James Copyright Material.
Reprinted by permission.
Studies in Short Fiction: Excerpt from "James's *In the Cage:*
A New Interpretation," by Stuart Hutchinson, from *Studies in Short Fiction,*
Vol. 19, No. 1, Winter 1982, pp. 19–25. Reprinted by permission of
Studies in Short Fiction, Newberry College, Newberry, SC.

Library of Congress Cataloging-in-Publication Data
James, Henry, 1843–1916.
[Turn of the screw]
The turn of the screw, and In the cage / Henry James.
p.   cm.
ISBN 0-375-75740-6
1. Telegraphers—Fiction.   2. Governesses—Fiction.   3. England—Fiction.
I. Title: In the cage.   II. James, Henry, 1843–1916. In the cage.   III. Title.
PS2116 .T8 2001
813'.4—dc21   00-066229

Modern Library website address: www.modernlibrary.com

Printed in the United States of America

6 8 9 7

HENRY JAMES

Henry James was born in New York City on April 15, 1843, of Scottish and Irish ancestry. His father, Henry James, Sr., was a whimsical, utterly charming, maddeningly open-minded parent—a Swedenborgian philosopher of considerable wealth who believed in a universal but wholly unformed society. He gave both Henry and his elder son, William, an infant baptism by taking them to Europe before they could even speak. In fact, Henry James later claimed that his first memory, dating from the age of two, was a glimpse of the column of the Place Vendôme framed by the window of the carriage in which he was riding. His peripatetic childhood took him to experimental schools in Geneva, Paris, and London. Even back in the United States he was shuffled from New York City to Albany to Newport to Boston and finally to Cambridge, where in 1862 he briefly attended Harvard Law School. "An obscure hurt," probably to his back, exempted him from service in the Civil War, and James felt he had failed as a man when it counted most to be one and he vowed never to marry.

In search of a possible occupation, the young James turned to literature; within five years it had become his profession. His earliest story appeared in *The Atlantic Monthly* in 1865, when he was twenty-two. From the start of his career James supported himself as a writer, and over the next ten years he produced book reviews, drama and art criticism, newspaper columns, travel pieces and travel books, short stories, novelettes, a biography, and his first novel—*Roderick Hudson* (1876). Late in 1875, following two recent trips to Europe, James settled in Paris, where he met Turgenev, Flaubert, and Zola, and wrote *The American* (1877). In December 1876 he moved to London, where he produced *The Europeans* (1878). Soon afterward he achieved fame on both sides of the Atlantic with the publication of *Daisy Miller* (1879), the book that forever identified him with the "international theme" of the effect of Americans and Europeans on one another.

Yet Henry James aspired to more than the success of *Daisy Miller*. Determined to scale new literary heights, James abandoned the intense social life of his earlier years and, with Balzac as his role model, devoted himself all out to the craft of fiction. Although *The Portrait of a Lady* (1881) was critically acclaimed and sold well, the other novels of James's "Balzac" period—*Washington Square* (1881), *The Bostonians* (1886), *The Princess Casamassima* (1886), and *The Tragic Muse* (1890)—were not popular with the public. As a result, he decided to redirect his efforts and began writing for the stage. In 1895, the disastrous opening night of his play *Guy Domville*—when James came onstage only to be hissed and booed by the London audience—forever ended his career as a playwright.

Rededicating himself to fiction, he wrote *The Spoils of Poynton* (1897), *What Maisie Knew* (1897), *The Turn of the Screw* (1898), and *The Awkward Age* (1899). Then, as he approached and passed the age of sixty James's three greatest novels appeared in rapid succession: *The Wings of the Dove* (1902), *The Ambassadors* (1903), and *The Golden Bowl* (1904). He spent most of his remaining years at Lamb House, his ivy-covered home in Rye, writing his memoirs and revising his novels for the twenty-four-volume New York Edition of his life-work. When World War I broke out, he was eager to serve his adopted country and threw himself into the civilian war effort. In

1915, after four decades of living in England, James became a British subject, and King George V conferred the Order of Merit on him in January 1916. Henry James died in London on February 28, 1916, and his ashes were buried in the James family plot in Cambridge, Massachusetts.

CONTENTS

INTRODUCTION

Hortense Calisher

Among the one hundred and three shorter works that Henry James is said to have written, these including the stories and those longer stretches he liked to call "nouvelles," no two are more opposite—in subject, tone, or even critical acceptance—than the pair reprinted here. "The Turn of the Screw," still perhaps the most popularly known, became so during his lifetime, an acclaim that would annoy him, as ignoring his wider range. "In the Cage," a sly bit of peripheral observation of how the "upper" and "lower" strata of British society actually ride tandem, was not included in the standard American anthologies edited either by Leon Edel, James's magisterial biographer, or by other critics who reigned during the mid-twentieth-century boom that hailed James's complexities as a fine answer to any of Europe's, and meant to keep him most on the American scene he had deserted.

Reading these two facets of his work side by side is like watching a rather small flint strike quite a spark when brushed against a comfortably entrenched stone. Both stories were written during that amazing burst of production of 1896–1901, after his failure as a playwright had admittedly cast him back on the element natural to him (during which there appeared five full-scale novels as well) and he had set himself up in his permanent home at Rye. Both stories are laid in Britain, though in vastly different locales. Each follows a recognizable tradition of English literature, though again from opposite poles—the gothic and the domestic. They are part of James's continuing tribute to the nation whose *Cornhill* magazine had published his first great success, *Daisy Miller* (initially turned down by an American publisher, later pirated). In Britain he might anticipate a readership schooled to cope with Dickens's occasional paragraph-long sentences, as well as a populace, not always educated, that still flocked to Shakespeare. While at home, Edith Wharton, introducing James to Finley Peter Dunne, humorist author of *Mr. Dooley,* had reported Dunne's later comment, "What a pity it takes him so long to say anything."

"The Turn of the Screw" comes on like a gothic opera whose cadences one has heard before, from Ann Radcliffe's *Mysteries of Udolpho* to Matthew Gregory "Monk" Lewis's late-eighteenth-century play *The Castle Spectre,* and on to a whole galaxy of nineteenth-century governesses who, enticed to lonely houses on wuthering moors, often by well-to-do, attractive male patrons, were sure to find, in a first chapter, that all was not as it should be. There might be a kindly disposed servant, isolated also and only partially leaking the true state of things. No near neighbors appear, and no farcical local Bottoms. The cast of a gothic tale is intentionally limited; that way the "shades," when seen, are the more distinct. The routine claptrap of dailiness is also to be avoided—meals, say, or furnishings. The governess in "The Turn of the Screw" partakes of bread-and-milk when she first meets the children, and later eats once, formally and in the dining room, with the boy. Each meal has a point to make in the narrative. Her bed is as big as a state bed. The house has a "machicolated tower." Given this scale we are then left to imagine room after empty room, wide windows, and a stair—all venues suitable for apparitions.

The outdoors is carefully inserted, from shrubbed expanses to the lake with its boat, to the slab of gravestone on which the governess sits at a crucial event—each sector of nature sufficient to the unfolding story, in a rhythm that both lulls and warns. Mrs. Grose, the housekeeper, has no apparatus of duty around her to confuse her functions as confidante, confirmer of the evil "relationship" of the two dead personae, and lastly to witness the shocking change in little Flora, in which damnation can be seen and heard. As in James's "The Pupil," a story of a more mundanely put-upon boy, Miles is awarded a more saintly ending, perhaps as the one who, of all in this story, has been the most aware. As often in the novels, we have been walked through unspecified horrors, in order to identify the "good."

By the end one has forgotten that "The Turn of the Screw" begins with that creaky device, the fireside story, here even third-hand as relayed from the governess's manuscript to its discloser, Douglas. He is evasive to the end but no match for the author, who despite all the tricksy atmospherics—or because of these?—has achieved what James always intends, and what all apostles of the imagination crave. He has floated his marvels, allowing them to hover undefined. He himself has done a bunk.

Meanwhile, at any rereading, red-haired Quint stares again through a window and Miss Jessel crouches at the stair bottom, both with the satirical visages of ghosts that last. All the arias have once again been sung.

———

"In the Cage" is a delicious story the more so because it confounds what we expect from James, who in spite of the quick-changes and voice-overs we have known him capable of, infrequently deserts the upstairs society whose citizen he is, in and out of books. Oh yes, he can "do" Mrs. Grose with a few flicks: her pillowy deference, warm sentiments, plus an occasional "Oh, laws." His usual society knows its servant class very well—or fancies it does. But to all of a sudden desert the parade of minds he normally inhabits—sophisticates, frauds, marriageable naïfs, genteel conspirators hanging on by their money thumbs, intellectualized villains and too honorable gentlemen—for a brief, perhaps tongue-in-cheek but loyal allegiance with a winning young woman from "downstairs"?

Who wouldn't be amazed by a James prancing about in the soulful dreams and rebellious ambitions of a pretty telegraphist, she affianced to a butcher whose curls and ponderous good nature just about distinguish him from his beef? He is so winning a portrait of the British tradesman, thick with his own opinions but no fool, that at the end we will wish to have heard more of him.

We never know the name of this heroine, sole support of a mother slipped from "lady" (this questionable) who nips whiskey. The girl, as she is known throughout, is defined by her cage and her function: "To sit there with two young men, the other telegraphist and the counter-clerk, to mind the 'sounder,' which was always going, to dole out stamps and postal-orders, weigh letters, answer stupid questions, give difficult change and, more than anything else, count ... the words of the telegrams thrust, from morning to night, through the gap left in the high lattice, across the encumbered shelf that her forearm ached with rubbing.... She knows a great many persons without their recognising the acquaintance.... That made it an emotion ... to see anyone come in whom she knew, as she called it, outside, and who could add something to the poor identity of her function."

So the stage is set, and we know that James is fond of her. So will we be, as in the easiest manner he adds a dab here—she's not stupid; a touch there—if she's innocent, it's worlds away from the tennis matches and tea-gowned mamas of wealth. This girl works for a living. Her cloister is the meek-shrewd pretension of the not quite lower-middle class, into which she and her mother, if ever they were born otherwise, which becomes doubtful, have dropped. In fact, the postal unit, where she sits with a clerk on either side, is in a grocery shop, august on that level perhaps, but smelling of ham and cheese and other provender. What can her creator be thinking of?—he who in the past has treated us to Florentine palaces, and hotels surely the Crillon? No wonder this story has been ignored, while the authorities build their own edifices. One can hear them whispering in the wings, like family butlers: "Mr. Henry has gone into trade."

The girl's seat is opposite the shop's door, allowing her to note every exit and entrance. Each time she serves a particular couple, the lady and gentleman who come to post their messages (all but once separately, but, as the girl comes to suspect, almost certainly to reach each other), their arrivals and departures are stagily produced: they are whipped in, do their business, which the girl competes to handle herself, and are whipped off. The technique can't but remind us that the author, now more calmly resident in Lamb House, has gone through a rough patch in the theater, via plays that when read seem to court ridicule, and got it. Yet he has been brushed by a technique, and isn't above using it.

Accordingly, the scenes in the shop have almost the pace of farce, that snap-snap come-and-go. Some sort of comedy this is, then, though not a "musical"; the girl likely knows nothing of that shake of skirts and song, and she is controlling things. If "In the Cage" is not merely cameo, this will be owed to her. What we are watching is the growth of her own imagination. An indigenous one, entirely suited to her station in life.

What she derives from the couple's onslaught of telegrams is quite correct. The lady of the couple is a titled one, and married; the gentleman her lover. Using false names, a practice the girl is sagely familiar with, they have been arranging assignations. In the telegrams there are breezy intimations of their world, evoked by the slyest of tokens, nicknames and meeting places from James's own métier. There, to the girl, the lady would be enveloped in the silks and flounces of her station, and the man, known to the occasional men who accompany him as "the Pink 'Un" or "the Count," is the handsome, debonair lover the ha'penny novels the girl feeds on would decree. These wouldn't be the penny-dreadfuls, versions of our pulp fiction, but the so-called kitchenmaid novels, an airily shrewd term surely coined by the employers of those maids. Still heard late into twentieth-century conversation, the phrase evokes the whole staircase underpinning the British "system," and must have sounded now and then in James's ear. The girl, drawn by the lover's image as much socially as sexually, meanwhile delaying her marriage, manages to meet him, in a scene almost tenderly evasive on both sides, and on hers plaintively clear. She knows her "position," and that she must see this as her strength, whether or not it is so. He has the myopia of his kind when so oddly challenged, yet the manners that will "see it through."

Even such a small drama has its chorus; here it's Mrs. Jordan, widow of a minister, reduced to earning her keep by arranging flowers for the high occasions of the noble rich, and to feigning to the girl and to herself that her own "intended" is a lord who employs her services. So providing a parable rather "low" in comparison to the girl's. But each obviously understands the kind of dreaming that is permissible, according to who she is, and where they are, on the scale. Everyone they know has a cage. Flying out and up has been known to happen. But it takes more than a ha'penny.

The story ends with a confusion of telegrams to be searched for a detail of one that the guilty couple must for their own safety recover, for which rescue the girl, to her own satisfaction, is the instrument.

It's not her fault if, by means of a twist here, a poke there, everybody in her story ends up perhaps too neatly tied to his or her proper destiny. Or that the slight backstage noise you may have heard throughout is the rustle of plot. What else do you expect of a telegraph office? As for the person most responsible here, she and all the cast quite agree with him. Dreams or no dreams, for God and for country there'll always be an upstairs and a downstairs. Where everyone knows his place.

———

At Rye, an old seaside town full of writers and artists, and the tourists who came looking for them, James was said to be content. During his working hours one or another of the neighbors who often dropped by, or the continuous stream of house guests, or the servants who at times numbered five, could hear his voice through the study door. After which he might take a walk.

In English country life, a tower is never far—one or two of those perhaps around which dramatic prose-poems (a form he was said to love) could accumulate. Or he might take a walk, dropping in at the golf club for company, though he did not play, or going into town, donning one of the hats and caps neighbor H. G. Wells had seen on the hall table. "A tweed cap and a stout stick for the marsh, a short, comfortable deerstalker ... a light brown felt hat for a morning walk down to the harbor, a grey felt hat with a black band and a gold-headed cane if afternoon calling in the town was afoot." According to F. W. Dupee, who provides these details, "Lamb House dominated a narrow thoroughfare in the upper town ... so full of easels and traffic that he could get out of his door, as he said, 'only by taking a flying leap over Art and Industry.'" Perhaps he walked there more than once to post a letter on his own, and thereby enjoy one of the pleasures—indeed, obligations—of a landowner: to chat with the democracy.

"In the Cage" belongs to the period when he had begun to dictate. That process would later be blamed for worsening his habit of qualifying the originally stated idea with a train of parentheses. Following such a sentence can indeed be like trying to partner a fan dancer. (If you succeed, you get to see the dancer.) Yet "In the Cage," barring a sortie or two, is fairly simple speech for James. Emigrating will not tame this tiger-trainer of the obvious, but for the moment it has domesticated him, down from London's snob-tables. "For the moment" is how a novelist intimately and fiercely sees time, and its environments. James, not yet a British citizen but soon to be so legally, is like the man in his "The Jolly Corner," between two states of being: Europe and home. What latent Americanism allowed him to nip the British class system so neatly between his own democratic pincers? Lightly, lightly it would have to be done, for his own sentiments are as double as any around. But as an employer of "service" himself, he has perhaps sniffed out why there are no revolutions, or not yet—the real secret of how the British class system survives. Because the "downstairs," caught in its own snobbery and romanced by it, collaborates.

He won't indict; he never does. He'll picture it. As so often, his vehicle will be a woman. The gallery is nearly endless: Isabel, Millie, Daisy, Fleda, Maisie, "Mrs. Brook," Mrs.... This nameless one, whose thought processes he tracks like a guardian angel, is so accurate in her perceptions, and yet so winningly lost in them. Thanks to him, we have her, and a piece of her nation as well.

—

These two stories have never before been juxtaposed. To see them so is gratifying. What to say of the writer who can float a surreal balloon across the haunted fields of Bly, only to warm us up at Crockers' emporium? Is it that nobody appreciates a mystery more than the realist?

James's formidable power of observation, his stance as a kind of bachelor recorder of human doings in which he is not involved, plus an avid interest in the social order, make him a first-class documentarian, joining him to that great body of storytellers who amass what formal history cannot.

No doubt he was wedded to showing us the facts as he saw them, or thought he did. As a writer he could stand aside as he seemed to in life, a family friend to all human circumstance. Or, as with most, to all that experience permitted him. He was born into a world where the emotions were stipulated, and the facts not always revealed. This would foster in him an innate hunger, to ferret out and display the concealed.

Is "The Turn of the Screw," concededly the greatest of James's "ghost stories," to be taken literally, as it would be by believers in the afterlife? Most marvelous is the language cover—each time the "presences" appear—so that the "visions," so plain to narrator and reader both, might be actual or not. Author has sucked out the ordinary. Yet the "ghosts" are as clear as fashion plates. While the governess, her overwhelming gestures to the children, and the very outline of her consciousness, take the stage. Is James at last allowing himself the exquisite relief of acknowledging evil as an actual presence in human life aboveground? Or, as to those Freudians who, mid-century, would embrace James as the arch-expressionist of their own analyses—is she a letter-perfect picture of obsession, as it advances upon a mind unaware?

It may help to look at James himself historically. The late nineteenth century rattled with supernatural concerns. Toward its end the great neurologist Charcot, on whose conclusions at his

Salpetrière clinic Freud would base his theory of hysteria, had an influence filtering into fashionable weekends, wherein via table-tipping séances or Ouija boards one sought communication with the dead. Professional mediums drew on home groups, or in the lecture hall.

James was always interested in children, often as both precocious and victim. "Child abuse," that tinny sociological phrase, scarcely inherits the way the Victorians both sentimentalized and confronted what "the little ones" might expect from their progenitors, in public or in private. Dickens exposed this for the poor. James, in his feinting, nuanced style, often did the same for the rich, who while pressing the social context on their young delegated any responsibility for it. The total abdication of Flora and Miles's benefactor is an exaggeration. As the screw turns, everything is. Orphans, like bastards, can be too beautiful. In a strictly moral age, and often in James, one does not merely have beauty; one suffers it. The governess's harping on the children's "unearthly beauty" is like a motif. James will never do more than hint of the sexual. Yet in certain affrighted posturings the children's doomed craving to be near their haunters does suggest.

One might well imply that the girl of "In the Cage" has far more than "just a crush" on the noble lover, outside whose chambers she daily walks, toward a scene that skirts outright mention of sex yet almost breathes of it, and that her chumminess with the butcher hides a certain reluctance. One could thump the evidence to show that the cage bars her sexually from ... the other space. Let's not.

Rather, see James as an artist on the cusp of his two centuries. An elitist, is he? Who doesn't like to read about those? A polysyllabist in common-denominator-educated America? If so, quite a few so reared seem able to handle that, readers down the decades doing him proud.

The exertions of the human beings in his world may be distant, strange, to our raucous, trendy lingo, but the minds of his people seem to move—well, in the nervous, truth-seeking, qualifying way that our minds, ordinary or not, seem to move. He gives us the language for it. Movies may have helped him, as they have us. Noting how each of his stories is like a film seen through a single lens. Every past is peculiar to itself. That's what we buffs like to see. And he could boast, meanwhile, that he got most of his ideas from ladies sitting next to him at dinner parties. Joke? And that he thought the phrase "summer afternoon" the most sublime.

One can never fully explain why one cleaves to some writers of the past, tattered with their eras as they must inevitably be. Except that to see them, these severed spirits, poised like carrier pigeons on the rooftops of their centuries, ready to fly us their modern messages, is mortal fun. Immortal, maybe.

———

HORTENSE CALISHER is the author of twenty-two books; her novels include *False Entry,* a National Book Award nominee; *The New Yorkers,* a sequel; *Age; On Keeping Women; Mysteries of Motion; Standard Dreaming; The Bobby-Soxer,* winner of the Kafka Prize; *In the Slammer with Carol Smith;* and *Journal from Ellipsia.* Her other works include *Herself: Autobiography of a Writer,* a National Book Award nominee; *Collected Stories of Hortense Calisher,* also a National Book Award nominee; and *The Novellas of Hortense Calisher,* a Modern Library hardcover. She is a past president of the American Academy and Institute of Arts and Letters and of the American PEN, a Guggenheim Fellow, and a recipient of the National Endowment for the Arts Lifetime Achievement Award. She lives in Manhattan and in a farmhouse on the New York–Vermont border with her husband, the writer Curtis Harnack.

THE TURN OF THE SCREW

The story had held us, round the fire, sufficiently breathless, but except the obvious remark that it was gruesome, as on Christmas Eve[1] in an old house a strange tale should essentially be, I remember no comment uttered till somebody happened to note it as the only case he had met in which such a visitation had fallen on a child. The case, I may mention, was that of an apparition in just such an old house as had gathered us for the occasion—an appearance, of a dreadful kind, to a little boy sleeping in the room with his mother and waking her up in the terror of it; waking her not to dissipate his dread and soothe him to sleep again, but to encounter also herself, before she had succeeded in doing so, the same sight that had shocked him. It was this observation that drew from Douglas—not immediately, but later in the evening—a reply that had the interesting consequence to which I call attention. Some one else told a story not particularly effective, which I saw he was not following. This I took for a sign that he had himself something to produce and that we should only have to wait. We waited in fact till two nights later; but that same evening, before we scattered, he brought out what was in his mind.

"I quite agree—in regard to Griffin's ghost, or whatever it was— that its appearing first to the little boy, at so tender an age, adds a particular touch. But it's not the first occurrence of its charming kind that I know to have been concerned with a child. If the child gives the effect another turn of the screw,[2] what do you say to *two* children—?"

"We say of course," somebody exclaimed, "that two children give two turns! Also that we want to hear about them."

I can see Douglas there before the fire, to which he had got up to present his back, looking down at this converser with his hands in his pockets. "Nobody but me, till now, has ever heard. It's quite too horrible." This was naturally declared by several voices to give the thing the utmost price, and our friend, with quiet art, prepared his triumph by turning his eyes over the rest of us and going on: "It's beyond everything. Nothing at all that I know touches it."

"For sheer terror?" I remember asking.

He seemed to say it wasn't so simple as that; to be really at a loss how to qualify it. He passed his hand over his eyes, made a little wincing grimace. "For dreadful—dreadfulness!"

"Oh how delicious!" cried one of the women.

He took no notice of her; he looked at me, but as if, instead of me, he saw what he spoke of. "For general uncanny ugliness and horror and pain."

"Well then," I said, "just sit right down and begin."

He turned round to the fire, gave a kick to a log, watched it an instant. Then as he faced us again: "I can't begin. I shall have to send to town."[3] There was a unanimous groan at this, and much reproach; after which, in his preoccupied way, he explained. "The story's written. It's in a locked drawer—it has not been out for years. I could write to my man and enclose the key; he could send down the packet as he finds it." It was to me in particular that he appeared to propound this—appeared almost to appeal for aid not to hesitate. He had broken a thickness of ice, the formation of many a winter; had had his reasons for a long silence. The others resented postponement, but it was just his scruples that charmed me. I adjured him to write by the first post and to agree with us for an early hearing; then I asked him if the experience in question had been his own. To this his answer was prompt. "Oh thank God, no!"

"And is the record yours? You took the thing down?"

"Nothing but the impression. I took that *here*"—he tapped his heart. "I've never lost it."

"Then your manuscript—?"

"Is in old faded ink and in the most beautiful hand." He hung fire again.[4] "A woman's. She has been dead these twenty years. She sent me the pages in question before she died." They were all listening now, and of course there was somebody to be arch, or at any rate to draw the inference. But if he put the inference by without a smile it was also without irritation. "She was a most charming person, but she was ten years older than I. She was my sister's governess," he quietly said. "She was the most agreeable woman I've ever known in her position; she'd have been worthy of any whatever. It was long ago, and this episode was long before. I was at Trinity,[5] and I found her at home on my coming down the second summer. I was much there that year—it was a beautiful one; and we had, in her off-hours, some strolls and talks in the garden—talks in which she struck me as awfully clever and nice. Oh yes; don't grin: I liked her extremely and am glad to this day to think she liked me too. If she hadn't she wouldn't have told me. She had never told any one. It wasn't simply that she said so, but that I knew she hadn't. I was sure; I could see. You'll easily judge why when you hear."

"Because the thing had been such a scare?"

He continued to fix me. "You'll easily judge," he repeated: "*you* will."

I fixed him too. "I see. She was in love."

He laughed for the first time. "You *are* acute. Yes, she was in love. That is she *had* been. That came out—she couldn't tell her story without its coming out. I saw it, and she saw I saw it; but neither of us spoke of it. I remember the time and the place—the corner of the lawn, the shade of the great beeches and the long hot summer afternoon. It wasn't a scene for a shudder; but oh—!" He quitted the fire and dropped back into his chair.

"You'll receive the packet Thursday morning?" I said.

"Probably not till the second post."

"Well then; after dinner—"

"You'll all meet me here?" He looked us round again. "Isn't anybody going?" It was almost the tone of hope.

"Everybody will stay!"

"*I* will—and *I* will!" cried the ladies whose departure had been fixed. Mrs. Griffin, however, expressed the need for a little more light. "Who was it she was in love with?"

"The story will tell," I took upon myself to reply.

"Oh I can't wait for the story!"

"The story *won't* tell," said Douglas; "not in any literal vulgar way."

"More's the pity then. That's the only way I ever understand."

"Won't *you* tell, Douglas?" somebody else inquired.

He sprang to his feet again. "Yes—to-morrow. Now I must go to bed. Good-night." And, quickly catching up a candlestick, he left us slightly bewildered. From our end of the great brown hall we heard his step on the stair; whereupon Mrs. Griffin spoke. "Well, if I don't know who she was in love with I know who *he* was."

"She was ten years older," said her husband.

"*Raison de plus*⁶—at that age! But it's rather nice, his long reticence."

"Forty years!" Griffin put in.

"With this outbreak at last."

"The outbreak," I returned, "will make a tremendous occasion of Thursday night"; and every one so agreed with me that in the light of it we lost all attention for everything else. The last story, however incomplete and like the mere opening of a serial, had been told; we handshook and "candlestuck,"⁷ as somebody said, and went to bed.

I knew the next day that a letter containing the key had, by the first post, gone off to his London apartments; but in spite of—or perhaps just on account of—the eventual diffusion of this knowledge we quite let him alone till after dinner, till such an hour of the evening in fact as might best accord with the kind of emotion on which our hopes were fixed. Then he became as communicative as we could desire, and indeed gave us his best reason for being so. We had it from him again before the fire in the hall, as we had had our mild wonders of the previous night. It appeared that the narrative he had promised to read us really required for a proper intelligence a few words of prologue. Let me say here distinctly, to have done with it, that this narrative, from an exact transcript of my own made much later, is what I shall presently give. Poor Douglas, before his death—when it was in sight—committed to me the manuscript that reached him on the third of these days and that, on the same spot, with immense effect, he began to read to our hushed little circle on the night of the fourth. The departing ladies who had said they would stay didn't, of course, thank heaven, stay: they departed, in consequence of arrangements made, in a rage of curiosity, as they professed, produced by the touches with which he had already worked us up. But that only made his little final auditory more compact and select, kept it, round the hearth, subject to a common thrill.

The first of these touches conveyed that the written statement took up the tale at a point after it had, in a manner, begun. The fact to be in possession of was therefore that his old friend, the youngest of several daughters of a poor country parson, had at the age of twenty, on taking service for the first time in the schoolroom, come up to London, in trepidation, to answer in person an advertisement that had already placed her in brief correspondence with the advertiser. This person proved, on her presenting herself for judgement at a house in Harley Street[8] that impressed her as vast and imposing—this prospective patron proved a gentleman, a bachelor in the prime of life, such a figure as had never risen, save in a dream or an old novel, before a fluttered anxious girl out of a Hampshire[9] vicarage. One could easily fix his type; it never, happily, dies out. He was handsome and bold and pleasant, off-hand and gay and kind. He struck her, inevitably, as gallant and splendid, but what took her most of all and gave her the courage she afterwards showed was that he put the whole thing to her as a favour, an obligation he should gratefully incur. She figured him as rich, but as fearfully extravagant—saw him all in a glow of high fashion, of good looks, of expensive habits, of charming ways with women. He had for his town residence a big house filled with the spoils of travel and the trophies of the chase; but it was to his country home, an old family place in Essex,[10] that he wished her immediately to proceed.

He had been left, by the death of his parents in India, guardian to a small nephew and a small niece, children of a younger, a military brother whom he had lost two years before. These children were, by the strangest of chances for a man in his position—a lone man without the right sort of experience or a grain of patience—very heavy on his hands. It had all been a great worry and, on his own part doubtless, a series of blunders, but he immensely pitied the poor chicks and had done all he could; had in particular sent them down to his other house, the proper place for them being of course the country, and kept them there from the first with the best people he could find to look after them, parting even with his own servants to wait on them and going down himself, whenever he might, to see how they were doing. The awkward thing was that they had practically no other relations and that his own affairs took up all his time. He had put them in possession of Bly, which was healthy and secure, and had placed at the head of their little establishment—but belowstairs only—an excellent woman, Mrs. Grose, whom he was sure his visitor would like and who had formerly been maid to his mother. She was now housekeeper and was also acting for the time as superintendent to the little girl, of whom, without children of her own, she was by good luck extremely fond. There were plenty of people to help, but of course the young lady who should go down as governess would be in supreme authority. She would also have, in holidays, to look after the small boy, who had been for a term at school—young as he was to be sent, but what else could be done?—and who, as the holidays were about to begin, would be back from one day to the other. There had been for the two children at first a young lady whom they had had the misfortune to lose. She had done for them quite beautifully—she was a most respectable person—till her death, the great awkwardness of which had, precisely, left no alternative but the school for little Miles. Mrs. Grose, since then, in the way of manners and things, had done as she could for Flora; and there were, further, a cook, a housemaid, a dairywoman, an old pony, an old groom, and an old gardener, all likewise thoroughly respectable.

So far had Douglas presented his picture when some one put a question. "And what did the former governess die of? Of so much respectability?"

Our friend's answer was prompt. "That will come out. I don't anticipate."

"Pardon me—I thought that was just what you *are* doing."

"In her successor's place," I suggested, "I should have wished to learn if the office brought with it—"

"Necessary danger to life?" Douglas completed my thought. "She did wish to learn, and she did learn. You shall hear to-morrow what she learnt. Meanwhile of course the prospect struck her as slightly grim. She was young, untried, nervous: it was a vision of serious duties and little company, of really great loneliness. She hesitated—took a couple of days to consult and consider. But the salary offered much exceeded her modest measure, and on a second interview she faced the music, she engaged." And Douglas, with this, made a pause that, for the benefit of the company, moved me to throw in—

"The moral of which was of course the seduction exercised by the splendid young man. She succumbed to it."

He got up and, as he had done the night before, went to the fire, gave a stir to a log with his foot, then stood a moment with his back to us. "She saw him only twice."

"Yes, but that's just the beauty of her passion."

A little to my surprise, on this, Douglas turned round to me. "It *was* the beauty of it. There were others," he went on, "who hadn't succumbed. He told her frankly all his difficulty—that for several applicants the conditions had been prohibitive. They were somehow simply afraid. It sounded dull—it sounded strange; and all the more so because of his main condition."

"Which was—?"

"That she should never trouble him—but never, never: neither appeal nor complain nor write about anything; only meet all questions herself, receive all moneys from his solicitor, take the whole thing over and let him alone. She promised to do this, and she mentioned to me that when, for a moment, disburdened, delighted, he held her hand, thanking her for the sacrifice, she already felt rewarded."

"But was that all her reward?" one of the ladies asked.

"She never saw him again."

"Oh!" said the lady; which, as our friend immediately again left us, was the only other word of importance contributed to the subject till, the next night, by the corner of the hearth, in the best chair, he opened the faded red cover of a thin old-fashioned gilt-edged album. The whole thing took indeed more nights than one, but on the first occasion the same lady put another question. "What's your title?"

"I haven't one."

"Oh *I* have!" I said. But Douglas, without heeding me, had begun to read with a fine clearness that was like a rendering to the ear of the beauty of his author's hand.

I

I remember the whole beginning as a succession of flights and drops, a little see-saw of the right throbs and the wrong. After rising, in town, to meet his appeal I had at all events a couple of very bad days—found all my doubts bristle again, felt indeed sure I had made a mistake. In this state of mind I spent the long hours of bumping swinging coach that carried me to the stopping-place at which I was to be met by a vehicle from the house. This convenience, I was told, had been ordered, and I found, toward the close of the June afternoon, a commodious fly[11] in waiting for me. Driving at that hour, on a lovely day, through a country the summer sweetness of which served as a friendly welcome, my fortitude revived and, as we turned into the avenue, took a flight that was probably but a proof of the point to which it had sunk. I suppose I had expected, or had dreaded, something so dreary that what greeted me was a good surprise. I remember as a thoroughly pleasant impression the broad clear front, its open windows and fresh curtains and the pair of maids looking out; I remember the lawn and the bright flowers and the crunch of my wheels on the gravel and the clustered tree-tops over which the rooks circled and cawed in the golden sky. The scene had a greatness that made it a different affair from my own scant home, and there immediately appeared at the door, with a little girl in her hand, a civil person who dropped me as decent a curtsey as if I had been the mistress or a distinguished visitor. I had received in Harley Street a narrower notion of the place, and that, as I recalled it, made me think the proprietor still more of a gentleman, suggested that what I was to enjoy might be a matter beyond his promise.

I had no drop again till the next day, for I was carried triumphantly through the following hours by my introduction to the younger of my pupils. The little girl who accompanied Mrs. Grose affected me on the spot as a creature too charming not to make it a great fortune to have to do with her. She was the most beautiful child I had ever seen, and I afterwards wondered why my employer hadn't made more of a point to me of this. I slept little that night— I was too much excited; and this astonished me too, I recollect, remained with me, adding to my sense of the liberality with which I was treated. The large impressive room, one of the best in the house, the great state bed, as I almost felt it, the figured full draperies, the long glasses in which, for the first time, I could see myself from head to foot, all struck me—like the wonderful appeal of my small charge—as so many things thrown in. It was thrown in as well, from the first moment, that I should get on with Mrs. Grose in a relation over which, on my way, in the coach, I fear I had rather brooded. The one appearance indeed that in this early outlook might have made me shrink again was that of her being so inordinately glad to see me. I felt within half an hour that she was so glad—stout simple plain clean wholesome woman—as to be positively on her guard against showing it too much. I wondered even then a little why she should wish *not* to show it, and that, with reflexion, with suspicion, might of course have made me uneasy.

But it was a comfort that there could be no uneasiness in a connexion with anything so beatific as the radiant image of my little girl, the vision of whose angelic beauty had probably more than anything else to do with the restlessness that, before morning, made me several times rise and wander about my room to take in the whole picture and prospect; to watch from my open window the faint summer dawn, to look at such stretches of the rest of the house as I could catch, and to listen, while in the fading dusk the first birds began to twitter, for the possible recurrence of a sound or two, less natural and not without but within, that I had fancied I heard.

There had been a moment when I believed I recognised, faint and far, the cry of a child; there had been another when I found myself just consciously starting as at the passage, before my door, of a light footstep. But these fancies were not marked enough not to be thrown off, and it is only in the light, or the gloom, I should rather say, of other and subsequent matters that they now come back to me. To watch, teach, "form" little Flora would too evidently be the making of a happy and useful life. It had been agreed between us downstairs that after this first occasion I should have her as a matter of course at night, her small white bed being already arranged, to that end, in my room. What I had undertaken was the whole care of her, and she had remained just this last time with Mrs. Grose only as an effect of our consideration for my inevitable strangeness and her natural timidity. In spite of this timidity—which the child herself, in the oddest way in the world, had been perfectly frank and brave about, allowing it, without a sign of uncomfortable consciousness, with the deep sweet serenity indeed of one of Raphael's holy infants,[12] to be discussed, to be imputed to her and to determine us—I felt quite sure she would presently like me. It was part of what I already liked Mrs. Grose herself for, the pleasure I could see her feel in my admiration and wonder as I sat at supper with four tall candles and with my pupil, in a high chair and a bib, brightly facing me between them over bread and milk. There were naturally things that in Flora's presence could pass between us only as prodigious and gratified looks, obscure and round-about allusions.

"And the little boy—does he look like her? Is he too so very remarkable?"

One wouldn't, it was already conveyed between us, too grossly flatter a child. "Oh Miss, *most* remarkable. If you think well of this one!"—and she stood there with a plate in her hand, beaming at our companion, who looked from one of us to the other with placid heavenly eyes that contained nothing to check us.

"Yes; if I do—?"

"You *will* be carried away by the little gentleman!"

"Well, that, I think, is what I came for—to be carried away. I'm afraid, however," I remember feeling the impulse to add, "I'm rather easily carried away. I was carried away in London!"

I can still see Mrs. Grose's broad face as she took this in. "In Harley Street?"

"In Harley Street."

"Well, Miss, you're not the first—and you won't be the last."

"Oh I've no pretensions," I could laugh, "to being the only one. My other pupil, at any rate, as I understand, comes back to-morrow?"

"Not to-morrow—Friday, Miss. He arrives, as you did, by the coach, under care of the guard, and is to be met by the same carriage."

I forthwith wanted to know if the proper as well as the pleasant and friendly thing wouldn't therefore be that on the arrival of the public conveyance I should await him with his little sister; a proposition to which Mrs. Grose assented so heartily that I somehow took her manner as a kind of comforting pledge—never falsified, thank heaven!—that we should on every question be quite at one. Oh she was glad I was there!

What I felt the next day was, I suppose, nothing that could be fairly called a reaction from the cheer of my arrival; it was probably at the most only a slight oppression produced by a fuller measure of the scale, as I walked round them, gazed up at them, took them in, of my new circumstances. They had as it were, an extent and mass for which I had not been prepared and in the presence of which I found myself, freshly, a little scared not less than a little proud. Regular lessons, in this agitation, certainly suffered some wrong; I reflected that my first duty was, by the gentlest arts I could contrive, to win the child into the sense of knowing me. I spent the day with her out of doors; I arranged with her, to her great satisfaction, that it should be she, she only, who might show me the place. She showed it step by step and room by room and secret by secret, with droll delightful childish talk about it and with the result, in half an hour, of our becoming tremendous friends. Young as she was I was struck, throughout our little tour, with her confidence and courage, with the way, in empty chambers and dull corridors, on crooked staircases that made me pause and even on the summit of an old machicolated[13] square tower that made me dizzy, her morning music, her disposition to tell me so many more things than she asked, rang out and led me on. I have not seen Bly since the day I left it, and I daresay that to my present older and more informed eyes it would show a very reduced importance. But as my little conductress, with her hair of gold and her frock of blue, danced before me round corners and pattered down passages, I had the view of a castle of romance inhabited by a rosy sprite, such a place as would somehow, for diversion of the young idea, take all colour out of story-books and fairy-tales. Wasn't it just a story-book over which I had fallen a-doze and a-dream? No; it was a big ugly antique but convenient house, embodying a few features of a building still older, half-displaced and half-utilised, in which I had the fancy of our being almost as lost as a handful of passengers in a great drifting ship. Well, I was strangely at the helm!

I I

This came home to me when, two days later, I drove over with Flora to meet, as Mrs. Grose said, the little gentleman; and all the more for an incident that, presenting itself the second evening, had deeply disconcerted me. The first day had been, on the whole, as I have expressed, reassuring; but I was to see it wind up to a change of note. The postbag that evening—it came late—contained a letter for me which, however, in the hand of my employer, I found to be composed but of a few words enclosing another, addressed to himself, with a seal still unbroken. "This, I recognise, is from the head-master, and the head-master's an awful bore. Read him, please; deal with him; but mind you don't report. Not a word. I'm off!" I broke the seal with a great effort—so great a one that I was a long time coming to it; took the unopened missive at last up to my room and only attacked it just before going to bed. I had better have let it wait till morning, for it gave me a second sleepless night. With no counsel to take, the next day, I was full of distress; and it finally got so the better of me that I determined to open myself at least to Mrs. Grose.

"What does it mean? The child's dismissed his school."

She gave me a look that I remarked at the moment; then visibly, with a quick blankness, seemed to try to take it back. "But aren't they all—?"

"Sent home—yes. But only for the holidays. Miles may never go back at all."

Consciously, under my attention, she reddened. "They won't take him?"

"They absolutely decline."

At this she raised her eyes, which she had turned from me; I saw them fill with good tears. "What has he done?"

I cast about; then I judged best simply to hand her my document—which, however, had the effect of making her, without taking it, simply put her hands behind her. She shook her head sadly. "Such things are not for me, Miss."

My counsellor couldn't read! I winced at my mistake, which I attenuated as I could, and opened the letter again to repeat it to her; then, faltering in the act and folding it up once more, I put it back in my pocket. "Is he really *bad*?"

The tears were still in her eyes. "Do the gentlemen say so?"

"They go into no particulars. They simply express their regret that it should be impossible to keep him. That can have but one meaning." Mrs. Grose listened with dumb emotion; she forbore to ask me what this meaning might be; so that, presently, to put the thing with some coherence and with the mere aid of her presence to my own mind, I went on: "That he's an injury to the others."

At this, with one of the quick turns of simple folk, she suddenly flamed up. "Master Miles!—*him* an injury?"

There was such a flood of good faith in it that, though I had not yet seen the child, my very fears made me jump to the absurdity of the idea. I found myself, to meet my friend the better, offering it, on the spot, sarcastically. "To his poor little innocent mates!"

"It's too dreadful," cried Mrs. Grose, "to say such cruel things! Why, he's scarce ten years old."

"Yes, yes; it would be incredible."

She was evidently grateful for such a profession. "See him, Miss, first. *Then* believe it!" I felt forthwith a new impatience to see him; it was the beginning of a curiosity that, all the next hours, was to deepen almost to pain. Mrs. Grose was aware, I could judge, of what she had produced in me, and she followed it up with assurance. "You might as well believe it of the little lady. Bless her," she added the next moment—"*look* at her!"

I turned and saw that Flora, whom, ten minutes before, I had established in the schoolroom with a sheet of white paper, a pencil, and a copy of nice "round O's," now presented herself to view at the open door. She expressed in her little way an extraordinary detachment from disagreeable duties, looking at me, however, with a great childish light that seemed to offer it as a mere result of the affection she had conceived for my person, which had rendered necessary that she should follow me. I needed nothing more than this to feel the full force of Mrs. Grose's comparison, and, catching my pupil in my arms, covered her with kisses in which there was a sob of atonement.

None the less, the rest of the day, I watched for further occasion to approach my colleague, especially as, toward evening, I began to fancy she rather sought to avoid me. I overtook her, I remember, on the staircase; we went down together and at the bottom I detained her, holding her there with a hand on her arm. "I take what you said to me at noon as a declaration that *you've* never known him to be bad."

She threw back her head; she had clearly by this time, and very honestly, adopted an attitude. "Oh never known him—I don't pretend *that!*"

I was upset again. "Then you *have* known him—?"

"Yes indeed, Miss, thank God!"

On reflexion I accepted this. "You mean that a boy who never is—?"

"Is no boy for *me*!"

I held her tighter. "You like them with the spirit to be naughty?" Then, keeping pace with her answer, "So do I!" I eagerly brought out. "But not to the degree to contaminate—"

"To contaminate?"—my big word left her at a loss.

I explained it. "To corrupt."

She stared, taking my meaning in; but it produced in her an odd laugh. "Are you afraid he'll corrupt *you*?" She put the question with such a fine bold humour that with a laugh, a little silly doubtless, to match her own, I gave way for the time to the apprehension of ridicule.

But the next day, as the hour for my drive approached, I cropped up in another place. "What was the lady who was here before?"

"The last governess? She was also young and pretty—almost as young and almost as pretty, Miss, even as you."

"Ah then I hope her youth and her beauty helped her!" I recollect throwing off. "He seems to like us young and pretty!"

"Oh he *did*," Mrs. Grose assented: "it was the way he liked every one!" She had no sooner spoken indeed than she caught herself up. "I mean that's *his* way—the master's."

I was struck. "But of whom did you speak first?"

She looked blank, but she coloured. "Why of *him*."

"Of the master?"

"Of who else?"

There was so obviously no one else that the next moment I had lost my impression of her having accidentally said more than she meant; and I merely asked what I wanted to know. "Did *she* see anything in the boy—?"

"That wasn't right? She never told me."

I had a scruple, but I overcame it. "Was she careful—particular?"

Mrs. Grose appeared to try to be conscientious. "About some things—yes."

"But not about all?"

Again she considered. "Well, Miss—she's gone. I won't tell tales."

"I quite understand your feeling," I hastened to reply; but I thought it after an instant not opposed to this concession to pursue: "Did she die here?"

"No—she went off."

I don't know what there was in this brevity of Mrs. Grose's that struck me as ambiguous. "Went off to die?" Mrs. Grose looked straight out of the window, but I felt that, hypothetically, I had a right to know what young persons engaged for Bly were expected to do. "She was taken ill, you mean, and went home?"

"She was not taken ill, so far as appeared, in this house. She left it, at the end of the year, to go home, as she said, for a short holiday, to which the time she had put in had certainly given her a right. We had then a young woman—a nursemaid who had stayed on and who was a good girl and clever; and *she* took the children altogether for the interval. But our young lady never came back, and at the very moment I was expecting her I heard from the master that she was dead."

I turned this over. "But of what?"

"He never told me! But please, Miss," said Mrs. Grose, "I must get to my work."

III

Her thus turning her back on me was fortunately not, for my just preoccupations, a snub that could check the growth of our mutual esteem. We met, after I had brought home little Miles, more intimately than ever on the ground of my stupefaction, my general emotion: so monstrous was I then ready to pronounce it that such a child as had now been revealed to me should be under an interdict. I was a little late on the scene of his arrival, and I felt, as he stood wistfully looking out for me before the door of the inn at which the coach had put him down, that I had seen him on the instant, without and within, in the great glow of freshness, the same positive fragrance of purity, in which I had from the first moment seen his little sister. He was incredibly beautiful, and Mrs. Grose had put her finger on it: everything but a sort of passion of tenderness for him was swept away by his presence. What I then and there took him to my heart for was something divine that I have never found to the same degree in any child—his indescribable little air of knowing nothing in the world but love. It would have been impossible to carry a bad name with a greater sweetness of innocence, and by the time I had got back to Bly with him I remained merely bewildered—so far, that is, as I was not outraged—by the sense of the horrible letter locked up in one of the drawers of my room. As soon as I could compass a private word with Mrs. Grose I declared to her that it was grotesque.

She promptly understood me. "You mean the cruel charge—?"

"It doesn't live an instant. My dear woman, *look* at him!"

She smiled at my pretension to have discovered his charm. "I assure you, Miss, I do nothing else! What will you say then?" she immediately added.

"In answer to the letter?" I had made up my mind. "Nothing at all."

"And to his uncle?"

I was incisive. "Nothing at all."

"And to the boy himself?"

I was wonderful. "Nothing at all."

She gave with her apron a great wipe to her mouth. "Then I'll stand by you. We'll see it out."

"We'll see it out!" I ardently echoed, giving her my hand to make it a vow.

She held me there a moment, then whisked up her apron again with her detached hand. "Would you mind, Miss, if I used the freedom—"

"To kiss me? No!" I took the good creature in my arms and after we had embraced like sisters felt still more fortified and indignant.

This at all events was for the time: a time so full that as I recall the way it went it reminds me of all the art I now need to make it a little distinct. What I look back at with amazement is the situation I accepted. I had undertaken, with my companion, to see it out, and I was under a charm apparently that could smooth away the extent and the far and difficult connexions of such an effort. I was lifted aloft on a great wave of infatuation and pity. I found it simple, in my ignorance, my confusion, and perhaps my conceit, to assume that I could deal with a boy whose education for the world was all on the point of beginning. I am unable even to remember at this day what proposal I framed for the end of his holidays and the resumption of his studies. Lessons with me indeed, that charming summer, we all had a theory that he was to have; but I now feel that for weeks the lessons must have been rather my own. I learnt something—at first certainly—that had not been one of the teachings of my small smothered life; learnt to be amused, and even amusing, and not to think for the morrow. It was the first time, in a manner, that I had known space and air and freedom, all the music of summer and all the mystery of nature. And then there was consideration—and consideration was sweet. Oh it was a trap—not designed but deep—to my imagination, to my delicacy, perhaps to my vanity; to whatever in me was most excitable. The best way to picture it all is to say that I was off my guard. They gave me so little trouble—they were of a gentleness so extraordinary. I used to speculate—but even this with a dim disconnectedness—as to how the rough future (for all futures are rough!) would handle them and might bruise them. They had the bloom of health and happiness; and yet, as if I had been in charge of a pair of little grandees, of princes of the blood, for whom everything, to be right, would have to be fenced about and ordered and arranged, the only form that in my fancy the after-years could take for them was that of a romantic, a really royal extension of the garden and the park. It may be of course above all that what suddenly broke into this gives the previous time a charm of stillness—that hush in which something gathers or crouches. The change was actually like the spring of a beast.

In the first weeks the days were long; they often, at their finest, gave me what I used to call my own hour, the hour when, for my pupils, tea-time and bed-time having come and gone, I had before my final retirement a small interval alone. Much as I liked my companions this hour was the thing in the day I liked most; and I liked it best of all when, as the light faded—or rather, I should say, the day lingered and the last calls of the last birds sounded, in a flushed sky, from the old trees—I could take a turn into the grounds and enjoy, almost with a sense of property that amused and flattered me, the beauty and dignity of the place. It was a pleasure at these moments to feel myself tranquil and justified; doubtless perhaps also to reflect that by my discretion, my quiet good sense and general high propriety, I was giving pleasure—if he ever thought of it!—to the person to whose pressure I had yielded. What I was doing was what he had earnestly hoped and directly asked of me, and that I *could*, after all, do it proved even a greater joy than I had expected. I daresay I fancied myself in short a remarkable young woman and took comfort in the faith that this would more publicly appear. Well, I needed to be remarkable to offer a front to the remarkable things that presently gave their first sign.

It was plump, one afternoon, in the middle of my very hour: the children were tucked away and I had come out for my stroll. One of the thoughts that, as I don't in the least shrink now from noting, used to be with me in these wanderings was that it would be as charming as a charming story suddenly to meet some one. Some one would appear there at the turn of a path and would stand before me and smile and approve. I didn't ask more than that—I only asked that he should *know;* and the only way to be sure he knew would be to see it, and the kind light of it, in his handsome face. That was exactly present to me—by which I mean the face was—when, on the first of these occasions, at the end of a long June day, I stopped short on emerging from one of the plantations and coming into view of the house. What arrested me on the spot—and with a shock much greater than any vision had allowed for—was the sense that my imagination had, in a flash, turned real. He did stand there!—but high up, beyond the lawn and at the very top of the tower to which, on that first morning, little Flora had conducted me. This tower was one of a pair—square incongruous crenellated structures—that were distinguished, for some reason, though I could see little difference, as the new and the old. They flanked opposite ends of the house and were probably architectural absurdities, redeemed in a measure indeed by not being wholly disengaged nor of a height too pretentious, dating, in their gingerbread antiquity, from a romantic revival that was already a respectable past. I admired them, had fancies about them, for we could all profit in a degree, especially when they loomed through the dusk, by the grandeur of their actual battlements; yet it was not at such an elevation that the figure I had so often invoked seemed most in place.

It produced in me, this figure, in the clear twilight, I remember, two distinct gasps of emotion, which were, sharply, the shock of my first and that of my second surprise. My second was a violent perception of the mistake of my first: the man who met my eyes was not the person I had precipitately supposed. There came to me thus a bewilderment of vision of which, after these years, there is no living view that I can hope to give. An unknown man in a lonely place is a permitted object of fear to a young woman privately bred; and the figure that faced me was—a few more seconds assured me—as little any one else I knew as it was the image that had been in my mind. I had not seen it in Harley Street—I had not seen it anywhere. The place, moreover, in the strangest way in the world, had on the instant and by the very fact of its appearance become a solitude. To me at least, making my statement here with a deliberation with which I have never made it, the whole feeling of the moment returns. It was as if, while I took in what I did take in, all the rest of the scene had been stricken with death. I can hear again, as I write, the intense hush in which the sounds of evening dropped. The rooks stopped cawing in the golden sky and the friendly hour lost for the unspeakable minute all its voice. But there was no other change in nature, unless indeed it were a change that I saw with a stranger sharpness. The gold was still in the sky, the clearness in the air, and the man who looked at me over the battlements was as definite as a picture in a frame. That's how I thought, with extraordinary quickness, of each person he might have been and that he wasn't. We were confronted across our distance quite long enough for me to ask myself with intensity who then he was and to feel, as an effect of my inability to say, a wonder that in a few seconds more became intense.

The great question, or one of these, is afterwards, I know, with regard to certain matters, the question of how long they have lasted.

Well, this matter of mine, think what you will of it, lasted while I caught at a dozen possibilities, none of which made a difference for the better, that I could see, in there having been in the house—and for how long, above all?—a person of whom I was in ignorance. It lasted while I just bridled a little with the sense of how my office seemed to require that there should be no such ignorance and no such person. It lasted while this visitant, at all event—and there was a touch of the strange freedom, as I remember, in the sign of familiarity of his wearing no hat—seemed to fix me, from his position, with just the question, just the scrutiny through the fading light, that his own presence provoked. We were too far apart to call to each other, but there was a moment at which, at shorter range, some challenge between us, breaking the hush, would have been the right result of our straight mutual stare. He was in one of the angles, the one away from the house, very erect, as it struck me, and with both hands on the ledge. So I saw him as I see the letters I form on this page; then, exactly, after a minute, as if to add to the spectacle, he slowly changed his place—passed, looking at me hard all the while, to the opposite corner of the platform. Yes, it was intense to me that during this transit he never took his eyes from me, and I can see at this moment the way his hand, as he went, moved from one of the crenellations to the next. He stopped at the other corner, but less long, and even as he turned away still markedly fixed me. He turned away; that was all I knew.

IV

It was not that I didn't wait, on this occasion, for more, since I was as deeply rooted as shaken. Was there a "secret" at Bly—a mystery of Udolpho[14] or an insane, an unmentionable relative kept in unsuspected confinement? I can't say how long I turned it over, or how long, in a confusion of curiosity and dread, I remained where I had had my collision; I only recall that when I re-entered the house darkness had quite closed in. Agitation, in the interval, certainly had held me and driven me, for I must, in circling about the place, have walked three miles; but I was to be later on so much more overwhelmed that this mere dawn of alarm was a comparatively human chill. The most singular part of it in fact—singular as the rest had been—was the part I became, in the hall, aware of in meeting Mrs. Grose. This picture comes back to me in the general train—the impression, as I received it on my return, of the wide white panelled space, bright in the lamplight and with its portraits and red carpet, and of the good surprised look of my friend, which immediately told me she had missed me. It came to me straightway, under her contact, that, with plain heartiness, mere relieved anxiety at my appearance, she knew nothing whatever that could bear upon the incident I had there ready for her. I had not suspected in advance that her comfortable face would pull me up, and I somehow measured the importance of what I had seen by my thus finding myself hesitate to mention it. Scarce anything in the whole history seems to me so odd as this fact that my real beginning of fear was one, as I may say, with the instinct of sparing my companion. On the spot, accordingly, in the pleasant hall and with her eyes on me, I, for a reason that I couldn't then have phrased, achieved an inward revolution—offered a vague pretext for my lateness and, with the plea of the beauty of the night and of the heavy dew and wet feet, went as soon as possible to my room.

Here it was another affair; here, for many days after, it was a queer affair enough. There were hours, from day to day—or at least there were moments, snatched even from clear duties—when I had to shut myself up to think. It wasn't so much yet that I was more nervous than I could bear to be as that I was remarkably afraid of becoming so; for the truth I had now to turn over was simply and clearly the truth that I could arrive at no account whatever of the visitor with whom I had been so inexplicably and yet, as it seemed to me, so intimately concerned. It took me little time to see that I might easily sound, without forms of inquiry and without exciting remark, any domestic complication. The shock I had suffered must have sharpened all my senses; I felt sure, at the end of three days and as the result of mere closer attention, that I had not been practised upon by the servants nor made the object of any "game." Of whatever it was that I knew nothing was known around me. There was but one sane inference: some one had taken a liberty rather monstrous. That was what, repeatedly, I dipped into my room and locked the door to say to myself. We had been, collectively, subject to an intrusion; some unscrupulous traveller, curious in old houses, had made his way in unobserved, enjoyed the prospect from the best point of view and then stolen out as he came. If he had given me such a bold hard stare, that was but a part of his indiscretion. The good thing, after all, was that we should surely see no more of him.

This was not so good a thing, I admit, as not to leave me to judge that what, essentially, made nothing else much signify was simply my charming work. My charming work was just my life with Miles and Flora, and through nothing could I so like it as through feeling that to throw myself into it was to throw myself out of my trouble. The attraction of my small charges was a constant joy, leading me to wonder afresh at the vanity of my original fears, the distaste I had begun by entertaining for the probable grey prose of my office. There was to be no grey prose, it appeared, and no long grind; so how could work not be charming that presented itself as daily beauty? It was all the romance of the nursery and the poetry of the schoolroom. I don't mean by this of course that we studied only fiction and verse; I mean that I can express no otherwise the sort of interest my companions inspired. How can I describe that except by saying that instead of growing deadly used to them—and it's a marvel for a governess: I call the sisterhood to witness!—I made constant fresh discoveries. There was one direction, assuredly, in which these discoveries stopped: deep obscurity continued to cover the region of the boy's conduct at school. It had been promptly given me, I have noted, to face that mystery without a pang. Perhaps even it would be nearer the truth to say that—without a word—he himself had cleared it up. He had made the whole charge absurd. My conclusion bloomed there with the real rose-flush of his innocence: he was only too fine and fair for the little horrid unclean schoolworld, and he had paid a price for it. I reflected acutely that the sense of such individual differences, such superiorities of quality, always, on the part of the majority—which could include even stupid sordid head-masters—turns infallibly to the vindictive.

Both the children had a gentleness—it was their only fault, and it never made Miles a muff[15]—that kept them (how shall I express it?) almost impersonal and certainly quite unpunishable. They were like those cherubs of the anecdote who had—morally at any rate—nothing to whack![16] I remember feeling with Miles in especial as if he had had, as it were, nothing to call even an infinitesimal history. We expect of a small child scant enough "antecedents," but there was in this beautiful little boy something extraordinarily sensitive, yet extraordinarily happy, that, more than in any creature of his age I have seen, struck me as beginning anew each day. He had never for a second suffered. I took this as a direct disproof of his having really been chastised. If he had been wicked he would have "caught" it, and I should have caught it by the rebound—I should have found the trace, should have felt the wound and the dishonour. I could reconstitute nothing at all, and he was therefore an angel. He never spoke of his school, never mentioned a comrade or a master; and I, for my part, was quite too much disgusted to allude to them. Of course I was under the spell, and the wonderful part is that, even at the time, I perfectly knew I was. But I gave myself up to it; it was an antidote to any pain, and I had more pains than one. I was in receipt in these days of disturbing letters from home, where things were not going well. But with this joy of my children what things in the world mattered? That was the question I used to put to my scrappy retirements. I was dazzled by their loveliness.

There was a Sunday—to get on—when it rained with such force and for so many hours that there could be no procession to church; in consequence of which, as the day declined, I had arranged with Mrs. Grose that, should the evening show improvement, we would attend together the late service. The rain happily stopped, and I prepared for our walk, which, through the park and by the good road to the village, would be a matter of twenty minutes. Coming downstairs to meet my colleague in the hall, I remembered a pair of gloves that had required three stitches and that had received them—with a publicity perhaps not edifying—while I sat with the children at their tea, served on Sundays, by exception, in that cold clean temple of mahogany and brass, the "grown-up" dining-room. The gloves had been dropped there, and I turned in to recover them. The day was grey enough, but the afternoon light still lingered, and it enabled me, on crossing the threshold, not only to recognise, on a chair near the wide window, then closed, the articles I wanted, but to become aware of a person on the other side of the window and looking straight in. One step into the room had sufficed; my vision was instantaneous; it was all there. The person looking straight in was the person who had already appeared to me. He appeared thus again with I won't say greater distinctness, for that was impossible, but with a nearness that represented a forward stride in our intercourse and made me, as I met him, catch my breath and turn cold. He was the same—he was the same, and seen, this time, as he had been seen before, from the waist up, the window, though the dining-room was on the ground floor, not going down to the terrace on which he stood. His face was close to the glass, yet the effect of this better view was, strangely, just to show me how intense the former had been. He remained but a few seconds—long enough to convince me he also saw and recognised; but it was as if I had been looking at him for years and had known him always. Something, however, happened this time that had not happened before; his stare into my face, through the glass and across the room, was as deep and hard as then, but it quitted me for a moment during which I could still watch it, see it fix successively several other things. On the spot there came to me the added shock of a certitude that it was not for me he had come. He had come for some one else.

The flash of this knowledge—for it was knowledge in the midst of dread—produced in me the most extraordinary effect, starting, as I stood there, a sudden vibration of duty and courage. I say courage because I was beyond all doubt already far gone. I bounded straight out of the door again, reached that of the house, got in an instant upon the drive and, passing along the terrace as fast as I could rush, turned a corner and came full in sight. But it was in sight of nothing now—my visitor had vanished. I stopped, almost

dropped, with the real relief of this; but I took in the whole scene—
I gave him time to reappear. I call it time, but how long was it? I
can't speak to the purpose to-day of the duration of these things.
That kind of measure must have left me: they couldn't have lasted
as they actually appeared to me to last. The terrace and the whole
place, the lawn and the garden beyond it, all I could see of the park,
were empty with a great emptiness. There were shrubberies and
big trees, but I remember the clear assurance I felt that none of
them concealed him. He was there or was not there: not there if I
didn't see him. I got hold of this; then, instinctively, instead of returning as I had come, went to the window. It was confusedly present to me that I ought to place myself where he had stood. I did so;
I applied my face to the pane and looked, as he had looked, into the
room. As if, at this moment, to show me exactly what his range had
been, Mrs. Grose, as I had done for himself just before, came in
from the hall. With this I had the full image of a repetition of what
had already occurred. She saw me as I had seen my own visitant;
she pulled up short as I had done; I gave her something of the shock
that I had received. She turned white, and this made me ask myself
if I had blanched as much. She stared, in short, and retreated just on
my lines, and I knew she had then passed out and come round to me
and that I should presently meet her. I remained where I was, and
while I waited I thought of more things than one. But there's only
one I take space to mention. I wondered why *she* should be scared.

V

Oh she let me know as soon as, round the corner of the house,
she loomed again into view. "What in the name of goodness is the
matter—?" She was now flushed and out of breath.

I said nothing till she came quite near. "With me?" I must have
made a wonderful face. "Do I show it?"

"You're as white as a sheet. You look awful."

I considered; I could meet on this, without scruple, any degree
of innocence. My need to respect the bloom of Mrs. Grose's had

dropped, without a rustle, from my shoulders, and if I wavered for the instant it was not with what I kept back. I put out my hand to her and she took it; I held her hard a little, liking to feel her close to me. There was a kind of support in the shy heave of her surprise. "You came for me for church, of course, but I can't go."

"Has anything happened?"

"Yes. You must know now. Did I look very queer?"

"Through this window? Dreadful!"

"Well," I said, "I've been frightened." Mrs. Grose's eyes expressed plainly that *she* had no wish to be, yet also that she knew too well her place not to be ready to share with me any marked inconvenience. Oh it was quite settled that she *must* share! "Just what you saw from the dining-room a minute ago was the effect of that. What *I* saw—just before—was much worse."

Her hand tightened. "What was it?"

"An extraordinary man. Looking in."

"What extraordinary man?"

"I haven't the least idea."

Mrs. Grose gazed round us in vain. "Then where is he gone?"

"I know still less."

"Have you seen him before?"

"Yes—once. On the old tower."

She could only look at me harder. "Do you mean he's a stranger?"

"Oh very much!"

"Yet you didn't tell me?"

"No—for reasons. But now that you've guessed—"

Mrs. Grose's round eyes encountered this charge. "Ah I haven't guessed!" she said very simply. "How can I if *you* don't imagine?"

"I don't in the very least."

"You've seen him nowhere but on the tower?"

"And on this spot just now."

Mrs. Grose looked round again. "What was he doing on the tower?"

"Only standing there and looking down at me."

She thought a minute. "Was he a gentleman?"

I found I had no need to think. "No." She gazed in deeper wonder. "No."

"Then nobody about the place? Nobody from the village?"

"Nobody—nobody. I didn't tell you, but I made sure."

She breathed a vague relief: this was, oddly, so much to the good. It only went indeed a little way. "But if he isn't a gentleman—"

"What *is* he? He's a horror."

"A horror?"

"He's—God help me if I know *what* he is!"

Mrs. Grose looked round once more; she fixed her eyes on the duskier distance and then, pulling herself together, turned to me with full inconsequence. "It's time we should be at church."

"Oh I'm not fit for church!"

"Won't it do you good?"

"It won't do *them*—!" I nodded at the house.

"The children?"

"I can't leave them now."

"You're afraid—?"

I spoke boldly. "I'm afraid of *him*."

Mrs. Grose's large face showed me, at this, for the first time, the far-away faint glimmer of a consciousness more acute: I somehow made out in it the delayed dawn of an idea I myself had not given her and that was as yet quite obscure to me. It comes back to me that I thought instantly of this as something I could get from her; and I felt it to be connected with the desire she presently showed to know more. "When was it—on the tower?"

"About the middle of the month. At this same hour."

"Almost at dark," said Mrs. Grose.

"Oh no, not nearly. I saw him as I see you."

"Then how did he get in?"

"And how did he get out?" I laughed. "I had no opportunity to ask him! This evening, you see," I pursued, "he has not been able to get in."

"He only peeps?"

"I hope it will be confined to that!" She had now let go my hand; she turned away a little. I waited an instant; then I brought out: "Go to church. Good-bye. I must watch."

Slowly she faced me again. "Do you fear for them?"

We met in another long look. "Don't *you?*" Instead of answering she came nearer to the window and, for a minute, applied her face to the glass. "You see how he could see," I meanwhile went on.

She didn't move. "How long was he here?"

"Till I came out. I came to meet him."

Mrs. Grose at last turned round, and there was still more in her face. "*I* couldn't have come out."

"Neither could I!" I laughed again. "But I did come. I've my duty."

"So have I mine," she replied; after which she added: "What's he like?"

"I've been dying to tell you. But he's like nobody."

"Nobody?" she echoed.

"He has no hat." Then seeing in her face that she already, in this, with a deeper dismay, found a touch of picture, I quickly added stroke to stroke. "He has red hair, very red, close-curling, and a pale face, long in shape, with straight good features and little rather queer whiskers that are as red as his hair. His eyebrows are somehow darker; they look particularly arched and as if they might move a good deal. His eyes are sharp, strange—awfully; but I only know clearly that they're rather small and very fixed. His mouth's wide, and his lips are thin, and except for his little whiskers he's quite clean-shaven. He gives me a sort of sense of looking like an actor."

"An actor!" It was impossible to resemble one less, at least, than Mrs. Grose at that moment.

"I've never seen one, but so I suppose them. He's tall, active, erect," I continued, "but never—no, never!—a gentleman."

My companion's face had blanched as I went on; her round eyes started and her mild mouth gaped. "A gentleman?" she gasped, confounded, stupefied: "a gentleman *he?*"

"You know him, then?"

She visibly tried to hold herself. "But he *is* handsome?"

I saw the way to help her. "Remarkably!"

"And dressed—?"

"In somebody's clothes. They're smart, but they're not his own."

She broke into a breathless affirmative groan. "They're the master's!"

I caught it up. "You *do* know him?"

She faltered but a second. "Quint!" she cried.[17]

"Quint?"

"Peter Quint—his own man, his valet, when he was here!"

"When the master was?"

Gaping still, but meeting me, she pieced it all together. "He never wore his hat, but he did wear—well, there were waistcoats missed! They were both here—last year. Then the master went, and Quint was alone."

I followed, but halting a little. "Alone?"

"Alone with *us*." Then as from a deeper depth, "In charge," she added.

"And what became of him?"

She hung fire so long that I was still more mystified. "He went too," she brought out at last.

"Went where?"

Her expression, at this, became extraordinary. "God knows where! He died."

"Died?" I almost shrieked.

She seemed fairly to square herself, plant herself more firmly to express the wonder of it. "Yes. Mr. Quint's dead."

VI

It took, of course, more than that particular passage to place us together in presence of what we had now to live with as we could, my dreadful liability to impressions of the order so vividly exemplified, and my companion's knowledge henceforth—a knowledge half consternation and half compassion—of that liability. There had been this evening, after the revelation that left me for an hour so prostrate—there had been for either of us no attendance on any service but a little service of tears and vows, of prayers and promises, a climax to the series of mutual challenges and pledges that had straightway ensued on our retreating together to the schoolroom and shutting ourselves up there to have everything out. The result of our having everything out was simply to reduce our situation to the last rigour of its elements. She herself had seen nothing, not the shadow of a shadow, and nobody in the house but the governess was in the governess's plight; yet she accepted without directly impugning my sanity the truth as I gave it to her, and ended by showing me on this ground an awe-stricken tenderness, a deference to my more than questionable privilege, of which the very breath has remained with me as that of the sweetest of human charities.

What was settled between us accordingly that night was that we thought we might bear things together; and I was not even sure that in spite of her exemption it was she who had the best of the burden. I knew at this hour, I think, as well as I knew later, what I was capable of meeting to shelter my pupils; but it took me some time to be wholly sure of what my honest comrade was prepared for to keep terms with so stiff an agreement. I was queer company enough—quite as queer as the company I received; but as I trace over what we went through I see how much common ground we must have found in the one idea that, by good fortune, *could* steady us. It was the idea, the second movement, that led me straight out, as I may say, of the inner chamber of my dread. I could take the air in the court, at least, and there Mrs. Grose could join me. Perfectly can I recall now the particular way strength came to me before we separated for the night. We had gone over and over every feature of what I had seen.

"He was looking for some one else, you say—some one who was not you?"

"He was looking for little Miles." A portentous clearness now possessed me. "*That's* whom he was looking for."

"But how do you know?"

"I know, I know, I know!" My exaltation grew. "And *you* know, my dear!"

She didn't deny this, but I required, I felt, not even so much telling as that. She took it up again in a moment. "What if *he* should see him?"

"Little Miles? That's what he wants!"

She looked immensely scared again. "The child?"

"Heaven forbid! The man. He wants to appear to *them*." That he might was an awful conception, and yet somehow I could keep it at bay; which, moreover, as we lingered there, was what I succeeded in practically proving. I had an absolute certainty that I should see again what I had already seen, but something within me said that by offering myself bravely as the sole subject of such experience, by accepting, by inviting, by surmounting it all, I should serve as an expiatory victim and guard the tranquillity of the rest of the household. The children in especial I should thus fence about and absolutely save. I recall one of the last things I said that night to Mrs. Grose.

"It does strike me that my pupils have never mentioned—!"

She looked at me hard as I musingly pulled up. "His having been here and the time they were with him?"

"The time they were with him, and his name, his presence, his history, in any way. They've never alluded to it."

"Oh the little lady doesn't remember. She never heard or knew."

"The circumstances of his death?" I thought with some intensity. "Perhaps not. But Miles would remember—Miles would know."

"Ah don't try him!" broke from Mrs. Grose.

I returned her the look she had given me. "Don't be afraid." I continued to think. "It *is* rather odd."

"That he has never spoken of him?"

"Never by the least reference. And you tell me they were 'great friends.'"

"Oh it wasn't *him*!" Mrs. Grose with emphasis declared. "It was Quint's own fancy. To play with him, I mean—to spoil him." She paused a moment; then she added: "Quint was much too free."

This gave me, straight from my vision of his face—*such* a face!— a sudden sickness of disgust. "Too free with *my* boy?"

"Too free with every one!"

I forbore for the moment to analyse this description further than by the reflexion that a part of it applied to several of the members of the household, of the half-dozen maids and men who were still of our small colony. But there was everything, for our apprehension, in the lucky fact that no discomfortable legend, no perturbation of scullions, had ever, within any one's memory, attached to the kind old place. It had neither bad name nor ill fame, and Mrs. Grose, most apparently, only desired to cling to me and to quake in silence. I even put her, the very last thing of all, to the test. It was when, at midnight, she had her hand on the schoolroom door to take leave. "I *have* it from you then—for it's of great importance— that he was definitely and admittedly bad?"

"Oh not admittedly. *I* knew it—but the master didn't."

"And you never told him?"

"Well, he didn't like tale-bearing—he hated complaints. He was terribly short with anything of that kind, and if people were all right to *him*—"

"He wouldn't be bothered with more?" This squared well enough with my impression of him: he was not a trouble-loving gentleman, nor so very particular perhaps about some of the company he himself kept. All the same, I pressed my informant. "I promise you *I* would have told!"

She felt my discrimination. "I daresay I was wrong. But really I was afraid."

"Afraid of what?"

"Of things that man could do. Quint was so clever—he was so deep."

I took this in still more than I probably showed. "You weren't afraid of anything else? Not of his effect—?"

"His effect?" she repeated with a face of anguish and waiting while I faltered.

"On innocent little precious lives. They were in your charge."

"No, they weren't in mine!" she roundly and distressfully returned. "The master believed in him and placed him here because he was supposed not to be quite in health and the country air so good for him. So he had everything to say. Yes"—she let me have it—"even about *them*."

"Them—that creature?" I had to smother a kind of howl. "And you could bear it?"

"No. I couldn't—and I can't now!" And the poor woman burst into tears.

A rigid control, from the next day, was, as I have said, to follow them; yet how often and how passionately, for a week, we came back together to the subject! Much as we had discussed it that Sunday night, I was, in the immediate later hours in especial—for it may be imagined whether I slept—still haunted with the shadow of something she had not told me. I myself had kept back nothing, but there was a word Mrs. Grose had kept back. I was sure, moreover, by morning that this was not from a failure of frankness, but because on every side there were fears. It seems to me indeed, in raking it all over, that by the time the morrow's sun was high I had restlessly read into the facts before us almost all the meaning they were to receive from subsequent and more cruel occurrences. What they gave me above all was just the sinister figure of the living man—the dead one would keep a while!—and of the months he had continuously passed at Bly, which, added up, made a formidable stretch. The limit of this evil time had arrived only when, on the dawn of a winter's morning, Peter Quint was found, by a labourer going to early work, stone dead on the road from the village: a catastrophe explained—superficially at least—by a visible wound to his head; such a wound as might have been produced (and as, on the final evidence, *had* been) by a fatal slip, in the dark and after leaving the public-house, on the steepish icy slope, a wrong path altogether, at the bottom of which he lay. The icy slope, the turn mistaken at night and in liquor, accounted for much—practically, in the end and after the inquest and boundless chatter, for everything; but there had been matters in his life, strange passages and perils, secret disorders, vices more than suspected, that would have accounted for a good deal more.

I scarce know how to put my story into words that shall be a credible picture of my state of mind; but I was in these days literally able to find a joy in the extraordinary flight of heroism the occasion demanded of me. I now saw that I had been asked for a service admirable and difficult; and there would be a greatness in letting it be seen—oh in the right quarter!—that I could succeed where many another girl might have failed. It was an immense help to me—I confess I rather applaud myself as I look back!—that I saw my response so strongly and so simply. I was there to protect and defend the little creatures in the world the most bereaved and the most lovable, the appeal of whose helplessness had suddenly become only too explicit, a deep constant ache of one's own engaged affection. We were cut off, really, together; we were united in our danger. They had nothing but me, and I—well, I had *them*. It was in short a magnificent chance. This chance presented itself to me in an image richly material. I was a screen—I was to stand before them. The more I saw the less they would. I began to watch them in a stifled suspense, a disguised tension, that might well, had it continued too long, have turned to something like madness. What saved me, as I now see, was that it turned to another matter altogether. It didn't last as suspense—it was superseded by horrible proofs. Proofs, I say, yes—from the moment I really took hold.

This moment dated from an afternoon hour that I happened to spend in the grounds with the younger of my pupils alone. We had left Miles indoors, on the red cushion of a deep window-seat; he had wished to finish a book, and I had been glad to encourage a purpose so laudable in a young man whose only defect was a certain ingenuity of restlessness. His sister, on the contrary, had been alert to come out, and I strolled with her half an hour, seeking the shade, for the sun was still high and the day exceptionally warm. I was aware afresh with her, as we went, of how, like her brother, she contrived—it was the charming thing in both children—to let me alone without appearing to drop me and to accompany me without appearing to oppress. They were never importunate and yet never listless. My attention to them all really went to seeing them amuse themselves immensely without me: this was a spectacle they seemed actively to prepare and that employed me as an active admirer. I walked in a world of their invention—they had no occasion whatever to draw upon mine; so that my time was taken only with being for them some remarkable person or thing that the game of the moment required and that was merely, thanks to my superior, my exalted stamp, a happy and highly distinguished sinecure. I forget what I was on the present occasion; I only remember that I was something very important and very quiet and that Flora was playing very hard. We were on the edge of the lake, and, as we had lately begun geography, the lake was the Sea of Azof.[18]

Suddenly, amid these elements, I became aware that on the other side of the Sea of Azof we had an interested spectator. The way this knowledge gathered in me was the strangest thing in the world—the strangest, that is, except the very much stranger in which it quickly merged itself. I had sat down with a piece of work—for I was something or other that could sit—on the old stone bench which overlooked the pond; and in this position I began to take in with certitude and yet without direct vision the presence, a good way off, of a third person. The old trees, the thick shrubbery, made a great and pleasant shade, but it was all suffused with the brightness of the hot still hour. There was no ambiguity in anything; none whatever at least in the conviction I from one moment to another found myself forming as to what I should see straight before me and across the lake as a consequence of raising my eyes. They were attached at this juncture to the stitching in which I was engaged, and I can feel once more the spasm of my effort not to move them till I should so have steadied myself as to be able to make up my mind what to do. There was an alien object in view—a figure whose right of presence I instantly and passionately questioned. I recollect counting over perfectly the possibilities, reminding myself that nothing was more natural, for instance, than the appearance of one of the men about the place, or even of a messenger, a postman or a tradesman's boy, from the village. That reminder had as little effect on my practical certitude as I was conscious—still even without looking—of its having upon the character and attitude of our visitor. Nothing was more natural than that these things should be the other things they absolutely were not.

Of the positive identity of the apparition I would assure myself as soon as the small clock of my courage should have ticked out the right second; meanwhile, with an effort that was already sharp enough, I transferred my eyes straight to little Flora, who, at the moment, was about ten yards away. My heart had stood still for an instant with the wonder and terror of the question whether she too would see; and I held my breath while I waited for what a cry from her, what some sudden innocent sign either of interest or of alarm, would tell me. I waited, but nothing came; then in the first place— and there is something more dire in this, I feel, than in anything I have to relate—I was determined by a sense that within a minute all spontaneous sounds from her had dropped; and in the second by the circumstance that also within the minute she had, in her play, turned her back to the water. This was her attitude when I at last looked at her—looked with the confirmed conviction that we were still, together, under direct personal notice. She had picked up a small flat piece of wood which happened to have in it a little hole that had evidently suggested to her the idea of sticking in another fragment that might figure as a mast and make the thing a boat. This second morsel, as I watched her, she was very markedly and intently attempting to tighten in its place. My apprehension of what she was doing sustained me so that after some seconds I felt I was ready for more. Then I again shifted my eyes—I faced what I had to face.

VII

I got hold of Mrs. Grose as soon after this as I could; and I can give no intelligible account of how I fought out the interval. Yet I still hear myself cry as I fairly threw myself into her arms: "They *know*—it's too monstrous: they know, they know!"

"And what on earth—?" I felt her incredulity as she held me.

"Why all that *we* know—and heaven knows what more besides!" Then as she released me I made it out to her, made it out perhaps only now with full coherency even to myself. "Two hours ago, in the garden"—I could scarce articulate—"Flora *saw!*"

Mrs. Grose took it as she might have taken a blow in the stomach. "She has told you?" she panted.

"Not a word—that's the horror. She kept it to herself! The child of eight, *that* child!" Unutterable still for me was the stupefaction of it.

Mrs. Grose of course could only gape the wider. "Then how do you know?"

"I was there—I saw with my eyes: saw she was perfectly aware."

"Do you mean aware of *him*?"

"No—of *her*." I was conscious as I spoke that I looked prodigious things, for I got the slow reflexion of them in my companion's face. "Another person—this time; but a figure of quite as unmistakable horror and evil: a woman in black, pale and dreadful—with such an air also, and such a face!—on the other side of the lake. I was there with the child—quiet for the hour; and in the midst of it she came."

"Came how—from where?"

"From where they come from! She just appeared and stood there—but not so near."

"And without coming nearer?"

"Oh for the effect and the feeling she might have been as close as you!"

My friend, with an odd impulse, fell back a step. "Was she some one you've never seen?"

"Never. But some one the child has. Some one *you* have." Then to show how I had thought it all out: "My predecessor—the one who died."

"Miss Jessel?"[19]

"Miss Jessel. You don't believe me?" I pressed.

She turned right and left in her distress. "How can you be sure?"

This drew from me, in the state of my nerves, a flash of impatience. "Then ask Flora—*she's* sure!" But I had no sooner spoken than I caught myself up. "No, for God's sake, *don't!* She'll say she isn't—she'll lie!"

Mrs. Grose was not too bewildered instinctively to protest. "Ah how *can* you?"

"Because I'm clear. Flora doesn't want me to know."

"It's only, then, to spare you."

"No, no—there are depths, depths! The more I go over it the more I see in it, and the more I see in it the more I fear. I don't know what I *don't* see, what I *don't* fear!"

Mrs. Grose tried to keep up with me. "You mean you're afraid of seeing her again?"

"Oh no; that's nothing—now!" Then I explained. "It's of *not* seeing her."

But my companion only looked wan. "I don't understand."

"Why, it's that the child may keep it up—and that the child assuredly *will*—without my knowing it."

At the image of this possibility Mrs. Grose for a moment collapsed, yet presently to pull herself together again as from the positive force of the sense of what, should we yield an inch, there would really be to give away. "Dear, dear—we must keep our heads! And after all, if she doesn't mind it—!" She even tried a grim joke. "Perhaps she likes it!"

"Like *such* things—a scrap of an infant!"

"Isn't it just a proof of her blest innocence?" my friend bravely inquired.

She brought me, for the instant, almost round. "Oh, we must clutch at *that*—we must cling to it! If it isn't a proof of what you say, it's a proof of—God knows what! For the woman's a horror of horrors."

Mrs. Grose, at this, fixed her eyes a minute on the ground; then at last raising them, "Tell me how you know," she said.

"Then you admit it's what she was?" I cried.

"Tell me how you know," my friend simply repeated.

"Know? By seeing her! By the way she looked."

"At you, do you mean—so wickedly?"

"Dear me, no—I could have borne that. She gave me never a glance. She only fixed the child."

Mrs. Grose tried to see it. "Fixed her?"

"Ah, with such awful eyes!"

She stared at mine as if they might really have resembled them. "Do you mean of dislike?"

"God help us, no. Of something much worse."

"Worse than dislike?"—this left her indeed at a loss.

"With a determination—indescribable. With a kind of fury of intention."

I made her turn pale. "Intention?"

"To get hold of her." Mrs. Grose—her eyes just lingering on mine—gave a shudder and walked to the window; and while she stood there looking out I completed my statement. "*That's* what Flora knows."

After a little she turned round. "The person was in black, you say?"

"In mourning—rather poor, almost shabby. But—yes—with extraordinary beauty." I now recognised to what I had at last, stroke by stroke, brought the victim of my confidence, for she quite visibly weighed this. "Oh handsome—very, very," I insisted; "wonderfully handsome. But infamous."

She slowly came back to me. "Miss Jessel—*was* infamous." She once more took my hand in both her own, holding it as tight as if to fortify me against the increase of alarm I might draw from this disclosure. "They were both infamous," she finally said.

So for a little we faced it once more together; and I found absolutely a degree of help in seeing it now so straight. "I appreciate," I said, "the great decency of your not having hitherto spoken; but the time has certainly come to give me the whole thing." She appeared to assent to this, but still only in silence; seeing which I went on: "I must have it now. Of what did she die? Come, there was something between them."

"There was everything."

"In spite of the difference——?"

"Oh of their rank, their condition"—she brought it woefully out. "*She* was a lady."

"I turned it over; I again saw. "Yes—she was a lady."

"And he so dreadfully below," said Mrs. Grose.

I felt that I doubtless needn't press too hard, in such company, on the place of a servant in the scale; but there was nothing to prevent an acceptance of my companion's own measure of my predecessor's abasement. There was a way to deal with that, and I dealt; the more readily for my full vision—on the evidence—of our employer's late clever good-looking "own" man; impudent, assured, spoiled, depraved. "The fellow was a hound."

Mrs. Grose considered as if it were perhaps a little a case for a sense of shades. "I've never seen one like him. He did what he wished."

"With *her*?"

"With them all."

It was as if now in my friend's own eyes Miss Jessel had again appeared. I seemed at any rate for an instant to trace their evocation of her as distinctly as I had seen her by the pond; and I brought out with decision: "It must have been also what *she* wished!"

Mrs. Grose's face signified that it had been indeed, but she said at the same time: "Poor woman—she paid for it!"

"Then you do know what she died of?" I asked.

"No—I know nothing. I wanted not to know; I was glad enough I didn't; and I thanked heaven she was well out of this!"

"Yet you had, then, your idea—"

"Of her real reason for leaving? Oh yes—as to that. She couldn't have stayed. Fancy it here—for a governess! And afterwards I imagined—and I still imagine. And what I imagine is dreadful."

"Not so dreadful as what *I* do," I replied; on which I must have shown her—as I was indeed but too conscious—a front of miserable defeat. It brought out again all her compassion for me, and at the renewed touch of her kindness my power to resist broke down. I burst, as I had the other time made her burst, into tears; she took me to her motherly breast, where my lamentation overflowed. "I don't do it!" I sobbed in despair; "I don't save or shield them! It's far worse than I dreamed. They're lost!"

VIII

What I had said to Mrs. Grose was true enough: there were in the matter I had put before her depths and possibilities that I lacked resolution to sound; so that when we met once more in the wonder of it we were of a common mind about the duty of resistance to extravagant fancies. We were to keep our heads if we should keep nothing else—difficult indeed as that might be in the face of all that, in our prodigious experience, seemed least to be questioned. Late that night, while the house slept, we had another talk in my room; when she went all the way with me as to its being beyond doubt that I had seen exactly what I had seen. I found that to keep her thoroughly in the grip of this I had only to ask her how, if I had "made it up," I came to be able to give, of each of the persons appearing to me, a picture disclosing, to the last detail, their special marks—a portrait on the exhibition of which she had instantly recognised and named them. She wished, of course—small blame to her!—to sink the whole subject; and I was quick to assure her that my own interest in it had now violently taken the form of a search for the way to escape from it. I closed with her cordially on the article of the likelihood that with recurrence—for recurrence we took for granted—I should get used to my danger; distinctly professing that my personal exposure had suddenly become the least of my discomforts. It was my new suspicion that was intolerable; and yet even to this complication the later hours of the day had brought a little ease.

On leaving her, after my first outbreak, I had of course returned to my pupils, associating the right remedy for my dismay with that sense of their charm which I had already recognised as a resource I could positively cultivate and which had never failed me yet. I had simply, in other words, plunged afresh into Flora's special society and there become aware—it was almost a luxury!—that she could put her little conscious hand straight upon the spot that ached. She had looked at me in sweet speculation and then had accused me to my face of having "cried." I had supposed the ugly signs of it brushed away; but I could literally—for the time at all event—rejoice, under this fathomless charity, that they had not entirely disappeared. To gaze into the depths of blue of the child's eyes and pronounce their loveliness a trick of premature cunning was to be guilty of a cynicism in preference to which I naturally preferred to abjure my judgement and, so far as might be, my agitation. I couldn't abjure for merely wanting to, but I could repeat to Mrs. Grose—as I did there, over and over, in the small hours—that with our small friends' voices in the air, their pressure on one's heart and their fragrant faces against one's cheek, everything fell to the ground but their incapacity and their beauty. It was a pity that, somehow, to settle this once for all, I had equally to re-enumerate the signs of subtlety that, in the afternoon, by the lake, had made a miracle of my show of self-possession. It was a pity to be obliged to reinvestigate the certitude of the moment itself and repeat how it had come to me as a revelation that the inconceivable communion I then surprised must have been for both parties a matter of habit. It was a pity I should have had to quaver out again the reasons for my not having, in my delusion, so much as questioned that the little girl saw our visitant even as I actually saw Mrs. Grose herself, and that she wanted, by just so much as she did thus see, to make me suppose she didn't, and at the same time, without showing anything, arrive at a guess as to whether I myself did! It was a pity I needed to recapitulate the portentous little activities by which she sought to divert my attention—the perceptible increase of movement, the greater intensity of play, the singing, the gabbling of nonsense and the invitation to romp.

Yet if I had not indulged, to prove there was nothing in it, in this review, I should have missed the two or three dim elements of comfort that still remained to me. I shouldn't, for instance, have been able to asseverate to my friend that I was certain—which was so much to the good—that *I* at least had not betrayed myself. I shouldn't have been prompted, by stress of need, by desperation of mind—I scarce know what to call it—to invoke such further aid to intelligence as might spring from pushing my colleague fairly to the wall. She had told me, bit by bit, under pressure, a great deal; but a small shifty spot on the wrong side of it all still sometimes brushed my brow like the wing of a bat; and I remember how on this occasion—for the sleeping house and the concentration alike of our danger and our watch seemed to help—I felt the importance of giving the last jerk to the curtain. "I don't believe anything so horrible," I recollect saying; "no, let us put it definitely, my dear, that I don't. But if I did, you know, there's a thing I should require now, just without sparing you the least bit more—oh not a scrap, come!—to get out of you. What was it you had in mind when, in our distress, before Miles came back, over the letter from his school, you said, under my insistence, that you didn't pretend for him he hadn't literally *ever* been 'bad'? He has *not*, truly, 'ever,' in these weeks that I myself have lived with him and so closely watched him; he has been an imperturbable little prodigy of delightful lovable goodness. Therefore you might perfectly have made the claim for him if you had not, as it happened, seen an exception to take. What was your exception, and to what passage in your personal observation of him did you refer?"

It was a straight question enough, but levity was not our note, and in any case I had before the grey dawn admonished us to separate got my answer. What my friend had had in mind proved immensely to the purpose. It was neither more nor less than the particular fact that for a period of several months Quint and the boy had been perpetually together. It was indeed the very appropriate item of evidence of her having ventured to criticise the propriety, to hint at the incongruity, of so close an alliance, and even to go so far on the subject as a frank overture to Miss Jessel would take her. Miss Jessel had, with a very high manner about it, requested her to mind her business, and the good woman had on this directly approached little Miles. What she had said to him, since I pressed, was that *she* liked to see young gentlemen not forget their station.

I pressed again, of course, the closer for that. "You reminded him that Quint was only a base menial?"

"As you might say! And it was his answer, for one thing, that was bad."

"And for another thing?" I waited. "He repeated your words to Quint?"

"No, not that, It's just what he *wouldn't*!" she could still impress on me. "I was sure, at any rate," she added, "that he didn't. But he denied certain occasions."

"What occasions?"

"When they had been about together quite as if Quint were his tutor—and a very grand one—and Miss Jessel only for the little lady. When he had gone off with the fellow, I mean, and spent hours with him."

"He then prevaricated about it—he said he hadn't?" Her assent was clear enough to cause me to add in a moment: "I see. He lied."

"Oh!" Mrs. Grose mumbled. This was a suggestion that it didn't matter; which indeed she backed up by a further remark. "You see, after all, Miss Jessel didn't mind. She didn't forbid him."

I considered. "Did he put that to you as a justification?"

At this she dropped again. "No, he never spoke of it."

"Never mentioned her in connexion with Quint?"

She saw, visibly flushing, where I was coming out. "Well, he didn't show anything. He denied," she repeated; "he denied."

Lord, how I pressed her now! "So that you could see he knew what was between the two wretches?"

"I don't know—I don't know!" the poor woman wailed.

"You do know, you dear thing," I replied; "only you haven't my dreadful boldness of mind, and you keep back, out of timidity and modesty and delicacy, even the impression that in the past, when you had, without my aid, to flounder about in silence, most of all made you miserable. But I shall get it out of you yet! There was something in the boy that suggested to you," I continued, "his covering and concealing their relation."

"Oh he couldn't prevent—"

"Your learning the truth? I daresay! But, heavens," I fell, with vehemence, a-thinking, "what it shows that they must, to that extent, have succeeded in making of him!"

"Ah nothing that's not nice *now*!" Mrs. Grose lugubriously pleaded.

"I don't wonder you looked queer," I persisted, "when I mentioned to you the letter from his school!"

"I doubt if I looked as queer as you!" she retorted with homely force. "And if he was so bad then as that comes to, how is he such an angel now?"

"Yes indeed—and if he was a fiend at school! How, how, how? Well," I said in my torment, "you must put it to me again, though I shall not be able to tell you for some days. Only put it to me again!" I cried in a way that made my friend stare. "There are directions in which I mustn't for the present let myself go." Meanwhile I returned to her first example—the one to which she had just previously referred—of the boy's happy capacity for an occasional slip. "If Quint—on your remonstrance at the time you speak of—was a base menial, one of the things Miles said to you, I find myself guessing, was that you were another." Again her admission was so adequate that I continued: "And you forgave him that?"

"Wouldn't *you*?"

"Oh yes!" And we exchanged there, in the stillness, a sound of the oddest amusement. Then I went on: "At all events, while he was with the man—"

"Miss Flora was with the woman. It suited them all!"

It suited me too, I felt, only too well; by which I mean that it suited exactly the particular deadly view I was in the very act of forbidding myself to entertain. But I so far succeeded in checking the expression of this view that I will throw, just here, no further light on it than may be offered by the mention of my final observation to Mrs. Grose. "His having lied and been impudent are, I confess, less engaging specimens than I had hoped to have from you of the outbreak in him of the little natural man.[20] Still," I mused, "they must do, for they make me feel more than ever that I must watch."

It made me blush, the next minute, to see in my friend's face how much more unreservedly she had forgiven him than her anecdote struck me as pointing out to my own tenderness any way to do. This was marked when, at the schoolroom door, she quitted me. "Surely you don't accuse *him*—"

"Of carrying on an intercourse that he conceals from me? Ah remember that, until further evidence, I now accuse nobody." Then before shutting her out to go by another passage to her own place, "I must just wait," I wound up.

IX

I waited and waited, and the days took as they elapsed something from my consternation. A very few of them, in fact, passing, in constant sight of my pupils, without a fresh incident, sufficed to give to grievous fancies and even to odious memories a kind of brush of the sponge. I have spoken of the surrender to their extraordinary childish grace as a thing I could actively promote in myself, and it may be imagined if I neglected now to apply at this source for whatever balm it would yield. Stranger than I can express, certainly, was the effort to struggle against my new lights. It would doubtless have been a greater tension still, however, had it not been so frequently successful. I used to wonder how my little charges could help guessing that I thought strange things about them; and the circumstance that these things only made them more interesting was not by itself a direct aid to keeping them in the dark. I trembled lest they should see that they *were* so immensely more interesting. Putting things at the worst, at all events, as in meditation I so often did, any clouding of their innocence could only be—blameless and foredoomed as they were—a reason the more for taking risks. There were moments when I knew myself to catch them up by an irresistible impulse and press them to my heart. As soon as I had done so I used to wonder—"What will they think of that? Doesn't it betray too much?" It would have been easy to get into a sad wild tangle about how much I might betray; but the real account, I feel, of the hours of peace I could still enjoy was that the immediate charm of my companions was a beguilement still effective even under the shadow of the possibility that it was studied. For if it occurred to me that I might occasionally excite suspicion by the little outbreaks of my sharper passion for them, so too I remember asking if I mightn't see a queerness in the traceable increase of their own demonstrations.

They were at this period extravagantly and preternaturally fond of me; which, after all, I could reflect, was no more than a graceful response in children perpetually bowed down over and hugged. The homage of which they were so lavish succeeded in truth for my nerves quite as well as if I never appeared to myself, as I may say, literally to catch them at a purpose in it. They had never, I think, wanted to do so many things for their poor protectress; I mean—though they got their lessons better and better, which was naturally what would please her most—in the way of diverting, entertaining, surprising her; reading her passages, telling her stories, acting her charades, pouncing out at her, in disguises, as animals and historical characters, and above all astonishing her by the "pieces" they had secretly got by heart and could interminably recite. I should never get to the bottom—were I to let myself go even now—of the prodigious private commentary, all under still more private correction, with which I in these days overscored their full hours. They had shown me from the first a facility for everything, a general faculty which, taking a fresh start, achieved remarkable flights. They got their little tasks as if they loved them; they indulged, from the mere exuberance of the gift, in the most unimposed little miracles of memory. They not only popped out at me as tigers and as Romans, but as Shakespeareans, astronomers and navigators. This was so singularly the case that it had presumably much to do with the fact as to which, at the present day, I am at a loss for a different explanation: I allude to my unnatural composure on the subject of another school for Miles. What I remember is that I was content for the time not to open the question, and that contentment must have sprung from the sense of his perpetually striking show of cleverness. He was too clever for a bad governess, for a parson's daughter, to spoil; and the strangest if not the brightest thread in the pensive embroidery I just spoke of was the impression I might have got, if I had dared to work it out, that he was under some influence operating in his small intellectual life as a tremendous incitement.

If it was easy to reflect, however, that such a boy could postpone school, it was at least as marked that for such a boy to have been "kicked out" by a school-master was a mystification without end. Let me add that in their company now—and I was careful almost never to be out of it—I could follow no scent very far. We lived in a cloud of music and affection and success and private theatricals. The musical sense in each of the children was of the quickest, but the elder in especial had a marvellous knack of catching and repeating. The schoolroom piano broke into all gruesome fancies; and when that failed there were confabulations in corners, with a sequel of one of them going out in the highest spirits in order to "come in" as something new. I had had brothers myself, and it was no revelation to me that little girls could be slavish idolaters of little boys. What surpassed everything was that there was a little boy in the world who could have for the inferior age, sex and intelligence so fine a consideration. They were extraordinarily at one, and to say that they never either quarrelled or complained is to make the note of praise coarse for their quality of sweetness. Sometimes perhaps indeed (when I dropped into coarseness) I came across traces of little understandings between them by which one of them should keep me occupied while the other slipped away. There is a naïf side, I suppose, in all diplomacy; but if my pupils practised upon me it was surely with the minimum of grossness. It was all in the other quarter that, after a lull, the grossness broke out.

I find that I really hang back; but I must take my horrid plunge. In going on with the record of what was hideous at Bly I not only challenge the most liberal faith—for which I little care; but (and this is another matter) I renew what I myself suffered, I again push my dreadful way through it to the end. There came suddenly an hour after which, as I look back, the business seems to me to have been all pure suffering; but I have at least reached the heart of it, and the straightest road out is doubtless to advance. One evening—with nothing to lead up or prepare it—I felt the cold touch of the impression that had breathed on me the night of my arrival and which, much lighter then as I have mentioned, I should probably have made little of in memory had my subsequent sojourn been less agitated. I had not gone to bed; I sat reading by a couple of candles. There was a roomful of old books at Bly—last-century fiction some of it, which, to the extent of a distinctly deprecated renown, but never to so much as that of a stray specimen, had reached the sequestered home and appealed to the unavowed curiosity of my youth. I remember that the book I had in my hand was Fielding's *Amelia*;[21] also that I was wholly awake. I recall further both a general conviction that it was horribly late and a particular objection to looking at my watch. I figure finally that the white curtain draping, in the fashion of those days, the head of Flora's little bed, shrouded, as I had assured myself long before, the perfection of childish rest. I recollect in short that though I was deeply interested in my author I found myself, at the turn of a page and with his spell all scattered, looking straight up from him and hard at the door of my room. There was a moment during which I listened, reminded of the faint sense I had had, the first night, of there being something undefinably astir in the house, and noted the soft breath of the open casement just move the half-drawn blind. Then, with all the marks of a deliberation that must have seemed magnificent had there been any one to admire it, I laid down my book, rose to my feet and, taking a candle, went straight out of the room and, from the passage, on which my light made little impression, noiselessly closed and locked the door.

I can say now neither what determined nor what guided me, but I went straight along the lobby, holding my candle high, till I came within sight of the tall window that presided over the great turn of the staircase. At this point I precipitately found myself aware of three things. They were practically simultaneous, yet they had flashes of succession. My candle, under a bold flourish, went out, and I perceived, by the uncovered window, that the yielding dusk of earliest morning rendered it unnecessary. Without it, the next instant, I knew that there was a figure on the stair. I speak of sequences, but I required no lapse of seconds to stiffen myself for a third encounter with Quint. The apparition had reached the landing half-way up and was therefore on the spot nearest the window, where, at sight of me, it stopped short and fixed me exactly as it had fixed me from the tower and from the garden. He knew me as well as I knew him; and so, in the cold faint twilight, with a glimmer in the high glass and another on the polish of the oak stair below, we faced each other in our common intensity. He was absolutely, on this occasion, a living detestable dangerous presence. But that was not the wonder of wonders; I reserve this distinction for quite another circumstance: the circumstance that dread had unmistakably quitted me and that there was nothing in me unable to meet and measure him.

I had plenty of anguish after that extraordinary moment, but I had, thank God, no terror. And he knew I hadn't—I felt myself at the end of an instant magnificently aware of this. I felt, in a fierce rigour of confidence, that if I stood my ground a minute I should cease—for the time at least—to have him to reckon with: and during the minute, accordingly, the thing was as human and hideous as a real interview: hideous just because it *was* human, as human as to have met alone, in the small hours, in a sleeping house, some enemy, some adventurer, some criminal. It was the dead silence of our long gaze at such close quarters that gave the whole horror, huge as it was, its only note of the unnatural. If I had met a murderer in such a place and at such an hour we still at least would have spoken. Something would have passed, in life, between us; if nothing had passed one of us would have moved. The moment was so prolonged that it would have taken but little more to make me doubt if even *I* were in life. I can't express what followed it save by saying that the silence itself—which was indeed in a manner an attestation of my strength—became the element into which I saw the figure disappear; in which I definitely saw it turn, as I might have seen the low wretch to which it had once belonged turn on receipt of an order, and pass, with my eyes on the villainous back that no hunch would have more disfigured, straight down the staircase and into the darkness in which the next bend was lost.

X

I remained a while at the top of the stair, but with the effect presently of understanding that when my visitor had gone, he had gone; then I returned to my room. The foremost thing I saw there by the light of the candle I had left burning was that Flora's little bed was empty; and on this I caught my breath with all the terror that, five minutes before, I had been able to resist. I dashed at the place in which I had left her lying and over which—for the small silk counterpane and the sheets were disarranged—the white curtains had been deceivingly pulled forward; then my step, to my unutterable relief, produced an answering sound: I noticed an agitation of the window-blind, and the child, ducking down, emerged rosily from the other side of it. She stood there in so much of her candour and so little of her nightgown, with her pink bare feet and the golden glow of her curls. She looked intensely grave, and I had never had such a sense of losing an advantage acquired (the thrill of which had just been so prodigious) as on my consciousness that she addressed me with a reproach—"You naughty: where *have* you been?" Instead of challenging her own irregularity I found myself arraigned and explaining. She herself explained, for that matter, with the loveliest eagerest simplicity. She had known suddenly as she lay there, that I was out of the room, and had jumped up to see what had become of me. I had dropped, with the joy of her reappearance, back into my chair—feeling then, and then only, a little faint; and she had pattered straight over to me, thrown herself upon my knee, given herself to be held with the flame of the candle full in the wonderful little face that was still flushed with sleep. I remember closing my eyes an instant, yielding, consciously, as before the excess of something beautiful that shone out of the blue of her own. "You were looking for me out of the window?" I said. "You thought I might be walking in the grounds?"

"Well, you know, I thought some one was"—she never blanched as she smiled out that at me.

Oh how I looked at her now! "And did you see any one?"

"Ah *no*!" she returned almost (with the full privilege of childish inconsequence) resentfully, though with a long sweetness in her little drawl of the negative.

At that moment, in the state of my nerves, I absolutely believed she lied; and if I once more closed my eyes it was before the dazzle of the three or four possible ways in which I might take this up. One of these for a moment tempted me with such singular force that, to resist it, I must have gripped my little girl with a spasm that, wonderfully, she submitted to without a cry or a sign of fright. Why not break out at her on the spot and have it all over?—give it to her straight in her lovely little lighted face? "You see, you see, you *know* that you do and that you already quite suspect I believe it; therefore why not frankly confess it to me, so that we may at least live with it together and learn perhaps, in the strangeness of our fate, where we are and what it means?" This solicitation dropped, alas, as it came: if I could immediately have succumbed to it I might have spared myself—well, you'll see what. Instead of succumbing I sprang again to my feet, looked at her bed and took a helpless middle way. "Why did you pull the curtain over the place to make me think you were still there?"

Flora luminously considered; after which, with her little divine smile: "Because I don't like to frighten you!"

"But if I had, by your idea, gone out—?"

She absolutely declined to be puzzled; she turned her eyes to the flame of the candle as if the question were as irrelevant, or at any rate as impersonal, as Mrs. Marcet[22] or nine-times-nine. "Oh but you know," she quite adequately answered, "that you might come back, you dear, and that you *have*!" And after a little, when she had got into bed, I had, a long time, by almost sitting on her for the retention of her hand, to show how I recognised the pertinence of my return.

You may imagine the general complexion, from that moment, of my nights. I repeatedly sat up till I didn't know when; I selected moments when my room-mate unmistakably slept, and, stealing out, took noiseless turns in the passage. I even pushed as far as to where I had last met Quint. But I never met him there again, and I may as well say at once that I on no other occasion saw him in the house. I just missed, on the staircase, nevertheless, a different adventure. Looking down it from the top I once recognised the presence of a woman seated on one of the lower steps with her back presented to me, her body half-bowed and her head, in an attitude of woe, in her hands. I had been there but an instant, however, when she vanished without looking round at me. I knew, for all that, exactly what dreadful face she had to show; and I wondered whether, if instead of being above I had been below, I should have had the same nerve for going up that I had lately shown Quint. Well, there continued to be plenty of call for nerve. On the eleventh night after my latest encounter with that gentleman—they were all numbered now—I had an alarm that perilously skirted it and that indeed, from the particular quality of its unexpectedness, proved quite my sharpest shock. It was precisely the first night during this series that, weary with vigils, I had conceived I might again without laxity lay myself down at my old hour. I slept immediately and, as I afterwards knew, till about one o'clock; but when I woke it was to sit straight up, as completely roused as if a hand had shaken me. I had left a light burning, but it was now out, and I felt an instant certainty that Flora had extinguished it. This brought me to my feet and straight, in the darkness, to her bed, which I found she had left. A glance at the window enlightened me further, and the striking of a match completed the picture.

The child had again got up—this time blowing out the taper, and had again, for some purpose of observation or response, squeezed in behind the blind and was peering out into the night. That she now saw—as she had not, I had satisfied myself, the previous time—was proved to me by the fact that she was disturbed neither by my re-illumination nor by the haste I made to get into slippers and into a wrap. Hidden, protected, absorbed, she evidently rested on the sill—the casement opened forward—and gave herself up. There was a great still moon to help her, and this fact had counted in my quick decision. She was face to face with the apparition we had met at the lake, and could now communicate with it as she had not then been able to do. What I, on my side, had to care for was, without disturbing her, to reach, from the corridor, some other window turned to the same quarter. I got to the door without her hearing me; I got out of it, closed it and listened, from the other side, for some sound from her. While I stood in the passage I had my eyes on her brother's door, which was but ten steps off and which, indescribably, produced in me a renewal of the strange impulse that I lately spoke of as my temptation. What if I should go straight in and march to *his* window?—what if, by risking to his boyish bewilderment a revelation of my motive, I should throw across the rest of the mystery the long halter of my boldness?

This thought held me sufficiently to make me cross to his threshold and pause again. I preternaturally listened; I figured to myself what might portentously be; I wondered if his bed were also empty and he also secretly at watch. It was a deep soundless minute, at the end of which my impulse failed. He was quiet; he might be innocent; the risk was hideous; I turned away. There was a figure in the grounds—a figure prowling for a sight, the visitor with whom Flora was engaged; but it wasn't the visitor most concerned with my boy. I hesitated afresh, but on other grounds and only a few seconds; then I had made my choice. There were empty rooms enough at Bly, and it was only a question of choosing the right one. The right one suddenly presented itself to me as the lower one—though high above the gardens—in the solid corner of the house that I have spoken of as the old tower. This was a large square chamber, arranged with some state as a bedroom, the extravagant size of which made it so inconvenient that it had not for years, though kept by Mrs. Grose in exemplary order, been occupied. I had often admired it and I knew my way about in it; I had only, after just faltering at the first chill gloom of its disuse, to pass across it and unbolt in all quietness one of the shutters. Achieving this transit I uncovered the glass without a sound and, applying my face to the pane, was able, in the darkness without being much less than within, to see that I commanded the right direction. Then I saw something more. The moon made the night extraordinarily penetrable and showed me on the lawn a person, diminished by distance, who stood there motionless and as if fascinated, looking up to where I had appeared—looking, that is, not so much straight at me as at something that was apparently above me. There was clearly another person above me—there was a person on the tower; but the presence on the lawn was not in the least what I had conceived and had confidently hurried to meet. The presence on the lawn—I felt sick as I made it out—was poor little Miles himself.

XI

It was not till late next day that I spoke to Mrs. Grose; the rigour with which I kept my pupils in sight making it often difficult to meet her privately: the more as we each felt the importance of not provoking—on the part of the servants quite as much as on that of the children—any suspicion of a secret flurry or of a discussion of mysteries. I drew a great security in this particular from her mere smooth aspect. There was nothing in her fresh face to pass on to others the least of my horrible confidences. She believed me, I was sure, absolutely: if she hadn't I don't know what would have become of me, for I couldn't have borne the strain alone. But she was a magnificent monument to the blessing of a want of imagination, and if she could see in our little charges nothing but their beauty and amiability, their happiness and cleverness, she had no direct communication with the sources of my trouble. If they had been at all visibly blighted or battered she would doubtless have grown, on tracing it back, haggard enough to match them; as matters stood, however, I could feel her, when she surveyed them with her large white arms folded and the habit of serenity in all her look, thank the Lord's mercy that if they were ruined the pieces would still serve. Flights of fancy gave place, in her mind, to a steady fireside glow, and I had already begun to perceive how, with the development of the conviction that—as time went on without a public accident—our young things could, after all, look out for themselves, she addressed her greatest solicitude to the sad case presented by the deputy-guardian. That, for myself, was a sound simplification: I could engage that, to the world, my face should tell no tales, but it would have been, in the conditions, an immense added worry to find myself anxious about hers.

At the hour I now speak of she had joined me, under pressure, on the terrace, where, with the lapse of the season, the afternoon sun was now agreeable; and we sat there together while before us and at a distance, yet within call if we wished, the children strolled to and fro in one of their most manageable moods. They moved slowly, in unison, below us, over the lawn, the boy, as they went, reading aloud from a story-book and passing his arm round his sister to keep her quite in touch. Mrs. Grose watched them with positive placidity; then I caught the suppressed intellectual creak with which she conscientiously turned to take from me a view of the back of the tapestry. I had made her a receptacle of lurid things, but there was an odd recognition of my superiority—my accomplishments and my function—in her patience under my pain. She offered her mind to my disclosures as, had I wished to mix a witch's broth and proposed it with assurance, she would have held out a large clean saucepan. This had become thoroughly her attitude by the time that, in my recital of the events of the night, I reached the point of what Miles had said to me when, after seeing him, at such a monstrous hour, almost on the very spot where he happened now to be, I had gone down to bring him in; choosing then, at the window, with a concentrated need of not alarming the house, rather that method than any noisier process. I had left her meanwhile in little doubt of my small hope of representing with success even to her actual sympathy my sense of the real splendour of the little inspiration with which, after I had got him into the house, the boy met my final articulate challenge. As soon as I appeared in the moonlight on the terrace he had come to me as straight as possible; on which I had taken his hand without a word and led him, through the dark spaces, up the staircase where Quint had so hungrily hovered for him, along the lobby where I had listened and trembled, and so to his forsaken room.

Not a sound, on the way, had passed between us, and I had wondered—oh *how* I had wondered!—if he were groping about in his dreadful little mind for something plausible and not too grotesque. It would tax his invention certainly, and I felt, this time, over his real embarrassment, a curious thrill of triumph. It was a sharp trap for any game hitherto successful. He could play no longer at perfect propriety, nor could he pretend to it; so how the deuce would he get out of the scrape? There beat in me indeed, with the passionate throb of this question, an equal dumb appeal as to how the deuce *I* should. I was confronted at last, as never yet, with all the risk attached even now to sounding my own horrid note. I remember in fact that as we pushed into his little chamber, where the bed had not been slept in at all and the window, uncovered to the moonlight, made the place so clear that there was no need of striking a match—I remember how I suddenly dropped, sank upon the edge of the bed from the force of the idea that he must know how he really, as they say, "had" me. He could do what he liked, with all his cleverness to help him, so long as I should continue to defer to the old tradition of the criminality of those caretakers of the young who minister to superstitions and fears. He "had" me indeed, and in a cleft stick; for who would ever absolve me, who would consent that I should go unhung, if, by the faintest tremor of an overture, I were the first to introduce into our perfect intercourse an element so dire? No, no: it was useless to attempt to convey to Mrs. Grose, just as it is scarcely less so to attempt to suggest here, how, during our short stiff brush there in the dark, he fairly shook me with admiration. I was of course thoroughly kind and merciful; never, never yet had I placed on his small shoulders hands of such tenderness as those with which, while I rested against the bed, I held him there well under fire. I had no alternative but, in form at least, to put it to him.

"You must tell me now—and all the truth. What did you go out for? What were you doing there?"

I can still see his wonderful smile, the whites of his beautiful eyes and the uncovering of his clear teeth, shine to me in the dusk. "If I tell you why, will you understand?" My heart, at this, leaped into my mouth. *Would* he tell me why? I found no sound on my lips to press it, and I was aware of answering only with a vague repeated grimacing nod. He was gentleness itself, and while I wagged my head at him he stood there more than ever a little fairy prince. It was his brightness indeed that gave me a respite. Would it be so great if he were really going to tell me? "Well," he said at last, "just exactly in order that you should do this."

"Do what?"

"Think me—for a change—*bad*!" I shall never forget the sweetness and gaiety with which he brought out the word, nor how, on top of it, he bent forward and kissed me. It was practically the end of everything. I met his kiss and I had to make, while I folded him for a minute in my arms, the most stupendous effort not to cry. He had given exactly the account of himself that permitted least my going behind it, and it was only with the effect of confirming my acceptance of it that, as I presently glanced about the room, I could say:

"Then you didn't undress at all?"

He fairly glittered in the gloom. "Not at all. I sat up and read."

"And when did you go down?"

"At midnight. When I'm bad I *am* bad!"

"I see, I see—it's charming. But how could you be sure I should know it?"

"Oh I arranged that with Flora." His answers rang out with a readiness! "She was to get up and look out."

"Which is what she did do." It was I who fell into the trap!

"So she disturbed you, and, to see what she was looking at, you also looked—you saw."

"While you," I concurred, "caught your death in the night air!"

He literally bloomed so from this exploit that he could afford radiantly to assent. "How otherwise should I have been bad enough?" he asked. Then, after another embrace, the incident and our interview closed on my recognition of all the reserves of goodness that, for his joke, he had been able to draw upon.

XII

The particular impression I had received proved in the morning light, I repeat, not quite successfully presentable to Mrs. Grose, though I re-enforced it with the mention of still another remark that he had made before we separated. "It all lies in half-a-dozen words," I said to her, "words that really settle the matter. 'Think, you know, what I *might* do!' He threw that off to show me how good he is. He knows down to the ground what he 'might do.' That's what he gave them a taste of at school."

"Lord, you do change!" cried my friend.

"I don't change—I simply make it out. The four, depend upon it, perpetually meet. If on either of these last nights you had been with either child you'd clearly have understood. The more I've watched and waited the more I've felt that if there were nothing else to make it sure it would be made so by the systematic silence of each. *Never,* by a slip of the tongue, have they so much as alluded to either of their old friends, any more than Miles has alluded to his expulsion. Oh yes, we may sit here and look at them, and they may show off to us there to their fill; but even while they pretend to be lost in their fairy-tale they're steeped in the vision of the dead restored to them. He's not reading to her," I declared; "they're talking of *them*— they're talking horrors! I go on, I know, as if I were crazy; and it's a wonder I'm not. What I've seen would have made *you* so; but it has only made me more lucid, made me get hold of still other things."

My lucidity must have seemed awful, but the charming creatures who were victims of it, passing and repassing in their interlocked sweetness, gave my colleague something to hold on by; and I felt how tight she held as, without stirring in the breath of my passion, she covered them still with her eyes. "Of what other things have you got hold?"

"Why, of the very things that have delighted, fascinated and yet, at bottom, as I now so strangely see, mystified and troubled me. Their more than earthly beauty, their absolutely unnatural goodness. It's a game," I went on; "it's a policy and a fraud!"

"On the part of little darlings—?"

"As yet mere lovely babies? Yes, mad as that seems!" The very act of bringing it out really helped me to trace it—follow it all up and piece it all together. "They haven't been good—they've only been absent. It has been easy to live with them because they're simply leading a life of their own. They're not mine—they're not ours. They're his and they're hers!"

"Quint's and that woman's?"

"Quint's and that woman's. They want to get to them."

Oh how, at this, poor Mrs. Grose appeared to study them! "But for what?"

"For the love of all the evil that, in those dreadful days, the pair put into them. And to ply them with that evil still, to keep up the work of demons, is what brings the others back."

"Laws!" said my friend under her breath. The exclamation was homely, but it revealed a real acceptance of my further proof of what, in the bad time—for there had been a worse even than this!—must have occurred. There could have been no such justification for me as the plain assent of her experience to whatever depth of depravity I found credible in our brace of scoundrels. It was in obvious submission of memory that she brought out after a moment: "They *were* rascals! But what can they now do?" she pursued.

"Do?" I echoed so loud that Miles and Flora, as they passed at their distance, paused an instant in their walk and looked at us. "Don't they do enough?" I demanded in a lower tone, while the children, having smiled and nodded and kissed hands to us, resumed their exhibition. We were held by it a minute; then I answered: "They can destroy them!" At this my companion did turn, but the appeal she launched was a silent one, the effect of which was to make me more explicit. "They don't know as yet quite how—but they're trying hard. They're seen only across, as it were, and beyond—in strange places and on high places, the top of towers, the roof of houses, the outside of windows, the further edge of pools; but there's a deep design, on either side, to shorten the distance and overcome the obstacle: so the success of the tempters is only a question of time. They've only to keep to their suggestions of danger."

"For the children to come?"

"And perish in the attempt!" Mrs. Grose slowly got up, and I scrupulously added: "Unless, of course, we can prevent!"

Standing there before me while I kept my seat she visibly turned things over. "Their uncle must do the preventing. He must take them away."

"And who's to make him?"

She had been scanning the distance, but she now dropped on me a foolish face. "You, Miss."

"By writing to him that his house is poisoned and his little nephew and niece mad?"

"But if they *are*, Miss?"

"And if I am myself, you mean? That's charming news to be sent him by a person enjoying his confidence and whose prime undertaking was to give him no worry."

Mrs. Grose considered, following the children again. "Yes, he do hate worry. That was the great reason—"

"Why those fiends took him in so long? No doubt, though his indifference must have been awful. As I'm not a fiend, at any rate, I shouldn't take him in."

My companion, after an instant and for all answer, sat down again and grasped my arm. "Make him at any rate come to you."

I stared. "To *me*?" I had a sudden fear of what she might do. "'Him'?"

"He ought to *be* here—he ought to help."

I quickly rose and I think I must have shown her a queerer face than ever yet. "You see me asking him for a visit?" No, with her eyes on my face she evidently couldn't. Instead of it even—as a woman reads another—she could see what I myself saw: his derision, his amusement, his contempt for the breakdown of my resignation at being left alone and for the fine machinery I had set in motion to attract his attention to my slighted charms. She didn't know—no one knew—how proud I had been to serve him and to stick to our terms; yet she none the less took the measure, I think, of the warning I now gave her. "If you should so lose your head as to appeal to him for me—"

She was really frightened. "Yes, Miss?"

"I would leave, on the spot, both him and you."

XIII

It was all very well to join them, but speaking to them proved quite as much as ever an effort beyond my strength—offered, in close quarters, difficulties as insurmountable as before. This situation continued a month, and with new aggravations and particular notes, the note above all, sharper and sharper, of the small ironic consciousness on the part of my pupils. It was not, I am as sure to-day as I was sure then, my mere infernal imagination: it was absolutely traceable that they were aware of my predicament and that this strange relation made, in a manner, for a long time, the air in which we moved. I don't mean that they had their tongues in their cheeks or did anything vulgar, for that was not one of their dangers: I do mean, on the other hand, that the element of the unnamed and untouched became, between us, greater than any other, and that so much avoidance couldn't have been made successful without a great deal of tacit arrangement. It was as if, at moments, we were perpetually coming into sight of subjects before which we must stop short, turning suddenly out of alleys that we perceived to be blind, closing with a little bang that made us look at each other— for, like all bangs, it was something louder than we had intended— the doors we had indiscreetly opened. All roads lead to Rome, and there were times when it might have struck us that almost every branch of study or subject of conversation skirted forbidden ground. Forbidden ground was the question of the return of the dead in general and of whatever, in especial, might survive, for memory, of the friends little children had lost. There were days when I could have sworn that one of them had, with a small invisible nudge, said to the other: "She thinks she'll do it this time—but she *won't!*" To "do it" would have been to indulge, for instance— and for once in a way—in some direct reference to the lady who had prepared them for my discipline. They had a delightful endless appetite for passages in my own history to which I had again and again treated them; they were in possession of everything that had ever happened to me, had had, with every circumstance the story of my smallest adventures and of those of my brothers and sisters and of the cat and the dog at home, as well as many particulars of the whimsical bent of my father, of the furniture and arrangement of our house and of the conversation of the old women of our village. There were things enough, taking one with another, to chatter about, if one went very fast and knew by instinct when to go round. They pulled with an art of their own the strings of my invention and my memory; and nothing else perhaps, when I thought of such occasions afterwards, gave me so the suspicion of being watched from under cover. It was in any case over *my* life, *my* past and *my* friends alone that we could take anything like our ease; a state of affairs that led them sometimes without the least pertinence to break out into sociable reminders. I was invited—with no visible connexion—to repeat afresh Goody Gosling's celebrated *mot*[23] or to confirm the details already supplied as to the cleverness of the vicarage pony.

It was partly at such junctures as these and partly at quite differ-ent ones that, with the turn my matters had now taken, my pre-dicament, as I have called it, grew most sensible. The fact that the days passed for me without another encounter ought, it would have appeared, to have done something toward soothing my nerves. Since the light brush, that second night on the upper landing, of the presence of a woman at the foot of the stair, I had seen nothing, whether in or out of the house, that one had better not have seen. There was many a corner round which I expected to come upon Quint, and many a situation that, in a merely sinister way, would have favoured the appearance of Miss Jessel. The summer had turned, the summer had gone; the autumn had dropped upon Bly and had blown out half our lights. The place, with its grey sky and withered garlands, its bared spaces and scattered dead leaves, was like a theatre after the performance—all strewn with crumpled playbills. There were exactly states of the air, conditions of sound and of stillness, unspeakable impressions of the *kind* of ministering moment, that brought back to me, long enough to catch it, the feeling of the medium in which, that June evening out of doors, I had had my first sight of Quint, and in which too, at those other instants, I had, after seeing him through the window, looked for him in vain in the circle of shrubbery. I recognised the signs, the portents—I recognised the moment, the spot. But they remained unaccompanied and empty, and I continued unmolested; if unmolested one could call a young woman whose sensibility had, in the most extraordinary fashion, not declined but deepened. I had said in my talk with Mrs. Grose on that horrid scene of Flora's by the lake—and had perplexed her by so saying—that it would from that moment distress me much more to lose my power than to keep it. I had then expressed what was vividly in my mind: the truth that, whether the children really saw or not—since, that is, it was not yet definitely proved—I greatly preferred, as a safeguard, the fulness of my own exposure. I was ready to know the very worst that was to be known. What I had then had an ugly glimpse of was that my eyes might be sealed just while theirs were most opened. Well, my eyes *were* sealed, it appeared, at present—a consummation for which it seemed blasphemous not to thank God. There was, alas, a difficulty about that: I would have thanked him with all my soul had I not had in a proportionate measure this conviction of the secret of my pupils.

How can I retrace to-day the strange steps of my obsession? There were times of our being together when I would have been ready to swear that, literally, in my presence, but with my direct sense of it closed, they had visitors who were known and were welcome. Then it was that, had I not been deterred by the very chance that such an injury might prove greater than the injury to be averted, my exaltation would have broken out. "They're here, they're here, you little wretches," I would have cried, "and you can't deny it now!" The little wretches denied it with all the added volume of their sociability and their tenderness, just in the crystal depths of which—like the flash of a fish in a stream—the mockery of their advantage peeped up. The shock had in truth sunk into me still deeper than I knew on the night when, looking out either for

Quint or for Miss Jessel under the stars, I had seen there the boy over whose rest I watched and who had immediately brought in with him—had straightway there turned on me—the lovely upward look with which, from the battlements above us, the hideous apparition of Quint had played. If it was a question of a scare my discovery on this occasion had scared me more than any other, and it was essentially in the scared state that I drew my actual conclusions. They harassed me so that sometimes, at odd moments, I shut myself up audibly to rehearse—it was at once a fantastic relief and a renewed despair—the manner in which I might come to the point. I approached it from one side and the other while, in my room, I flung myself about, but I always broke down in the monstrous utterance of names. As they died away on my lips I said to myself that I should indeed help them to represent something infamous if by pronouncing them I should violate as rare a little case of instinctive delicacy as any schoolroom probably had ever known. When I said to myself: "*They* have the manners to be silent, and you, trusted as you are, the baseness to speak!" I felt myself crimson and covered my face with my hands. After these secret scenes I chattered more than ever, going on volubly enough till one of our prodigious palpable hushes occurred—I can call them nothing else—the strange dizzy lift or swim (I try for terms!) into a stillness, a pause of all life, that had nothing to do with the more or less noise we at the moment might be engaged in making and that I could hear through any intensified mirth or quickened recitation or louder strum of the piano. Then it was that the others, the outsiders, were there. Though they were not angels they "passed," as the French say, causing me, while they stayed, to tremble with the fear of their addressing to their younger victims some yet more infernal message or more vivid image than they had thought good enough for myself.

What it was least possible to get rid of was the cruel idea that, whatever I had seen, Miles and Flora saw *more*—things terrible and unguessable and that sprang from dreadful passages of intercourse in the past. Such things naturally left on the surface, for the time, a chill that we vociferously denied we felt; and we had all three, with repetition, got into such splendid training that we went, each time, to mark the close of the incident, almost automatically through the very same movements. It was striking of the children at all events to kiss me inveterately with a wild irrelevance and never to fail—one or the other—of the precious question that had helped us through many a peril. "When do you think he *will* come? Don't you think we *ought* to write?"—there was nothing like that inquiry, we found by experience, for carrying off an awkwardness. "He" of course was their uncle in Harley Street; and we lived in much profusion of theory that he might at any moment arrive to mingle in our circle. It was impossible to have given less encouragement than he had administered to such a doctrine, but if we had not had the doctrine to fall back upon we should have deprived each other of some of our finest exhibitions. He never wrote to them—that may have been selfish, but it was a part of the flattery of his trust of myself; for the way in which a man pays his highest tribute to a woman is apt to be but by the more festal celebration of one of the sacred laws of his comfort. So I held that I carried out the spirit of the pledge given not to appeal to him when I let our young friends understand that their own letters were but charming literary exercises. They were too beautiful to be posted; I kept them myself; I have them all to this hour. This was a rule indeed which only added to the satiric effect of my being plied with the supposition that he might at any moment be among us. It was exactly as if our young friends knew how almost more awkward than anything else that might be for me. There appears to me, moreover, as I look back no note in all this more extraordinary than the mere fact that, in spite of my tension and of their triumph, I never lost patience with them. Adorable they must in truth have been, I now feel, since I didn't in these days hate them! Would exasperation, however, if relief had longer been postponed, finally have betrayed me? It little matters, for relief arrived. I call it relief though it was only the relief that a snap brings to a strain or the burst of a thunderstorm to a day of suffocation. It was at least change, and it came with a rush.

XIV

Walking to church a certain Sunday morning, I had little Miles at my side and his sister, in advance of us and at Mrs. Grose's, well in sight. It was a crisp clear day, the first of its order for some time; the night had brought a touch of frost and the autumn air, bright and sharp, made the church-bells almost gay. It was an odd accident of thought that I should have happened at such a moment to be particularly and very gratefully struck with the obedience of my little charges. Why did they never resent my inexorable, my perpetual society? Something or other had brought nearer home to me that I had all but pinned the boy to my shawl, and that in the way our companions were marshalled before me I might have appeared to provide against some danger of rebellion. I was like a gaoler[24] with an eye to possible surprises and escapes. But all this belonged—I mean their magnificent little surrender—just to the special array of the facts that were most abysmal. Turned out for Sunday by his uncle's tailor, who had had a free hand and a notion of pretty waistcoats and of his grand little air, Miles's whole title to independence, the rights of his sex and situation, were so stamped upon him that if he had suddenly struck for freedom I should have had nothing to say. I was by the strangest of chances wondering how I should meet him when the revolution unmistakably occurred. I call it a revolution because I now see how, with the word he spoke, the curtain rose on the last act of my dreadful drama and the catastrophe was precipitated. "Look here, my dear, you know," he charmingly said, "when in the world, please, am I going back to school?"

Transcribed here the speech sounds harmless enough, particularly as uttered in the sweet, high, casual pipe with which, at all interlocutors, but above all at his eternal governess, he threw off intonations as if he were tossing roses. There was something in them that always made one "catch," and I caught at any rate now so effectually that I stopped as short as if one of the trees of the park had fallen across the road. There was something new, on the spot, between us, and he was perfectly aware I recognised it, though to enable me to do so he had no need to look a whit less candid and charming than usual. I could feel in him how he already, from my at first finding nothing to reply, perceived the advantage he had gained. I was so slow to find anything that he had plenty of time, after a minute, to continue with his suggestive but inconclusive smile: "You know, my dear, that for a fellow to be with a lady *always*—!" His "my dear" was constantly on his lips for me, and nothing could have expressed more the exact shade of the sentiment with which I desired to inspire my pupils than its fond familiarity. It was so respectfully easy.

But oh how I felt that at present I must pick my own phrases! I remember that, to gain time, I tried to laugh, and I seemed to see in the beautiful face with which he watched me how ugly and queer I looked. "And always with the same lady?" I returned.

He neither blenched nor winked. The whole thing was virtually out between us. "Ah of course she's a jolly 'perfect' lady; but after all I'm a fellow, don't you see? who's—well, getting on."

I lingered there with him an instant ever so kindly. "Yes, you're getting on." Oh but I felt helpless!

I have kept to this day the heartbreaking little idea of how he seemed to know that and to play with it. "And you can't say I've not been awfully good, can you?"

I laid my hand on his shoulder, for though I felt how much better it would have been to walk on I was not yet quite able. "No, I can't say that, Miles."

"Except just that one night, you know—!"

"That one night?" I couldn't look as straight as he.

"Why, when I went down—went out of the house."

"Oh yes. But I forget what you did it for."

"You forget?"—he spoke with the sweet extravagance of childish reproach. "Why, it was just to show you I could!"

"Oh yes—you could."

"And I can again."

I felt I might perhaps after all succeed in keeping my wits about me. "Certainly. But you won't."

"No, not *that* again. It was nothing."

"It was nothing," I said. "But we must go on."

He resumed our walk with me, passing his hand into my arm. "Then when *am* I going back?"

I wore, in turning it over, my most responsible air. "Were you very happy at school?"

He just considered. "Oh I'm happy enough anywhere!"

"Well, then," I quavered, "if you're just as happy here—!"

"Ah but that isn't everything! Of course *you* know a lot—"

"But you hint that you know almost as much?" I risked as he paused.

"Not half I want to!" Miles honestly professed. "But it isn't so much that."

"What is it, then?"

"Well—I want to see more life."

"I see; I see." We had arrived within sight of the church and of various persons, including several of the household of Bly, on their way to it and clustered about the door to see us go in. I quickened our step; I wanted to get there before the question between us opened up much further; I reflected hungrily that he would have for more than an hour to be silent; and I thought with envy of the comparative dusk of the pew and of the almost spiritual help of the hassock on which I might bend my knees. I seemed literally to be running a race with some confusion to which he was about to reduce me, but I felt he had got in first when, before we had even entered the churchyard, he threw out:

"I want my own sort!"

It literally made me bound forward. "There aren't many of your own sort, Miles!" I laughed. "Unless perhaps dear little Flora!"

"You really compare me to a baby girl?"

This found me singularly weak. "Don't you, then, *love* our sweet Flora?"

"If I didn't—and you too; if I didn't—!" he repeated as if retreating for a jump, yet leaving his thought so unfinished that, after we had come into the gate, another stop, which he imposed on me by the pressure of his arm, had become inevitable. Mrs. Grose and Flora had passed into the church, the other worshippers had followed and we were, for the minute, alone among the old thick graves. We had paused, on the path from the gate, by a low oblong table-like tomb.

"Yes, if you didn't—?"

He looked, while I waited, about at the graves. "Well, you know what!" But he didn't move, and he presently produced something that made me drop straight down on the stone slab as if suddenly to rest. "Does my uncle think what *you* think?"

I markedly rested. "How do you know what I think?"

"Ah well, of course I don't; for it strikes me you never tell me. But I mean does *he* know?"

"Know what, Miles?"

"Why, the way I'm going on."

I recognised quickly enough that I could make, to this inquiry, no answer that wouldn't involve something of a sacrifice of my employer. Yet it struck me that we were all, at Bly, sufficiently sacrificed to make that venial. "I don't think your uncle much cares."

Miles, on this, stood looking at me. "Then don't you think he can be made to?"

"In what way?"

"Why, by his coming down."

"But who'll get him to come down?"

"*I* will!" the boy said with extraordinary brightness and emphasis. He gave me another look charged with that expression and then marched off alone into church.

XV

The business was practically settled from the moment I never followed him. It was a pitiful surrender to agitation, but my being aware of this had somehow no power to restore me. I only sat there on my tomb and read into what our young friend had said to me the fulness of its meaning; by the time I had grasped the whole of which I had also embraced, for absence, the pretext that I was ashamed to offer my pupils and the rest of the congregation such an example of delay. What I said to myself above all was that Miles had got something out of me and that the gage of it for him would be just this awkward collapse. He had got out of me that there was something I was much afraid of, and that he should probably be able to make use of my fear to gain, for his own purpose, more freedom. My fear was of having to deal with the intolerable question of the grounds of his dismissal from school, since that was really but the question of the horrors gathered behind. That his uncle should arrive to treat with me of these things was a solution that, strictly speaking, I ought now to have desired to bring on; but I could so little face the ugliness and the pain of it that I simply procrastinated and lived from hand to mouth. The boy, to my deep discomposure, was immensely in the right, was in a position to say to me: "Either you clear up with my guardian the mystery of this interruption of my studies, or you cease to expect me to lead with you a life that's so unnatural for a boy." What was so unnatural for the particular boy I was concerned with was this sudden revelation of a consciousness and a plan.

That was what really overcame me, what prevented my going in. I walked round the church, hesitating, hovering; I reflected that I had already, with him, hurt myself beyond repair. Therefore I could patch up nothing and it was too extreme an effort to squeeze beside him into the pew: he would be so much more sure than ever to pass his arm into mine and make me sit there for an hour in close mute contact with his commentary on our talk. For the first minute since his arrival I wanted to get away from him. As I paused beneath the high east window and listened to the sounds of worship I was taken with an impulse that might master me, I felt, and completely, should I give it the least encouragement. I might easily put an end to my ordeal by getting away altogether. Here was my chance; there was no one to stop me; I could give the whole thing up—turn my back and bolt. It was only a question of hurrying again, for a few preparations, to the house which the attendance at church of so many of the servants would practically have left unoccupied. No one, in short, could blame me if I should just drive desperately off. What was it to get away if I should get away only till dinner? That would be in a couple of hours, at the end of which—I had the acute prevision—my little pupils would play at innocent wonder about my non-appearance in their train.

"What *did* you do, you naughty bad thing? Why in the world, to worry us so—and take our thoughts off too, don't you know?—did you desert us at the very door?" I couldn't meet such questions nor, as they asked them, their false little lovely eyes; yet it was all so exactly what I should have to meet that, as the prospect grew sharp to me, I at last let myself go.

I got, so far as the immediate moment was concerned, away; I came straight out of the churchyard and, thinking hard, retraced my steps through the park. It seemed to me that by the time I reached the house I had made up my mind to cynical flight. The Sunday stillness both of the approaches and of the interior, in which I met no one, fairly stirred me with a sense of opportunity. Were I to get off quickly this way I should get off without a scene, without a word. My quickness would have to be remarkable, however, and the question of a conveyance was the great one to settle. Tormented, in the hall, with difficulties and obstacles, I remember sinking down at the foot of the staircase—suddenly collapsing there on the lowest step and then, with a revulsion, recalling that it was exactly where, more than a month before, in the darkness of night and just so bowed with evil things, I had seen the spectre of the most horrible of women. At this I was able to straighten myself; I went the rest of the way up; I made, in my turmoil, for the school-room, where there were objects belonging to me that I should have to take. But I opened the door to find again, in a flash, my eyes unsealed. In the presence of what I saw I reeled straight back upon resistance.

Seated at my own table in the clear noonday light I saw a person whom, without my previous experience, I should have taken at the first blush for some housemaid who might have stayed at home to look after the place and who, availing herself of rare relief from observation and of the schoolroom table and my pens, ink and paper, had applied herself to the considerable effort of a letter to her sweetheart. There was an effort in the way that, while her arms rested on the table, her hands, with evident weariness, supported her head; but at the moment I took this in I had already become aware that, in spite of my entrance, her attitude strangely persisted. Then it was—with the very act of its announcing itself—that her identity flared up in a change of posture. She rose, not as if she had heard me, but with an indescribable grand melancholy of indifference and detachment, and, within a dozen feet of me, stood there as my vile predecessor. Dishonoured and tragic, she was all before me; but even as I fixed and, for memory, secured it, the awful image passed away. Dark as midnight in her black dress, her haggard beauty and her unutterable woe, she had looked at me long enough to appear to say that her right to sit at my table was as good as mine to sit at hers. While these instants lasted indeed I had the extraordinary chill of a feeling that it was I who was the intruder. It was as a wild protest against it that, actually addressing her—"You terrible miserable woman!"—I heard myself break into a sound that, by the open door, rang through the long passage and the empty house. She looked at me as if she heard me, but I had recovered myself and cleared the air. There was nothing in the room the next minute but the sunshine and the sense that I must stay.

XVI

I had so perfectly expected the return of the others to be marked by a demonstration that I was freshly upset at having to find them merely dumb and discreet about my desertion. Instead of gaily denouncing and caressing me they made no allusion to my having failed them, and I was left, for the time, on perceiving that she too said nothing, to study Mrs. Grose's odd face. I did this to such purpose that I made sure they had in some way bribed her to silence; a silence that, however, I would engage to break down on the first private opportunity. This opportunity came before tea: I secured five minutes with her in the housekeeper's room, where, in the twilight, amid a smell of lately-baked bread, but with the place all swept and garnished, I found her sitting in pained placidity before the fire. So I see her still, so I see her best: facing the flame from her straight chair in the dusky shining room, a large clean picture of the "put away"—of drawers closed and locked and rest without a remedy.

"Oh yes, they asked me to say nothing; and to please them—so long as they were there—of course I promised. But what had happened to you?"

"I only went with you for the walk," I said. "I had then to come back to meet a friend."

She showed her surprise. "A friend—*you?*"

"Oh yes, I've a couple!" I laughed. "But did the children give you a reason?"

"For not alluding to your leaving us? Yes; they said you'd like it better. *Do* you like it better?"

My face had made her rueful. "No, I like it worse!" But after an instant I added: "Did they say why I should like it better?"

"No; Master Miles only said 'We must do nothing but what she likes!' "

"I wish indeed he would! And what did Flora say?"

"Miss Flora was too sweet. She said 'Oh of course, of course!'— and I said the same."

I thought a moment. "You were too sweet too—I can hear you all. But none the less, between Miles and me, it's now all out."

"All out?" My companion stared. "But what, Miss?"

"Everything. It doesn't matter. I've made up my mind. I came home, my dear," I went on, "for a talk with Miss Jessel."

I had by this time formed the habit of having Mrs. Grose literally well in hand in advance of my sounding that note; so that even now, as she bravely blinked under the signal of my word, I could keep her comparatively firm. "A talk! Do you mean she spoke?"

"It came to that. I found her, on my return, in the schoolroom."

"And what did she say?" I can hear the good woman still, and the candour of her stupefaction.

"That she suffers the torments—!"

It was this, of a truth, that made her, as she filled out my picture, gape. "Do you mean," she faltered "—of the lost?"

"Of the lost. Of the damned. And that's why, to share them—" I faltered myself with the horror of it.

But my companion, with less imagination, kept me up. "To share them—?"

"She wants Flora." Mrs. Grose might, as I gave it to her, fairly have fallen away from me had I not been prepared. I still held her there, to show I was. "As I've told you, however, it doesn't matter."

"Because you've made up your mind? But to what?"

"To everything."

"And what do you call 'everything'?"

"Why, to sending for their uncle."

"Oh Miss, in pity do," my friend broke out.

"Ah but I will, I *will*! I see it's the only way. What's 'out,' as I told you, with Miles is that if he thinks I'm afraid to—and has ideas of what he gains by that—he shall see he's mistaken. Yes, yes; his uncle shall have it here from me on the spot (and before the boy himself if necessary) that if I'm to be reproached with having done nothing again about more school—"

"Yes, Miss—" my companion pressed me.

"Well, there's that awful reason."

There were now clearly so many of these for my poor colleague that she was excusable for being vague. "But—a—which?"

"Why, the letter from his old place."

"You'll show it to the master?"

"I ought to have done so on the instant."

"Oh no!" said Mrs. Grose with decision.

"I'll put it before him," I went on inexorably, "that I can't undertake to work the question on behalf of a child who has been expelled—"

"For we've never in the least known what!" Mrs. Grose declared.

"For wickedness. For what else—when he's so clever and beautiful and perfect? Is he stupid? Is he untidy? Is he infirm? Is he ill-natured? He's exquisite—so it can be only *that;* and that would open up the whole thing. After all," I said, "it's their uncle's fault. If he left here such people—!"

"He didn't really in the least know them. The fault's mine." She had turned quite pale.

"Well, you shan't suffer," I answered.

"The children shan't!" she emphatically returned.

I was silent a while; we looked at each other. "Then what am I to tell him?"

"You needn't tell him anything. *I'll* tell him."

I measured this. "Do you mean you'll write—?" Remembering she couldn't, I caught myself up. "How do you communicate?"

"I tell the bailiff. *He* writes."

"And should you like him to write our story?"

My question had a sarcastic force that I had not fully intended, and it made her after a moment inconsequently break down. The tears were again in her eyes. "Ah Miss, *you* write!"

"Well—to-night," I at last returned; and on this we separated.

XVII

I went so far, in the evening, as to make a beginning. The weather had changed back, a great wind was abroad, and beneath the lamp, in my room, with Flora at peace beside me, I sat for a long time before a blank sheet of paper and listened to the lash of the rain and the batter of the gusts. Finally I went out, taking a candle; I crossed the passage and listened a minute at Miles's door. What, under my endless obsession, I had been impelled to listen for was some betrayal of his not being at rest, and I presently caught one, but not in the form I had expected. His voice tinkled out. "I say, you there—come in." It was gaiety in the gloom!

I went in with my light and found him in bed, very wide awake but very much at his ease. "Well, what are *you* up to?" he asked with a grace of sociability in which it occurred to me that Mrs. Grose, had she been present, might have looked in vain for proof that anything was "out."

I stood over him with my candle. "How did you know I was there?"

"Why of course I heard you. Did you fancy you made no noise? You're like a troop of cavalry!" he beautifully laughed.

"Then you weren't asleep?"

"Not much! I lie awake and think."

I had put my candle, designedly, a short way off, and then, as he held out his friendly old hand to me, had sat down on the edge of his bed. "What is it," I asked, "that you think of?"

"What in the world, my dear, but *you?*"

"Ah, the pride I take in your appreciation doesn't insist on that! I had so far rather you slept."

"Well, I think also, you know, of this queer business of ours."

I marked the coolness of his firm little hand. "Of what queer business, Miles?"

"Why, the way you bring me up. And all the rest!"

I fairly held my breath a minute, and even from my glimmering taper there was light enough to show how he smiled up at me from his pillow. "What do you mean by all the rest?"

"Oh you know, you know!"

I could say nothing for a minute, though I felt as I held his hand and our eyes continued to meet that my silence had all the air of admitting his charge and that nothing in the whole world of reality was perhaps at that moment so fabulous as our actual relation. "Certainly you shall go back to school," I said, "if it be that that troubles you. But not to the old place—we must find another, a better. How could I know it did trouble you, this question, when you never told me so, never spoke of it at all?" His clear listening face, framed in its smooth whiteness, made him for the minute as appealing as some wistful patient in a children's hospital; and I would have given, as the resemblance came to me, all I possessed on earth really to be the nurse or the sister of charity who might have helped to cure him. Well, even as it was I perhaps might help! "Do you know you've never said a word to me about your school—I mean the old one; never mentioned it in any way?"

He seemed to wonder; he smiled with the same loveliness. But he clearly gained time; he waited, he called for guidance. "Haven't I?" It wasn't for *me* to help him—it was for the thing I had met!

Something in his tone and the expression of his face, as I got this from him, set my heart aching with such a pang as it had never yet known; so unutterably touching was it to see his little brain puzzled and his little resources taxed to play, under the spell laid on him, a part of innocence and consistency. "No, never—from the hour you came back. You've never mentioned to me one of your masters, one of your comrades, nor the least little thing that ever happened to you at school. Never, little Miles—no, never—have you given me an inkling of anything that *may* have happened there. Therefore you can fancy how much I'm in the dark. Until you came out, that way, this morning, you had since the first hour I saw you scarce even made a reference to anything in your previous life. You seemed so perfectly to accept the present." It was extraordinary how my absolute conviction of his secret precocity—or whatever I might call the poison of an influence that I dared but half-phrase—made him, in spite of the faint breath of his inward trouble, appear as accessible as an older person, forced me to treat him as an intelligent equal. "I thought you wanted to go on as you are."

It struck me that at this he just faintly coloured. He gave, at any rate, like a convalescent slightly fatigued, a languid shake of his head. "I don't—I don't. I want to get away."

"You're tired of Bly?"

"Oh no, I like Bly."

"Well then—?"

"Oh *you* know what a boy wants!"

I felt I didn't know so well as Miles, and I took temporary refuge. "You want to go to your uncle?"

Again, at this, with his sweet ironic face, he made a movement on the pillow. "Ah you can't get off with that!"

I was silent a little, and it was I now, I think, who changed colour. "My dear, I don't want to get off!"

"You can't even if you do. You can't, you can't!"—he lay beautifully staring. "My uncle must come down and you must completely settle things."

"If we do," I returned with some spirit, "you may be sure it will be to take you quite away."

"Well, don't you understand that that's exactly what I'm working for? You'll have to *tell* him—about the way you've let it all drop: you'll have to tell him a tremendous lot!"

The exultation with which he uttered this helped me somehow for the instant to meet him rather more. "And how much will *you*, Miles, have to tell him? There are things he'll ask you!"

He turned it over. "Very likely. But what things?"

"The things you've never told me. To make up his mind what to do with you. He can't send you back—"

"I don't want to go back!" he broke in. "I want a new field."

He said it with admirable serenity, with positive unimpeachable gaiety; and doubtless it was that very note that most evoked for me the poignancy, the unnatural childish tragedy, of his probable reappearance at the end of three months with all this bravado and still more dishonour. It overwhelmed me now that I should never be able to bear that, and it made me let myself go. I threw myself upon him and in the tenderness of my pity I embraced him. "Dear little Miles, dear little Miles—!"

My face was close to his, and he let me kiss him, simply taking it with indulgent good humour. "Well, old lady?"

"Is there nothing—nothing at all that you want to tell me?"

He turned off a little, facing round toward the wall and holding up his hand to look at as one had seen sick children look. "I've told you—I told you this morning."

Oh I was sorry for him! "That you just want me not to worry you?"

He looked round at me now as if in recognition of my understanding him; then ever so gently, "To let me alone," he replied.

There was even a strange little dignity in it, something that made me release him, yet, when I had slowly risen, linger beside him. God knows *I* never wished to harass him, but I felt that merely, at this, to turn my back on him was to abandon or, to put it more truly, lose him. "I've just begun a letter to your uncle," I said.

"Well then, finish it!"

I waited a minute. "What happened before?"

He gazed up at me again. "Before what?"

"Before you came back. And before you went away."

For some time he was silent, but he continued to meet my eyes. "What happened?"

It made me, the sound of the words, in which it seemed to me I caught for the very first time a small faint quaver of consenting consciousness—it made me drop on my knees beside the bed and seize once more the chance of possessing him. "Dear little Miles, dear little Miles, if you *knew* how I want to help you! It's only that, it's nothing but that, and I'd rather die than give you a pain or do you a wrong—I'd rather die than hurt a hair of you. Dear little Miles"—oh I brought it out now even if I *should* go too far—"I just want you to help me to save you!" But I knew in a moment after this that I had gone too far. The answer to my appeal was instantaneous, but it came in the form of an extraordinary blast and chill, a gust of frozen air and a shake of the room as great as if, in the wild wind, the casement had crashed in. The boy gave a loud high shriek which, lost in the rest of the shock of sound, might have seemed, indistinctly, though I was so close to him, a note either of jubilation or of terror. I jumped to my feet again and was conscious of darkness. So for a moment we remained, while I stared about me and saw the drawn curtains unstirred and the window still tight. "Why, the candle's out!" I then cried.

"It was I who blew it, dear!" said Miles.

XVIII

The next day, after lessons, Mrs. Grose found a moment to say to me quietly: "Have you written, Miss?"

"Yes—I've written." But I didn't add—for the hour—that my letter, sealed and directed, was still in my pocket. There would be time enough to send it before the messenger should go to the village. Meanwhile there had been on the part of my pupils no more brilliant, more exemplary morning. It was exactly as if they had both had at heart to gloss over any recent little friction. They performed the dizziest feats of arithmetic, soaring quite out of *my* feeble range, and perpetrated, in higher spirits than ever, geographical and historical jokes. It was conspicuous of course in Miles in particular that he appeared to wish to show how easily he could let me down. This child, to my memory, really lives in a setting of beauty and misery that no words can translate; there was a distinction all his own in every impulse he revealed; never was a small natural creature, to the uninformed eye all frankness and freedom, a more ingenious, a more extraordinary little gentleman. I had perpetually to guard against the wonder of contemplation into which my initiated view betrayed me; to check the irrelevant gaze and discouraged sigh in which I constantly both attacked and renounced the enigma of what such a little gentleman could have done that deserved a penalty. Say that, by the dark prodigy I knew, the imagination of all evil *had* been opened up to him: all the justice within me ached for the proof that it could ever have flowered into an act.

He had never at any rate been such a little gentleman as when, after our early dinner on this dreadful day, he came round to me and asked if I shouldn't like him for half an hour to play to me. David playing to Saul could never have shown a finer sense of the occasion.[25] It was literally a charming exhibition of tact, of magnanimity, and quite tantamount to his saying outright: "The true knights we love to read about never push an advantage too far. I know what you mean now: you mean that—to be let alone yourself and not followed up—you'll cease to worry and spy upon me, won't keep me so close to you, will let me go and come. Well, I 'come,' you see—but I don't go! There'll be plenty of time for that. I do really delight in your society and I only want to show you that I contended for a principle." It may be imagined whether I resisted this appeal or failed to accompany him again, hand in hand, to the schoolroom. He sat down at the old piano and played as he had never played; and if there are those who think he had better have been kicking a football I can only say that I wholly agree with them. For at the end of a time that under his influence I had quite ceased to measure I started up with a strange sense of having literally slept at my post. It was after luncheon, and by the schoolroom fire, and yet I hadn't really in the least slept; I had only done something much worse—I had forgotten. Where all this time was Flora? When I put the question to Miles he played on a minute before answering, and then could only say: "Why, my dear, how do *I* know?"—

breaking, moreover, into a happy laugh which immediately after, as if it were a vocal accompaniment, he prolonged into incoherent extravagant song.

I went straight to my room, but his sister was not there; then, before going downstairs, I looked into several others. As she was nowhere about she would surely be with Mrs. Grose, whom in the comfort of that theory I accordingly proceeded in quest of. I found her where I had found her the evening before, but she met my quick challenge with blank scared ignorance. She had only supposed that, after the repast, I had carried off both the children; as to which she was quite in her right, for it was the very first time I had allowed the little girl out of my sight without some special provision. Of course now indeed she might be with the maids, so that the immediate thing was to look for her without an air of alarm. This we promptly arranged between us; but when, ten minutes later and in pursuance of our arrangement, we met in the hall, it was only to report on either side that after guarded inquiries we had altogether failed to trace her. For a minute there, apart from observation, we exchanged mute alarms, and I could feel with what high interest my friend returned me all those I had from the first given her.

"She'll be above," she presently said—"in one of the rooms you haven't searched."

"No; she's at a distance." I had made up my mind. "She has gone out."

Mrs. Grose stared. "Without a hat?"

I naturally also looked volumes. "Isn't that woman always without one?"

"She's with *her*?"

"She's with *her*!" I declared. "We must find them."

My hand was on my friend's arm, but she failed for the moment, confronted with such an account of the matter, to respond to my pressure. She communed, on the contrary, where she stood, with her uneasiness.

"And where's Master Miles?"

"Oh *he's* with Quint. They'll be in the schoolroom."

"Lord, Miss!" My view, I was myself aware—and therefore I suppose my tone—had never yet reached so calm an assurance.

"The trick's played," I went on; "they've successfully worked their plan. He found the most divine little way to keep me quiet while she went off."

" 'Divine'?" Mrs. Grose bewilderedly echoed.

"Infernal, then!" I almost cheerfully rejoined. "He has provided for himself as well. But come!"

She had helplessly gloomed at the upper regions. "You leave him—?"

"So long with Quint? Yes—I don't mind that now."

She always ended at these moments by getting possession of my hand, and in this manner she could at present still stay me. But after gasping an instant at my sudden resignation, "Because of your letter?" she eagerly brought out.

I quickly, by way of answer, felt for my letter, drew it forth, held it up, and then, freeing myself, went and laid it on the great hall-table. "Luke will take it," I said as I came back. I reached the house-door and opened it; I was already on the steps.

My companion still demurred: the storm of the night and the early morning had dropped, but the afternoon was damp and grey. I came down to the drive while she stood in the doorway. "You go with nothing on?"

"What do I care when the child has nothing? I can't wait to dress," I cried, "and if you must do so I leave you. Try meanwhile yourself upstairs."

"With *them?*" Oh on this the poor woman promptly joined me!

XIX

We went straight to the lake, as it was called at Bly, and I daresay rightly called, though it may have been a sheet of water less remarkable than my untravelled eyes supposed it. My acquaintance with sheets of water was small, and the pool of Bly, at all events on the few occasions of my consenting, under the protection of my pupils, to affront its surface in the old flat-bottomed boat moored there for our use, had impressed me both with its extent and its agitation. The usual place of embarkation was half a mile from the house, but I had an intimate conviction that, wherever Flora might be, she was not near home. She had not given me the slip for any small adventure, and, since the day of the very great one that I had shared with her by the pond, I had been aware, in our walks, of the quarter to which she most inclined. This was why I had now given to Mrs. Grose's steps so marked a direction—a direction making her, when she perceived it, oppose a resistance that showed me she was freshly mystified. "You're going to the water, Miss?—you think she's *in*—?"

"She may be, though the depth is, I believe, nowhere very great. But what I judge most likely is that she's on the spot from which, the other day, we saw together what I told you."

"When she pretended not to see—?"

"With that astounding self-possession! I've always been sure she wanted to go back alone. And now her brother has managed it for her."

Mrs. Grose still stood where she had stopped. "You suppose they really *talk* of them?"

I could meet this with an assurance! "They say things that, if we heard them, would simply appal us."

"And if she *is* there—?"

"Yes?"

"Then Miss Jessel is?"

"Beyond a doubt. You shall see."

"Oh thank you!" my friend cried, planted so firm that, taking it in, I went straight on without her. By the time I reached the pool, however, she was close behind me, and I knew that, whatever, to her apprehension, might befall me, the exposure of sticking to me struck her as her least danger. She exhaled a moan of relief as we at last came in sight of the greater part of the water without a sight of the child. There was no trace of Flora on that nearer side of the bank where my observation of her had been most startling, and none on the opposite edge, where, save for a margin of some twenty yards, a thick copse came down to the pond. This expanse, oblong in shape, was so narrow compared to its length that, with its ends out of view, it might have been taken for a scant river. We looked at the empty stretch, and then I felt the suggestion in my friend's eyes. I knew what she meant and I replied with a negative headshake.

"No, no; wait! She has taken the boat."

My companion stared at the vacant mooring-place and then again across the lake. "Then where is it?"

"Our not seeing it is the strongest of proofs. She has used it to go over, and then has managed to hide it."

"All alone—that child?"

"She's not alone, and at such times she's not a child: she's an old, old woman." I scanned all the visible shore while Mrs. Grose took again, into the queer element I offered her, one of her plunges of submission; then I pointed out that the boat might perfectly be in a small refuge formed by one of the recesses of the pool, an indentation masked, for the hither side, by a projection of the bank and by a clump of trees growing close to the water.

"But if the boat's there, where on earth's *she?*" my colleague anxiously asked.

"That's exactly what we must learn." And I started to walk further.

"By going all the way round?"

"Certainly, far as it is. It will take us but ten minutes, yet it's far enough to have made the child prefer not to walk. She went straight over."

"Laws!" cried my friend again: the chain of my logic was ever too strong for her. It dragged her at my heels even now, and when we had got halfway round—a devious tiresome process, on ground much broken and by a path choked with overgrowth—I paused to give her breath. I sustained her with a grateful arm, assuring her that she might hugely help me; and this started us afresh, so that in the course of but few minutes more we reached a point from which we found the boat to be where I had supposed it. It had been intentionally left as much as possible out of sight and was tied to one of the stakes of a fence that came, just there, down to the brink and that had been an assistance to disembarking. I recognised, as I looked at the pair of short thick oars, quite safely drawn up, the prodigious character of the feat for a little girl; but I had by this time lived too long among wonders and had panted to too many livelier measures. There was a gate in the fence, through which we passed, and that brought us after a trifling interval more into the open. Then "There she is!" we both exclaimed at once.

Flora, a short way off, stood before us on the grass and smiled as if her performance had now become complete. The next thing she did, however, was to stoop straight down and pluck—quite as if it were all she was there for—a big ugly spray of withered fern. I at once felt sure she had just come out of the copse. She waited for us, not herself taking a step, and I was conscious of the rare solemnity with which we presently approached her. She smiled and smiled, and we met; but it was all done in a silence by this time flagrantly ominous. Mrs. Grose was the first to break the spell: she threw herself on her knees and, drawing the child to her breast, clasped in a long embrace the little tender yielding body. While this dumb convulsion lasted I could only watch it—which I did the more intently when I saw Flora's face peep at me over our companion's shoulder. It was serious now—the flicker had left it; but it strengthened the pang with which I at that moment envied Mrs. Grose the simplicity of *her* relation. Still, all this while, nothing more passed between us save that Flora had let her foolish fern again drop to the ground. What she and I had virtually said to each other was that pretexts were useless now. When Mrs. Grose finally got up she kept the child's hand, so that the two were still before me; and the singular reticence of our communion was even more marked in the frank look she addressed me. "I'll be hanged," it said, "if *I'll* speak!"

It was Flora who, gazing all over me in candid wonder, was the first. She was struck with our bare-headed aspect. "Why, where are your things?"

"Where yours are, my dear!" I promptly returned.

She had already got back her gaiety and appeared to take this as an answer quite sufficient. "And where's Miles?" she went on.

There was something in the small valour of it that quite finished me: these three words from her were in a flash like the glitter of a drawn blade the jostle of the cup that my hand for weeks and weeks had held high and full to the brim and that now, even before speaking, I felt overflow in a deluge. "I'll tell you if you'll tell *me*—" I heard myself say, then heard the tremor in which it broke.

"Well, what?"

Mrs. Grose's suspense blazed at me, but it was too late now, and I brought the thing out handsomely. "Where, my pet, is Miss Jessel?"

XX

Just as in the churchyard with Miles, the whole thing was upon us. Much as I had made of the fact that this name had never once, between us, been sounded, the quick smitten glare with which the child's face now received it fairly likened my breach of the silence to the smash of a pane of glass. It added to the interposing cry, as if to stay the blow, that Mrs. Grose at the same instant uttered over my violence—the shriek of a creature scared, or rather wounded, which, in turn, within a few seconds, was completed by a gasp of my own. I seized my colleague's arm. "She's there, she's there!"

Miss Jessel stood before us on the opposite bank exactly as she had stood the other time, and I remember, strangely, as the first feeling now produced in me, my thrill of joy at having brought on a proof. She was there, so I was justified; she was there, so I was neither cruel nor mad. She was there for poor scared Mrs. Grose, but she was there most for Flora; and no moment of my monstrous time was perhaps so extraordinary as that in which I consciously threw out to her—with the sense that, pale and ravenous demon as she was, she would catch and understand it—an inarticulate message of gratitude. She rose erect on the spot my friend and I had lately quitted, and there wasn't in all the long reach of her desire an inch of her evil that fell short. This first vividness of vision and emotion were things of a few seconds, during which Mrs. Grose's dazed blink across to where I pointed struck me as showing that she too at last saw, just as it carried my own eyes precipitately to the child. The revelation then of the manner in which Flora was affected startled me in truth far more than it would have done to find her also merely agitated, for direct dismay was of course not what I had expected. Prepared and on her guard as our pursuit had actually made her, she would repress every betrayal; and I was therefore at once shaken by my first glimpse of the particular one for which I had not allowed. To see her, without a convulsion of her small pink face, not even feign to glance in the direction of the prodigy I announced, but only, instead of that, turn at *me* an expression of hard still gravity, an expression absolutely new and unprecedented and that appeared to read and accuse and judge me—this was a stroke that somehow converted the little girl herself into a figure portentous. I gaped at her coolness even though my certitude of her thoroughly seeing was never greater than at that instant, and then, in the immediate need to defend myself, I called her passionately to witness. "She's there, you little unhappy thing—there, there, *there,* and you know it as well as you know me!" I had said shortly before to Mrs. Grose that she was not at these times a child, but an old, old woman, and my description of her couldn't have been more strikingly confirmed than in the way in which, for all notice of this, she simply showed me, without an expressional concession or admission, a countenance of deeper and deeper, of indeed suddenly quite fixed reprobation. I was by this time—if I can put the whole thing at all together—more appalled at what I may properly call her manner than at anything else, though it was quite simultaneously that I became aware of having Mrs. Grose also, and very formidably, to reckon with. My elder companion, the next moment, at any rate, blotted out everything but her own flushed face and her loud shocked protest, a burst of high disapproval. "What a dreadful turn, to be sure, Miss! Where on earth do you see anything?"

I could only grasp her more quickly yet, for even while she spoke the hideous plain presence stood undimmed and undaunted. It had already lasted a minute, and it lasted while I continued, seizing my colleague, quite thrusting her at it and presenting her to it, to insist with my pointing hand. "You don't see her exactly as *we* see?—you mean to say you don't now—*now*? She's as big as a blazing fire! Only look, dearest woman, *look*—!" She looked, just as I did, and gave me, with her deep groan of negation, repulsion, compassion—the mixture with her pity of her relief at her exemption—a sense, touching to me even then, that she would have backed me up if she had been able. I might well have needed that, for with this hard blow of the proof that her eyes were hopelessly sealed I felt my own situation horribly crumble. I felt—I *saw*—my livid predecessor press, from her position, on my defeat, and I took the measure, more than all, of what I should have from this instant to deal with in the astounding little attitude of Flora. Into this attitude Mrs. Grose immediately and violently entered, breaking, even while there pierced through my sense of ruin a prodigious private triumph, into breathless reassurance.

"She isn't there, little lady, and nobody's there—and you never see nothing, my sweet! How can poor Miss Jessel—when poor Miss Jessel's dead and buried? *We* know, don't we, love?"—and she appealed, blundering in, to the child. "It's all a mere mistake and a worry and a joke—and we'll go home as fast as we can!"

Our companion, on this, had responded with a strange quick primness of propriety, and they were again, with Mrs. Grose on her feet, united, as it were, in shocked opposition to me. Flora continued to fix me with her small mask of disaffection, and even at that minute I prayed God to forgive me for seeming to see that, as she stood there holding tight to our friend's dress, her incomparable childish beauty had suddenly failed, had quite vanished. I've said it already—she was literally, she was hideously hard; she had turned common and almost ugly. "I don't know what you mean. I see nobody. I see nothing. I never *have*. I think you're cruel. I don't like you!" Then, after this deliverance, which might have been that of a vulgarly pert little girl in the street, she hugged Mrs. Grose more closely and buried in her skirts the dreadful little face. In this position she launched an almost furious wail. "Take me away, take me away—oh take me away from *her*!"

"From *me*?" I panted.

"From you—from you!" she cried.

Even Mrs. Grose looked across at me dismayed; while I had nothing to do but communicate again with the figure that, on the opposite bank, without a movement, as rigidly still as if catching, beyond the interval, our voices, was as vividly there for my disaster as it was not there for my service. The wretched child had spoken exactly as if she had got from some outside source each of her stabbing little words, and I could therefore, in the full despair of all I had to accept, but sadly shake my head at her. "If I had ever doubted all my doubt would at present have gone. I've been living with the miserable truth, and now it has only too much closed round me. Of course I've lost you: I've interfered, and you've seen, under *her* dictation"—with which I faced, over the pool again, our infernal witness—"the easy and perfect way to meet it. I've done my best, but I've lost you. Good-bye." For Mrs. Grose I had an imperative, an almost frantic "Go, go!" before which, in infinite distress, but mutely possessed of the little girl and clearly convinced, in spite of her blindness that something awful had occurred and some collapse engulfed us, she retreated, by the way we had come, as fast as she could move.

Of what first happened when I was left alone I had no subsequent memory. I only knew that at the end of, I suppose, a quarter of an hour, an odorous dampness and roughness, chilling and piercing my trouble, had made me understand that I must have thrown myself, on my face, to the ground and given way to a wildness of grief. I must have lain there long and cried and wailed, for when I raised my head the day was almost done. I got up and looked a moment, through the twilight, at the grey pool and its blank haunted edge, and then I took, back to the house, my dreary and difficult course. When I reached the gate in the fence the boat, to my surprise, was gone, so that I had a fresh reflexion to make on Flora's extraordinary command of the situation. She passed that night, by the most tacit and, I should add, were not the word so grotesque a false note, the happiest of arrangements, with Mrs. Grose. I saw neither of them on my return, but on the other hand I saw, as by an ambiguous compensation, a great deal of Miles.

I saw—I can use no other phrase—so much of him that it fairly measured more than it had ever measured. No evening I had passed at Bly was to have had the portentous quality of this one; in spite of which—and in spite also of the deeper depths of consternation that had opened beneath my feet—there was literally, in the ebbing actual, an extraordinarily sweet sadness. On reaching the house I had never so much as looked for the boy; I had simply gone straight to my room to change what I was wearing and to take in, at a glance, much material testimony to Flora's rupture. Her little belongings had all been removed. When later, by the schoolroom fire, I was served with tea by the usual maid, I indulged, on the article of my other pupil, in no inquiry whatever. He had his freedom now—he might have it to the end! Well, he did have it; and it consisted—in part at least—of his coming in at about eight o'clock and sitting down with me in silence. On the removal of the tea-things I had blown out the candles and drawn my chair closer: I was conscious of a mortal coldness and felt as if I should never again be warm. So when he appeared I was sitting in the glow with my thoughts. He paused a moment by the door as if to look at me; then—as if to share them—came to the other side of the hearth and sank into a chair. We sat there in absolute stillness; yet he wanted, I felt, to be with me.

XXI

Before a new day, in my room, had fully broken, my eyes opened to Mrs. Grose, who had come to my bedside with worse news. Flora was so markedly feverish that an illness was perhaps at hand; she had passed a night of extreme unrest, a night agitated above all by fears that had for their subject not in the least her former but wholly her present governess. It was not against the possible re-entrance of Miss Jessel on the scene that she protested—it was conspicuously and passionately against mine. I was at once on my feet, and with an immense deal to ask; the more that my friend had discernibly now girded her loins to meet me afresh. This I felt as soon as I had put to her the question of her sense of the child's sincerity as against my own. "She persists in denying to you that she saw, or has ever seen, anything?"

My visitor's trouble truly was great. "Ah Miss, it isn't a matter on which I can push her! Yet it isn't either, I must say, as if I much needed to. It has made her, every inch of her, quite old."

"Oh I see her perfectly from here. She resents, for all the world like some high little personage, the imputation on her truthfulness and, as it were, her respectability. 'Miss Jessel indeed—*she*!' Ah she's 'respectable,' the chit! The impression she gave me there yesterday was, I assure you, the very strangest of all: it was quite beyond any of the others. I *did* put my foot in it! She'll never speak to me again."

Hideous and obscure as it all was, it held Mrs. Grose briefly silent; then she granted my point with a frankness which, I made sure, had more behind it. "I think indeed, Miss, she never will. She do have a grand manner about it!"

"And that manner"—I summed it up—"is practically what's the matter with her now."

Oh that manner, I could see in my visitor's face, and not a little else besides! "She asks me every three minutes if I think you're coming in."

"I see—I see." I too, on my side, had so much more than worked it out. "Has she said to you since yesterday—except to repudiate her familiarity with anything so dreadful—a single other word about Miss Jessel?"

"Not one, Miss. And of course, you know," my friend added, "I took it from her by the lake that just then and there at least there *was* nobody."

"Rather! And naturally you take it from her still."

"I don't contradict her. What else can I do?"

"Nothing in the world! You've the cleverest little person to deal with. They've made them—their two friends, I mean—still cleverer even than nature did; for it was wondrous material to play on! Flora has now her grievance, and she'll work it to the end."

"Yes, Miss; but to *what* end?"

"Why that of dealing with me to her uncle. She'll make me out to him the lowest creature—!"

I winced at the fair show of the scene in Mrs. Grose's face; she looked for a minute as if she sharply saw them together. "And him who thinks so well of you!"

"He has an odd way—it comes over me now," I laughed, "—of proving it! But that doesn't matter. What Flora wants of course is to get rid of me."

My companion bravely concurred. "Never again to so much as look at you."

"So that what you've come to me now for," I asked, "is to speed me on my way?" Before she had time to reply, however, I had her in check. "I've a better idea—the result of my reflexions. My going *would* seem the right thing, and on Sunday I was terribly near it. Yet that won't do. It's *you* who must go. You must take Flora."

My visitor, at this, did speculate. "But where in the world—?"

"Away from here. Away from *them*. Away, even most of all, now, from me. Straight to her uncle."

"Only to tell on you—?"

"No, not 'only'! To leave me, in addition, with my remedy."

She was still vague. "And what *is* your remedy?"

"Your loyalty, to begin with. And then Miles's."

She looked at me hard. "Do you think he—?"

"Won't, if he has the chance, turn on me? Yes, I venture still to think it. At all events I want to try. Get off with his sister as soon as possible and leave me with him alone." I was amazed, myself, at the spirit I had still in reserve, and therefore perhaps a trifle the more disconcerted at the way in which, in spite of this fine example of it, she hesitated. "There's one thing, of course," I went on: "they mustn't, before she goes, see each other for three seconds." Then it came over me that, in spite of Flora's presumable sequestration from the instant of her return from the pool, it might already be too late. "Do you mean," I anxiously asked, "that they *have* met?"

At this she quite flushed. "Ah, Miss, I'm not such a fool as that! If

I've been obliged to leave her three or four times, it has been each time with one of the maids, and at present, though she's alone, she's locked in safe. And yet—and yet!" There were too many things.

"And yet what?"

"Well, are you so sure of the little gentleman?"

"I'm not sure of anything but *you.* But I have since last evening, a new hope. I think he wants to give me an opening. I do believe that—poor little exquisite wretch!—he wants to speak. Last evening, in the firelight and the silence, he sat with me for two hours as if it were just coming."

Mrs. Grose looked hard through the window at the grey gathering day. "And did it come?"

"No, though I waited and waited I confess it didn't, and it was without a breach of the silence, or so much as a faint allusion to his sister's condition and absence, that we at last kissed for good-night. All the same," I continued, "I can't, if her uncle sees her, consent to his seeing her brother without my having given the boy—and most of all because things have got so bad—a little more time."

My friend appeared on this ground more reluctant than I could quite understand. "What do you mean by more time?"

"Well, a day or two—really to bring it out. He'll then be on *my* side—of which you see the importance. If nothing comes I shall only fail, and you at the worst have helped me by doing on your arrival in town whatever you may have found possible." So I put it before her, but she continued for a little so lost in other reasons that I came again to her aid. "Unless indeed," I wound up, "you really want *not* to go."

I could see it, in her face, at last clear itself: she put out her hand to me as a pledge. "I'll go—I'll go. I'll go this morning."

I wanted to be very just. "If you *should* wish still to wait I'd engage she shouldn't see me."

"No, no: it's the place itself. She must leave it." She held me a moment with heavy eyes, then brought out the rest. "Your idea's the right one. I myself, Miss—"

"Well?"

"I can't stay."

The look she gave me with it made me jump at possibilities. "You mean that, since yesterday, you *have* seen—?"

She shook her head with dignity. "I've *heard*—!"

"Heard?"

"From that child—horrors! There!" she sighed with tragic relief. "On my honour, Miss, she says things—!" But at this evocation she broke down; she dropped with a sudden cry upon my sofa and, as I had seen her do before, gave way to all the anguish of it.

It was quite in another manner that I for my part let myself go. "Oh thank God!"

She sprang up again at this, drying her eyes with a groan. " 'Thank God'?"

"It so justifies me!"

"It does that, Miss!"

I couldn't have desired more emphasis, but I just waited. "She's so horrible?"

I saw my colleague scarce knew how to put it. "Really shocking."

"And about me?"

"About you, Miss—since you must have it. It's beyond everything, for a young lady; and I can't think wherever she must have picked up—"

"The appalling language she applies to me? I can, then!" I broke in with a laugh that was doubtless significant enough.

It only in truth left my friend still more grave. "Well, perhaps I ought to also—since I've heard some of it before! Yet I can't bear it," the poor woman went on while with the same movement she glanced, on my dressing-table, at the face of my watch. "But I must go back."

I kept her, however. "Ah if you can't bear it—!"

"How can I stop with her, you mean? Why just *for* that: to get her away. Far from this," she pursued, "far from *them*—"

"She may be different? She may be free?" I seized her almost with joy. "Then in spite of yesterday you *believe*—"

"In such doings?" Her simple description of them required, in the light of her expression, to be carried no farther, and she gave me the whole thing as she had never done. "I believe."

Yes, it was a joy, and we were still shoulder to shoulder: if I might continue sure of that I should care but little what else happened. My support in the presence of disaster would be the same as it had been in my early need of confidence, and if my friend would answer for my honesty I would answer for all the rest. On the point of taking leave of her, none the less, I was to some extent embarrassed. "There's one thing of course—it occurs to me—to remember. My letter giving the alarm will have reached town before you."

I now felt still more how she had been beating about the bush and how weary at last it had made her. "Your letter won't have got there. Your letter never went."

"What, then, became of it?"

"Goodness knows! Master Miles—"

"Do you mean *he* took it?" I gasped.

She hung fire, but she overcame her reluctance. "I mean that I saw yesterday, when I came back with Miss Flora, that it wasn't where you had put it. Later in the evening I had the chance to question Luke, and he declared that he had neither noticed nor touched it." We could only exchange, on this, one of our deeper mutual soundings, and it was Mrs. Grose who first brought up the plumb with an almost elate "You see!"

"Yes, I see that if Miles took it instead he probably will have read it and destroyed it."

"And don't you see anything else?"

I faced her a moment with a sad smile. "It strikes me that by this time your eyes are open even wider than mine."

They proved to be so indeed, but she could still almost blush to show it. "I make out now what he must have done at school." And she gave, in her simple sharpness, an almost droll disillusioned nod. "He stole!"

I turned it over—I tried to be more judicial. "Well—perhaps."

She looked as if she found me unexpectedly calm. "He stole *letters!*"

She couldn't know my reasons for a calmness after all pretty shallow; so I showed them off as I might. "I hope, then, it was to more purpose than in this case! The note, at all events, that I put on the table yesterday," I pursued, "will have given him so scant an advantage—for it contained only the bare demand for an interview— that he's already much ashamed of having gone so far for so little, and that what he had on his mind last evening was precisely the need of confession." I seemed to myself for the instant to have mastered it, to see it all. "Leave us, leave us"—I was already, at the door, hurrying her off. "I'll get it out of him. He'll meet me. He'll confess. If he confesses he's saved. And if he's saved—"

"Then *you* are?" The dear woman kissed me on this, and I took her farewell. "I'll save you without him!" she cried as she went.

XXII

Yet it was when she had got off—and I missed her on the spot—that the great pinch really came. If I had counted on what it would give me to find myself alone with Miles I quickly recognised that it would give me at least a measure. No hour of my stay in fact was so assailed with apprehensions as that of my coming down to learn that the carriage containing Mrs. Grose and my younger pupil had already rolled out of the gates. Now I *was,* I said to myself, face to face with the elements, and for much of the rest of the day, while I fought my weakness, I could consider that I had been supremely rash. It was a tighter place still than I had yet turned round in; all the more that, for the first time, I could see in the aspect of others a confused reflexion of the crisis. What had happened naturally caused them all to stare; there was too little of the explained, throw out whatever we might, in the suddenness of my colleague's act. The maids and the men looked blank; the effect of which on my nerves was an aggravation until I saw the necessity of making it a positive aid. It was in short by just clutching the helm that I avoided total wreck; and I daresay that, to bear up at all, I became that morning very grand and very dry. I welcomed the consciousness that I was charged with much to do, and I caused it to be known as well that, left thus to myself, I was quite remarkably firm. I wandered with that manner, for the next hour or two, all over the place and looked, I have no doubt, as if I were ready for any onset. So, for the benefit of whom it might concern, I paraded with a sick heart.

The person it appeared least to concern proved to be, till dinner, little Miles himself. My perambulations had given me meanwhile no glimpse of him, but they had tended to make more public the change taking place in our relation as a consequence of his having at the piano, the day before, kept me, in Flora's interest, so beguiled and befooled. The stamp of publicity had of course been fully given by her confinement and departure, and the change itself was now ushered in by our non-observance of the regular custom of the schoolroom. He had already disappeared when, on my way down, I pushed open his door, and I learned below that he had breakfasted—in the presence of a couple of the maids—with Mrs. Grose and his sister. He had then gone out, as he said, for a stroll; than which nothing, I reflected, could better have expressed his frank view of the abrupt transformation of my office. What he would now permit this office to consist of was yet to be settled: there was at the least a queer relief—I mean for myself in especial—in the renouncement of one pretension. If so much had sprung to the surface I scarce put it too strongly in saying that what had perhaps sprung highest was the absurdity of our prolonging the fiction that I had anything more to teach him. It sufficiently stuck out that, by tacit little tricks in which even more than myself he carried out the care for my dignity, I had had to appeal to him to let me off straining to meet him on the ground of his true capacity. He had at any rate his freedom now; I was never to touch it again: as I had amply shown, moreover, when, on his joining me in the schoolroom the previous night, I uttered, in reference to the interval just concluded, neither challenge nor hint. I had too much, from this moment, my other ideas. Yet when he at last arrived the difficulty of applying them, the accumulations of my problem, were brought straight home to me by the beautiful little presence on which what had occurred had as yet, for the eye, dropped neither stain nor shadow.

To mark, for the house, the high state I cultivated I decreed that my meals with the boy should be served, as we called it, downstairs; so that I had been awaiting him in the ponderous pomp of the room outside the window of which I had had from Mrs. Grose, that first scared Sunday, my flash of something it would scarce have done to call light. Here at present I felt afresh—for I had felt it again and again—how my equilibrium depended on the success of rigid will, the will to shut my eyes as tight as possible to the truth that what I had to deal with was, revoltingly, against nature. I could only get on at all by taking "nature" into my confidence and my account, by treating my monstrous ordeal as a push in a direction unusual, of course, and unpleasant, but demanding after all, for a fair front, only another turn of the screw of ordinary human virtue. No attempt, none the less, could well require more tact than just this attempt to supply, one's self, *all* the nature. How could I put even a little of that article into a suppression of reference to what had occurred? How, on the other hand, could I make a reference without a new plunge into the hideous obscure? Well, a sort of answer, after a time, had come to me, and it was so far confirmed as that I was met, incontestably, by the quickened vision of what was rare in my little companion. It was indeed as if he had found even now—as he had so often found at lessons—still some other delicate way to ease me off. Wasn't there light in the fact which, as we shared our solitude, broke out with a specious glitter it had never yet quite worn?—the fact that (opportunity aiding, precious opportunity which had now come) it would be preposterous, with a child so endowed, to forgo the help one might wrest from absolute intelligence? What had his intelligence been given him for but to save him? Mightn't one, to reach his mind, risk the stretch of a stiff arm across his character? It was as if, when we were face to face in the dining-room, he had literally shown me the way. The roast mutton was on the table and I had dispensed with attendance. Miles, before he sat down, stood a moment with his hands in his pockets and looked at the joint, on which he seemed on the point of passing some humorous judgement. But what he presently produced was: "I say, my dear, is she really very awfully ill?"

"Little Flora? Not so bad but that she'll presently be better. London will set her up. Bly had ceased to agree with her. Come here and take your mutton."

He alertly obeyed me, carried the plate carefully to his seat and, when he was established, went on: "Did Bly disagree with her so terribly all at once?"

"Not so suddenly as you might think. One had seen it coming on."

"Then why didn't you get her off before?"

"Before what?"

"Before she became too ill to travel."

I found myself prompt. "She's *not* too ill to travel; she only might have become so if she had stayed. This was just the moment to seize. The journey will dissipate the influence"—oh I was grand!—"and carry it off."

"I see, I see"—Miles, for that matter, was grand too. He settled to his repast with the charming little "table manner" that, from the day of his arrival, had relieved me of all grossness of admonition. Whatever he had been expelled from school for, it wasn't for ugly feeding. He was irreproachable, as always, to-day; but was unmistakably more conscious. He was discernibly trying to take for granted more things than he found, without assistance, quite easy; and he dropped into peaceful silence while he felt his situation. Our meal was of the briefest—mine a vain pretence, and I had the things immediately removed. While this was done Miles stood again with his hands in his little pockets and his back to me—stood and looked out of the wide window through which, that other day, I had seen what pulled me up. We continued silent while the maid was with us—as silent, it whimsically occurred to me, as some young couple who, on their wedding-journey, at the inn, feel shy in the presence of the waiter. He turned round only when the waiter had left us. "Well—so we're alone!"

XXIII

"Oh more or less." I imagine my smile was pale. "Not absolutely. We shouldn't like that!" I went on.

"No—I suppose we shouldn't. Of course we've the others."

"We've the others—we've indeed the others," I concurred.

"Yet even though we have them," he returned, still with his hands in his pockets and planted there in front of me, "they don't much count, do they?"

I made the best of it, but I felt wan. "It depends on what you call 'much'!"

"Yes"—with all accommodation—"everything depends!" On this, however, he faced to the window again and presently reached it with his vague restless cogitating step. He remained there a while with his forehead against the glass, in contemplation of the stupid shrubs I knew and the dull things of November. I had always my hypocrisy of "work," behind which I now gained the sofa. Steadying myself with it there as I had repeatedly done at those moments of torment that I have described as the moments of my knowing the children to be given to something from which I was barred, I sufficiently obeyed my habit of being prepared for the worst. But an extraordinary impression dropped on me as I extracted a meaning from the boy's embarrassed back—none other than the impression that I was not barred now. This inference grew in a few minutes to sharp intensity and seemed bound up with the direct perception that it was positively *he* who was. The frames and squares of the great window were a kind of image, for him, of a kind of failure. I felt that I saw him, in any case, shut in or shut out. He was admirable but not comfortable: I took it in with a throb of hope. Wasn't he looking through the haunted pane for something he couldn't see?—and wasn't it the first time in the whole business that he had known such a lapse? The first, the very first: I found it a splendid portent. It made him anxious, though he watched himself; he had been anxious all day and, even while in his usual sweet little manner he sat at table, had needed all his small strange genius to give it a gloss. When he at last turned round to meet me it was almost as if this genius had succumbed. "Well, I think I'm glad Bly agrees with *me*!"

"You'd certainly seem to have seen, these twenty-four hours, a good deal more of it than for some time before. I hope," I went on bravely, "that you've been enjoying yourself."

"Oh yes, I've been ever so far; all round about—miles and miles away. I've never been so free."

He had really a manner of his own, and I could only try to keep up with him. "Well, do you like it?"

He stood there smiling; then at last he put into two words—"Do *you*?"—more discrimination than I had ever heard two words contain. Before I had time to deal with that, however, he continued as if with the sense that this was an impertinence to be softened. "Nothing could be more charming than the way you take it, for of course if we're alone together now it's you that are alone most. But I hope," he threw in, "you don't particularly mind!"

"Having to do with you?" I asked. "My dear child, how can I help minding? Though I've renounced all claim to your company— you're so beyond me—I at least greatly enjoy it. What else should I stay on for?"

He looked at me more directly, and the expression of his face, graver now, struck me as the most beautiful I had ever found in it. "You stay on just for *that*?"

"Certainly. I stay on as your friend and from the tremendous interest I take in you till something can be done for you that may be more worth your while. That needn't surprise you." My voice trembled so that I felt it impossible to suppress the shake. "Don't you remember how I told you, when I came and sat on your bed the night of the storm, that there was nothing in the world I wouldn't do for you?"

"Yes, yes!" He, on his side, more and more visibly nervous, had a tone to master; but he was so much more successful than I that, laughing out through his gravity, he could pretend we were pleasantly jesting. "Only that, I think, was to get me to do something for *you*!"

"It was partly to get you to do something," I conceded. "But, you know, you didn't do it."

"Oh yes," he said with the brightest superficial eagerness, "you wanted me to tell you something."

"That's it. Out, straight out. What you have on your mind, you know."

"Ah, then, is *that* what you've stayed over for?"

He spoke with a gaiety through which I could still catch the finest little quiver of resentful passion; but I can't begin to express the effect upon me of an implication of surrender even so faint. It was as if what I had yearned for had come at last only to astonish me. "Well, yes—I may as well make a clean breast of it. It was precisely for that."

He waited so long that I supposed it for the purpose of repudiating the assumption on which my action had been founded; but what he finally said was: "Do you mean now—here?"

"There couldn't be a better place or time." He looked round him uneasily, and I had the rare—oh the queer! impression of the very first symptom I had seen in him of the approach of immediate fear. It was as if he were suddenly afraid of me—which struck me indeed as perhaps the best thing to make him. Yet in the very pang of the effort I felt it vain to try sternness, and I heard myself the next instant so gentle as to be almost grotesque. "You want so to go out again?"

"Awfully!" He smiled at me heroically, and the touching little bravery of it was enhanced by his actually flushing with pain. He had picked up his hat, which he had brought in, and stood twirling it in a way that gave me, even as I was just nearly reaching port, a perverse horror of what I was doing. To do it in *any* way was an act of violence, for what did it consist of but the obtrusion of the idea of grossness and guilt on a small helpless creature who had been for me a revelation of the possibilities of beautiful intercourse? Wasn't it base to create for a being so exquisite a mere alien awkwardness? I suppose I now read into our situation a clearness it couldn't have had at the time, for I seem to see our poor eyes already lighted with some spark of a prevision of the anguish that was to come. So we circled about with terrors and scruples, fighters not daring to close. But it was for each other we feared! That kept us a little longer suspended and unbruised. "I'll tell you everything," Miles said—"I mean I'll tell you anything you like. You'll stay on with me, and we shall both be all right, and I *will* tell you—I *will*. But not now."

"Why not now?"

My insistence turned him from me and kept him once more at his window in a silence during which, between us, you might have heard a pin drop. Then he was before me again with the air of a person for whom, outside, some one who had frankly to be reckoned with was waiting. "I have to see Luke."

I had not yet reduced him to quite so vulgar a lie, and I felt proportionately ashamed. But, horrible as it was, his lies made up my truth. I achieved thoughtfully a few loops of my knitting. "Well then, go to Luke, and I'll wait for what you promise. Only in return for that satisfy, before you leave me, one very much smaller request."

He looked as if he felt he had succeeded enough to be able still a little to bargain. "Very much smaller—?"

"Yes, a mere fraction of the whole. Tell me"—oh my work preoccupied me, and I was off-hand!—"if yesterday afternoon, from the table in the hall, you took, you know, my letter."

XXIV

My grasp of how he received this suffered for a minute from something that I can describe only as a fierce split of my attention—a stroke that at first, as I sprang straight up, reduced me to the mere blind movement of getting hold of him, drawing him close and, while I just fell for support against the nearest piece of furniture, instinctively keeping him with his back to the window. The appearance was full upon us that I had already had to deal with here: Peter Quint had come into view like a sentinel before a prison. The next thing I saw was that, from outside, he had reached the window, and then I knew that, close to the glass and glaring in through it, he offered once more to the room his white face of damnation. It represents but grossly what took place within me at the sight to say that on the second my decision was made; yet I believe that no woman so overwhelmed ever in so short a time recovered her command of the *act.* It came to me in the very horror of the immediate presence that the act would be, seeing and facing what I saw and faced, to keep the boy himself unaware. The inspiration—I can call it by no other name—was that I felt how voluntarily, how transcendently, I *might.* It was like fighting with a demon for a human soul, and when I had fairly so appraised it I saw how the human soul—held out, in the tremor of my hands, at arms' length—had a perfect dew of sweat on a lovely childish forehead. The face that was close to mine was as white as the face against the glass, and out of it presently came a sound, not low nor weak, but as if from much farther away, that I drank like a waft of fragrance.

"Yes—I took it."

At this, with a moan of joy, I enfolded, I drew him close; and while I held him to my breast, where I could feel in the sudden fever of his little body the tremendous pulse of his little heart, I kept my eyes on the thing at the window and saw it move and shift its posture. I have likened it to a sentinel, but its slow wheel, for a moment, was rather the prowl of a baffled beast. My present quickened courage, however, was such that, not too much to let it through, I had to shade, as it were, my flame. Meanwhile the glare of the face was again at the window, the scoundrel fixed as if to watch and wait. It was the very confidence that I might now defy him, as well as the positive certitude, by this time, of the child's unconsciousness, that made me go on. "What did you take it for?"

"To see what you said about me."

"You opened the letter?"

"I opened it."

My eyes were now, as I held him off a little again, on Miles's own face, in which the collapse of mockery showed me how complete was the ravage of uneasiness. What was prodigious was that at last, by my success, his sense was sealed and his communication stopped: he knew that he was in presence, but knew not of what, and knew still less that I also was and that I did know. And what did this strain of trouble matter when my eyes went back to the window only to see that the air was clear again and—by my personal triumph—the influence quenched? There was nothing there. I felt that the cause was mine and that I should surely get *all.* "And you found nothing!"—I let my elation out.

He gave the most mournful thoughtful little headshake. "Nothing."

"Nothing, nothing!" I almost shouted in my joy.

"Nothing, nothing," he sadly repeated.

I kissed his forehead; it was drenched. "So what have you done with it?"

"I've burnt it."

"Burnt it?" It was now or never. "Is that what you did at school?"

Oh what this brought up! "At school?"

"Did you take letters?—or other things?"

"Other things?" He appeared now to be thinking of something far off and that reached him only through the pressure of his anxiety. Yet it did reach him. "Did I *steal?*"

I felt myself redden to the roots of my hair as well as wonder if it were more strange to put to a gentleman such a question or to see him take it with allowances that gave the very distance of his fall in the world. "Was it for that you mightn't go back?"

The only thing he felt was rather a dreary little surprise. "Did you know I mightn't go back?"

"I know everything."

He gave me at this the longest and strangest look. "Everything?"

"Everything. Therefore *did* you—?" But I couldn't say it again.

Miles could, very simply. "No. I didn't steal."

My face must have shown him I believed him utterly; yet my hands—but it was for pure tenderness—shook him as if to ask him why, if it was all for nothing, he had condemned me to months of torment. "What, then, did you do?"

He looked in vague pain all round the top of the room and drew his breath, two or three times over, as if with difficulty. He might have been standing at the bottom of the sea and raising his eyes to some faint green twilight. "Well—I said things."

"Only that?"

"They thought it was enough!"

"To turn you out for?"

Never, truly, had a person "turned out" shown so little to explain it as this little person! He appeared to weigh my question, but in a manner quite detached and almost helpless. "Well, I suppose I oughtn't."

"But to whom did you say them?"

He evidently tried to remember, but it dropped—he had lost it. "I don't know!"

He almost smiled at me in the desolation of his surrender, which was indeed practically, by this time, so complete that I ought to have left it there. But I was infatuated—I was blind with victory, though even then the very effect that was to have brought him so much nearer was already that of added separation. "Was it to every one?" I asked.

"No; it was only to—" But he gave a sick little headshake. "I don't remember their names."

"Were they, then, so many?"

"No—only a few. Those I liked."

Those he liked? I seemed to float, not into clearness, but into a darker obscure, and within a minute there had come to me out of my very pity the appalling alarm of his being perhaps innocent. It was for the instant confounding and bottomless, for if he *were* innocent what then on earth was I? Paralysed, while it lasted, by the mere brush of the question, I let him go a little, so that, with a deep-drawn sigh, he turned away from me again; which, as he faced toward the clear window, I suffered, feeling that I had nothing now there to keep him from. "And did they repeat what you said?" I went on after a moment.

He was soon at some distance from me, still breathing hard and again with the air, though now without anger for it, of being confined against his will. Once more, as he had done before, he looked up at the dim day as if, of what had hitherto sustained him, nothing was left but an unspeakable anxiety. "Oh yes," he nevertheless replied—"they must have repeated them. To those *they* liked," he added.

There was somehow less of it than I had expected; but I turned it over. "And these things came round—?"

"To the masters? Oh yes!" he answered very simply. "But I didn't know they'd tell."

"The masters? They didn't—they've never told. That's why I ask you."

He turned to me again his little beautiful fevered face. "Yes, it was too bad."

"Too bad?"

"What I suppose I sometimes said. To write home."

I can't name the exquisite pathos of the contradiction given to such a speech by such a speaker; I only know that the next instant I heard myself throw off with homely force: "Stuff and nonsense!" But the next after that I must have sounded stern enough. "What *were* these things?"

My sternness was all for his judge, his executioner; yet it made him avert himself again, and that movement made *me,* with a single bound and an irrepressible cry, spring straight upon him. For there again, against the glass, as if to blight his confession and stay his answer, was the hideous author of our woe—the white face of damnation. I felt a sick swim at the drop of my victory and all the return of my battle, so that the wildness of my veritable leap only served as a great betrayal. I saw him, from the midst of my act, meet it with a divination, and on the perception that even now he only guessed, and that the window was still to his own eyes free, I let the impulse flame up to convert the climax of his dismay into the very proof of his liberation. "No more, no more, no more!" I shrieked to my visitant as I tried to press him against me.

"Is she *here?*" Miles panted as he caught with his sealed eyes the direction of my words. Then as his strange "she" staggered me and, with a gasp, I echoed it, "Miss Jessel, Miss Jessel!" he with sudden fury gave me back.

I seized, stupefied, his supposition—some sequel to what we had done to Flora, but this made me only want to show him that it was better still than that. "It's not Miss Jessel! But it's at the window—straight before us. It's *there*—the coward horror, there for the last time!"

At this, after a second in which his head made the movement of a baffled dog's on a scent and then gave a frantic little shake for air and light, he was at me in a white rage, bewildered, glaring vainly over the place and missing wholly, though it now, to my sense, filled the room like the taste of poison, the wide overwhelming presence. "It's *he?*"

I was so determined to have all my proof that I flashed into ice to challenge him. "Whom do you mean by 'he'?"

"Peter Quint—you devil!" His face gave again, round the room, its convulsed supplication. *"Where?"*

They are in my ears still, his supreme surrender of the name and his tribute to my devotion. "What does he matter now, my own?—what will he *ever* matter? *I* have you," I launched at the beast, "but he has lost you for ever!" Then for the demonstration of my work, "There, *there!*" I said to Miles.

But he had already jerked straight round, stared, glared again, and seen but the quiet day. With the stroke of the loss I was so proud of he uttered the cry of a creature hurled over an abyss, and the grasp with which I recovered him might have been that of catching him in his fall. I caught him, yes, I held him—it may be imagined with what a passion; but at the end of a minute I began to feel what it truly was that I held. We were alone with the quiet day, and his little heart, dispossessed, had stopped.

IN THE CAGE

I

It had occurred to her early that in her position—that of a young person spending, in framed and wired confinement, the life of a guinea-pig or a magpie—she should know a great many persons without their recognising the acquaintance. That made it an emotion the more lively—though singularly rare and always, even then, with opportunity still very much smothered—to see any one come in whom she knew, as she called it, outside, and who could add something to the poor identity of her function. Her function was to sit there with two young men—the other telegraphist and the counter-clerk; to mind the "sounder,"[1] which was always going, to dole out stamps and postal-orders, weigh letters, answer stupid questions, give difficult change and, more than anything else, count words as numberless as the sands of the sea, the words of the telegrams thrust, from morning to night, through the gap left in the high lattice, across the encumbered shelf that her forearm ached with rubbing. This transparent screen fenced out or fenced in, according to the side of the narrow counter on which the human lot was cast, the duskiest corner of a shop pervaded not a little, in winter, by the poison of perpetual gas, and at all times by the presence of hams, cheese, dried fish, soap, varnish, paraffin, and other solids and fluids that she came to know perfectly by their smells without consenting to know them by their names.

The barrier that divided the little post-and-telegraph-office from the grocery was a frail structure of wood and wire; but the social, the professional separation was a gulf that fortune, by a stroke quite remarkable, had spared her the necessity of contributing at all publicly to bridge. When Mr. Cocker's young men stepped over from behind the other counter to change a five-pound note—and Mr. Cocker's situation, with the cream of the "Court Guide"[2] and the dearest furnished apartments, Simpkin's, Ladle's, Thrupp's, just round the corner, was so select that his place was quite pervaded by the crisp rustle of these emblems—she pushed out the sovereigns as if the applicant were no more to her than one of the momentary appearances in the great procession; and this perhaps all the more from the very fact of the connection—only recognised outside indeed—to which she had lent herself with ridiculous inconsequence. She recognised the others the less because she had at last so unreservedly, so irredeemably, recognised Mr. Mudge. But she was a little ashamed, none the less, of having to admit to herself that Mr. Mudge's removal to a higher sphere—to a more commanding position, that is, though to a much lower neighbourhood—would have been described still better as a luxury than as the simplification that she contented herself with calling it. He had, at any rate, ceased to be all day long in her eyes, and this left something a little fresh for them to rest on of a Sunday. During the three months that he had remained at Cocker's after her consent to their engagement, she had often asked herself what it was that marriage would be able to add to a familiarity so final. Opposite there, behind the counter of which his superior stature, his whiter apron, his more clustering curls and more present, too present, h's had been for a couple of years the principal ornament, he had moved to and fro before her as on the small sanded floor of their contracted future. She was conscious now of the improvement of not having to take her present and her future at once. They were about as much as she could manage when taken separate.

She had, none the less, to give her mind steadily to what Mr. Mudge had again written her about, the idea of her applying for a transfer to an office quite similar—she couldn't yet hope for a place in a bigger—under the very roof where he was foreman, so that, dangled before her every minute of the day, he should see her, as he called it, "hourly," and in a part, the far N.W. district, where, with her mother, she would save, on their two rooms alone, nearly three shillings. It would be far from dazzling to exchange Mayfair for Chalk Farm,[3] and it was something of a predicament that he so kept at her; still, it was nothing to the old predicaments, those of the early times of their great misery, her own, her mother's, and her elder sister's—the last of whom had succumbed to all but absolute want when, as conscious, incredulous ladies, suddenly bereaved, betrayed, overwhelmed, they had slipped faster and faster down the steep slope at the bottom of which she alone had rebounded. Her mother had never rebounded any more at the bottom than on the way; had only rumbled and grumbled down and down, making, in respect of caps and conversation, no effort whatever, and too often, alas! smelling of whisky.

II

It was always rather quiet at Cocker's while the contingent from Ladle's and Thrupp's and all the other great places were at luncheon, or, as the young men used vulgarly to say, while the animals were feeding. She had forty minutes in advance of this to go home for her own dinner; and when she came back, and one of the young men took his turn, there was often half an hour during which she could pull out a bit of work[4] or a book—a book from the place where she borrowed novels, very greasy, in fine print and all about fine folks, at a ha'penny a day. This sacred pause was one of the numerous ways in which the establishment kept its finger on the pulse of fashion and fell into the rhythm of the larger life. It had something to do, one day, with the particular vividness marking the advent of a lady whose meals were apparently irregular, yet whom she was destined, she afterwards found, not to forget. The girl was *blasée;* nothing could belong more, as she perfectly knew, to the intense publicity of her profession; but she had a whimsical mind and wonderful nerves; she was subject, in short, to sudden flickers of antipathy and sympathy, red gleams in the grey, fitful awakings and followings, odd caprices of curiosity. She had a friend who had invented a new career for women—that of being in and out of people's houses to look after the flowers. Mrs. Jordan had a manner of her own of sounding this allusion; "the flowers," on her lips, were, in happy homes, as usual as the coals or the daily papers. She took charge of them, at any rate, in all the rooms, at so much a month, and people were quickly finding out what it was to make over this delicate duty to the widow of a clergyman. The widow, on her side, dilating on the initiations thus opened up to her, had been splendid to her young friend over the way she was made free of the greatest houses—the way, especially when she did the dinner-tables, set out so often for twenty, she felt that a single step more would socially, would absolutely, introduce her. On its being asked of her, then, if she circulated only in a sort of tropical solitude, with the upper servants for picturesque natives, and on her having to assent to this glance at her limitations, she had found a reply to the girl's invidious question. "You've no imagination, my dear!"—that was because the social door might at any moment open so wide.

Our young lady had not taken up the charge, had dealt with it good-humouredly, just because she knew so well what to think of it. It was at once one of her most cherished complaints and most secret supports that people didn't understand her, and it was accordingly a matter of indifference to her that Mrs. Jordan shouldn't; even though Mrs. Jordan, handed down from their early twilight of gentility and also the victim of reverses, was the only member of her circle in whom she recognised an equal. She was perfectly aware that her imaginative life was the life in which she spent most of her time; and she would have been ready, had it been at all worth while, to contend that, since her outward occupation didn't kill it, it must be strong indeed. Combinations of flowers and green-stuff, forsooth! What *she* could handle freely, she said to herself, was combinations of men and women. The only weakness in her faculty came from the positive abundance of her contact with the human herd; this was so constant, had the effect of becoming so cheap, that there were long stretches in which inspiration, divination and interest, quite dropped. The great thing was the flashes, the quick revivals, absolute accidents all, and neither to be counted on nor to be resisted. Some one had only sometimes to put in a penny for a stamp, and the whole thing was upon her. She was so absurdly constructed that these were literally the moments that made up—made up for the long stiffness of sitting there in the stocks, made up for the cunning hostility of Mr. Buckton and the importunate sympathy of the counter-clerk, made up for the daily, deadly, flourishy letter from Mr. Mudge, made up even for the most haunting of her worries, the rage at moments of not knowing how her mother did "get it."

She had surrendered herself moreover, of late, to a certain expansion of her consciousness; something that seemed perhaps vulgarly accounted for by the fact that, as the blast of the season roared louder and the waves of fashion tossed their spray further over the counter, there were more impressions to be gathered and really—for it came to that—more life to be led. Definite, at any rate, it was that by the time May was well started the kind of company she kept at Cocker's had begun to strike her as a reason—a reason she might almost put forward for a policy of procrastination. It sounded silly, of course, as yet, to plead such a motive, especially as the fascination of the place was, after all, a sort of torment. But she liked her torment; it was a torment she should miss at Chalk Farm. She was ingenious and uncandid, therefore, about leaving the breadth of London a little longer between herself and that austerity. If she had not quite the courage, in short, to say to Mr. Mudge that her actual chance for a play of mind was worth, any week, the three shillings he desired to help her to save, she yet saw something happen in the course of the month that, in her heart of hearts at least, answered the subtle question. This was connected precisely with the appearance of the memorable lady.

III

She pushed in three bescribbled forms which the girl's hand was quick to appropriate, Mr. Buckton having so frequent a perverse instinct for catching first any eye that promised the sort of entertainment with which she had her peculiar affinity. The amusements of captives are full of a desperate contrivance, and one of our young friend's ha'pennyworths had been the charming tale of *Picciola*.⁵ It was of course the law of the place that they were never to take no notice, as Mr. Buckton said, whom they served; but this also never prevented, certainly on the same gentleman's own part, what he was fond of describing as the underhand game. Both her companions, for that matter, made no secret of the number of favourites they had among the ladies; sweet familiarities in spite of which she had repeatedly caught each of them in stupidities and mistakes, confusions of identity and lapses of observation that never failed to remind her how the cleverness of men ended where the cleverness of women began. "Marguerite, Regent Street. Try on at six. All Spanish lace. Pearls. The full length." That was the first; it had no signature. "Lady Agnes Orme, Hyde Park Place.⁶ Impossible to-night, dining Haddon. Opera to-morrow, promised Fritz, but could do play Wednesday. Will try Haddon for Savoy, and anything in the world you like, if you can get Gussy. Sunday, Montenero. Sit Mason Monday, Tuesday. Marguerite awful. Cissy." That was the second. The third, the girl noted when she took it, was on a foreign form: "Everard, Hôtel Brighton, Paris. Only understand and believe. 22nd to 26th, and certainly 8th and 9th. Perhaps others. Come. Mary."

Mary was very handsome, the handsomest woman, she felt in a moment, she had ever seen—or perhaps it was only Cissy. Perhaps it was both, for she had seen stranger things than that—ladies wiring to different persons under different names. She had seen all sorts of things and pieced together all sorts of mysteries. There had once been one—not long before—who, without winking, sent off five over five different signatures. Perhaps these represented five different friends who had asked her—all women, just as perhaps now Mary and Cissy, or one or other of them, were wiring by deputy. Sometimes she put in too much—too much of her own sense; sometimes she put in too little; and in either case this often came round to her afterwards, for she had an extraordinary way of keeping clues. When she noticed, she noticed; that was what it came to. There were days and days, there were weeks sometimes, of vacancy. This arose often from Mr. Buckton's devilish and successful subterfuges for keeping her at the sounder whenever it looked as if anything might amuse; the sounder, which it was equally his business to mind, being the innermost cell of captivity, a cage within the cage, fenced off from the rest by a frame of ground glass. The counter-clerk would have played into her hands; but the counter-clerk was really reduced to idiocy by the effect of his passion for her. She flattered herself moreover, nobly, that with the unpleasant conspicuity of this passion she would never have consented to be obliged to him. The most she would ever do would be always to shove off on him whenever she could the registration of letters, a job she happened particularly to loathe. After the long stupors, at all events, there almost always suddenly would come a sharp taste of something; it was in her mouth before she knew it; it was in her mouth now.

To Cissy, to Mary, whichever it was, she found her curiosity going out with a rush, a mute effusion that floated back to her, like a returning tide, the living colour and splendour of the beautiful head, the light of eyes that seemed to reflect such utterly other things than the mean things actually before them; and, above all, the high, curt consideration of a manner that, even at bad moments, was a magnificent habit and of the very essence of the innumerable things—her beauty, her birth, her father and mother, her cousins, and all her ancestors—that its possessor couldn't have got rid of if she had wished. How did our obscure little public servant know that, for the lady of the telegrams, this was a bad moment? How did she guess all sorts of impossible things, such as, almost on the very spot, the presence of drama, at a critical stage, and the nature of the tie with the gentleman at the Hôtel Brighton? More than ever before it floated to her through the bars of the cage that this at last was the high reality, the bristling truth that she had hitherto only patched up and eked out—one of the creatures, in fine, in whom all the conditions for happiness actually met, and who, in the air they made, bloomed with an unwitting insolence. What came home to the girl was the way the insolence was tempered by something that was equally a part of the distinguished life, the custom of a flower-like bend to the less fortunate—a dropped fragrance, a mere quick breath, but which in fact pervaded and lingered. The apparition was very young, but certainly married, and our fatigued friend had a sufficient store of mythological comparison to recognise the port of Juno.[7] Marguerite might be "awful," but she knew how to dress a goddess.

Pearls and Spanish lace—she herself, with assurance, could see them, and the "full length" too, and also red velvet bows, which, disposed on the lace in a particular manner (she could have placed them with the turn of a hand), were of course to adorn the front of a black brocade that would be like a dress in a picture. However, neither Marguerite, nor Lady Agnes, nor Haddon, nor Fritz, nor Gussy was what the wearer of this garment had really come in for. She had come in for Everard—and that was doubtless not *his* true name either. If our young lady had never taken such jumps before, it was simply that she had never before been so affected. She went all the way. Mary and Cissy had been round together, in their single superb person, to see him—he must live round the corner; they had found that, in consequence of something they had come, precisely, to make up for or to have another scene about, he had gone off—gone off just on purpose to make them feel it; on which they had come together to Cocker's as to the nearest place; where they had put in the three forms partly in order not to put in the one alone. The two others, in a manner, covered it, muffled it, passed it off. Oh yes, she went all the way, and this was a specimen of how she often went. She would know the hand again any time. It was as handsome and as everything else as the woman herself. The woman herself had, on learning his flight, pushed past Everard's servant and into his room; she had written her missive at his table and with his pen. All this, every inch of it, came in the waft that she blew through and left behind her, the influence that, as I have said, lingered. And among the things the girl was sure of, happily, was that she should see her again.

IV

She saw her, in fact, and only ten days later; but this time she was not alone, and that was exactly a part of the luck of it. Being clever enough to know through what possibilities it could range, our young lady had ever since had in her mind a dozen conflicting theories about Everard's type; as to which, the instant they came into the place, she felt the point settled with a thump that seemed somehow addressed straight to her heart. That organ literally beat faster at the approach of the gentleman who was this time with Cissy, and who, as seen from within the cage, became on the spot the happiest of the happy circumstances with which her mind had invested the friend of Fritz and Gussy. He was a very happy circumstance indeed as, with his cigarette in his lips and his broken familiar talk caught by his companion, he put down the half-dozen telegrams which it would take them together some minutes to despatch. And here it occurred, oddly enough, that if, shortly before, the girl's interest in his companion had sharpened her sense for the messages then transmitted, her immediate vision of himself had the effect, while she counted his seventy words, of preventing intelligibility. *His* words were mere numbers, they told her nothing whatever; and after he had gone she was in possession of no name, of no address, of no meaning, of nothing but a vague, sweet sound and an immense impression. He had been there but five minutes, he had smoked in her face, and, busy with his telegrams, with the tapping pencil and the conscious danger, the odious betrayal that would come from a mistake, she had had no wandering glances nor roundabout arts to spare. Yet she had taken him in; she knew everything; she had made up her mind.

He had come back from Paris; everything was re-arranged; the pair were again shoulder to shoulder in their high encounter with life, their large and complicated game. The fine, soundless pulse of this game was in the air for our young woman while they remained in the shop. While they remained? They remained all day; their presence continued and abode with her, was in everything she did till nightfall, in the thousands of other words she counted, she transmitted, in all the stamps she detached and the letters she weighed and the change she gave, equally unconscious and unerring in each of these particulars, and not, as the run on the little office thickened with the afternoon hours, looking up at a single ugly face in the long sequence, nor really hearing the stupid questions that she patiently and perfectly answered. All patience was possible now, and all questions stupid after his—all faces ugly. She had been sure she should see the lady again; and even now she should perhaps, she should probably, see her often. But for him it was totally different; she should never, never see him. She wanted it too much. There was a kind of wanting that helped—she had arrived, with her rich experience, at that generalisation; and there was another kind that was fatal. It was this time the fatal kind; it would prevent.

Well, she saw him the very next day, and on this second occasion it was quite different; the sense of every syllable he despatched was fiercely distinct; she indeed felt her progressive pencil, dabbing as if with a quick caress the marks of his own, put life into every stroke. He was there a long time—had not brought his forms filled out, but worked them off in a nook on the counter; and there were other people as well—a changing, pushing cluster, with every one to mind at once and endless right change to make and information to produce. But she kept hold of him throughout; she continued, for herself, in a relation with him as close as that in which, behind the hated ground glass, Mr. Buckton luckily continued with the sounder. This morning everything changed, but with a kind of dreariness too; she had to swallow the rebuff to her theory about fatal desires, which she did without confusion and indeed with absolute levity; yet if it was now flagrant that he did live close at hand—at Park Chambers—and belonged supremely to the class that wired everything, even their expensive feelings (so that, as he never wrote, his correspondence cost him weekly pounds and pounds, and he might be in and out five times a day), there was, all the same, involved in the prospect, and by reason of its positive excess of light, a perverse melancholy, almost a misery. This was rapidly to give it a place in an order of feelings on which I shall presently touch.

Meanwhile, for a month, he was very constant. Cissy, Mary, never re-appeared with him; he was always either alone or accompanied only by some gentleman who was lost in the blaze of his glory. There was another sense, however—and indeed there was more than one—in which she mostly found herself counting in the splendid creature with whom she had originally connected him. He addressed this correspondent neither as Mary nor as Cissy; but the girl was sure of whom it was, in Eaton Square, that he was perpetually wiring to—and so irreproachably!—as Lady Bradeen. Lady Bradeen was Cissy, Lady Bradeen was Mary, Lady Bradeen was the friend of Fritz and of Gussy, the customer of Marguerite, and the close ally, in short (as was ideally right, only the girl had not yet found a descriptive term that was), of the most magnificent of men. Nothing could equal the frequency and variety of his communications to her ladyship but their extraordinary, their abysmal propriety. It was just the talk—so profuse sometimes that she wondered what was left for their real meetings—of the happiest people in the world. Their real meetings must have been constant, for half of it was appointments and allusions, all swimming in a sea of other allusions still, tangled in a complexity of questions that gave a wondrous image of their life. If Lady Bradeen was Juno, it was all certainly Olympian. If the girl, missing the answers, her ladyship's own outpourings, sometimes wished that Cocker's had only been one of the bigger offices where telegrams arrived as well as departed, there were yet ways in which, on the whole, she pressed the romance closer by reason of the very quantity of imagination that it demanded. The days and hours of this new friend, as she came to account him, were at all events unrolled, and however much more she might have known she would still have wished to go beyond. In fact she did go beyond; she went quite far enough.

But she could none the less, even after a month, scarce have told if the gentlemen who came in with him recurred or changed; and this in spite of the fact that they too were always posting and wiring, smoking in her face and signing or not signing. The gentlemen who came in with him were nothing, at any rate, when he was there. They turned up alone at other times—then only perhaps with a dim richness of reference. He himself, absent as well as present, was all. He was very tall, very fair, and had, in spite of his thick pre-occupations, a good-humour that was exquisite, particularly as it so often had the effect of keeping him on. He could have reached over anybody, and anybody—no matter who—would have let him; but he was so extraordinarily kind that he quite pathetically waited, never waggling things at her out of his turn or saying "Here!" with horrid sharpness. He waited for pottering old ladies, for gaping slaveys, for the perpetual Buttonses[8] from Thrupp's; and the thing in all this that she would have liked most unspeakably to put to the test was the possibility of her having for him a personal identity that might in a particular way appeal. There were moments when he actually struck her as on her side, arranging to help, to support, to spare her.

But such was the singular spirit of our young friend, that she could remind herself with a sort of rage that when people had awfully good manners—people of that class,—you couldn't tell. These manners were for everybody, and it might be drearily un-availing for any poor particular body to be overworked and un-usual. What he did take for granted was all sorts of facility; and his high pleasantness, his relighting of cigarettes while he waited, his unconscious bestowal of opportunities, of boons, of blessings, were all a part of his magnificent security, the instinct that told him there was nothing such an existence as his could ever lose by. He was, somehow, at once very bright and very grave, very young and im-mensely complete; and whatever he was at any moment, it was al-ways as much as all the rest the mere bloom of his beatitude. He was sometimes Everard, as he had been at the Hôtel Brighton, and he was sometimes Captain Everard. He was sometimes Philip with his surname and sometimes Philip without it. In some directions he was merely Phil, in others he was merely Captain. There were re-lations in which he was none of these things, but a quite different person—"the Count." There were several friends for whom he was William. There were several for whom, in allusion perhaps to his complexion, he was "the Pink 'Un." Once, once only by good luck, he had, coinciding comically, quite miraculously, with another person also near to her, been "Mudge." Yes, whatever he was, it was a part of his happiness—whatever he was and probably whatever he wasn't. And his happiness was a part—it became so little by little— of something that, almost from the first of her being at Cocker's, had been deeply with the girl.

V

This was neither more nor less than the queer extension of her experience, the double life that, in the cage, she grew at last to lead. As the weeks went on there she lived more and more into the world of whiffs and glimpses, and found her divinations work faster and stretch further. It was a prodigious view as the pressure heightened, a panorama fed with facts and figures, flushed with a torrent of colour and accompanied with wondrous world-music. What it mainly came to at this period was a picture of how London could amuse itself; and that, with the running commentary of a witness so exclusively a witness, turned for the most part to a hardening of the heart. The nose of this observer was brushed by the bouquet, yet she could never really pluck even a daisy. What could still remain fresh in her daily grind was the immense disparity, the difference and contrast, from class to class, of every instant and every motion. There were times when all the wires in the country seemed to start from the little hole-and-corner where she plied for a livelihood, and where, in the shuffle of feet, the flutter of "forms," the straying of stamps and the ring of change over the counter, the people she had fallen into the habit of remembering and fitting together with others, and of having her theories and interpretations of, kept up before her their long procession and rotation. What twisted the knife in her vitals was the way the profligate rich scattered about them, in extravagant chatter over their extravagant pleasures and sins, an amount of money that would have held the stricken household of her frightened childhood, her poor pinched mother and tormented father and lost brother and starved sister, together for a lifetime. During her first weeks she had often gasped at the sums people were willing to pay for the stuff they transmitted—the "much love"s, the "awful" regrets, the compliments and wonderments and vain, vague gestures that cost the price of a new pair of boots. She had had a way then of glancing at the people's faces, but she had early learned that if you became a telegraphist you soon ceased to be astonished. Her eye for types amounted nevertheless to genius, and there were those she liked and those she hated, her feeling for the latter of which grew to a positive possession, an instinct of observation and detection. There were the brazen women, as she called them, of the higher and the lower fashion, whose squanderings and graspings, whose struggles and secrets and love-affairs and lies, she tracked and stored up against them, till she had at moments, in private, a triumphant, vicious feeling of mastery and power, a sense of having their silly, guilty secrets in her pocket, her small retentive brain, and thereby knowing so much more about them than they suspected or would care to think. There were those she would have liked to betray, to trip up, to bring down with words altered and fatal; and all through a personal hostility provoked by the lightest signs, by their accidents of tone and manner, by the particular kind of relation she always happened instantly to feel.

There were impulses of various kinds, alternately soft and severe, to which she was constitutionally accessible and which were determined by the smallest accidents. She was rigid, in general, on the article of making the public itself affix its stamps, and found a special enjoyment in dealing, to that end, with some of the ladies who were too grand to touch them. She had thus a play of refinement and subtlety greater, she flattered herself, than any of which she could be made the subject; and though most people were too stupid to be conscious of this, it brought her endless little consolations and revenges. She recognised quite as much those of her sex whom she would have liked to help, to warn, to rescue, to see more of; and that alternative as well operated exactly through the hazard of personal sympathy, her vision for silver threads and moonbeams and her gift for keeping the clues and finding her way in the tangle. The moonbeams and silver threads presented at moments all the vision of what poor *she* might have made of happiness. Blurred and blank as the whole thing often inevitably, or mercifully, became, she could still, through crevices and crannies, be stupefied, especially by what, in spite of all seasoning, touched the sorest place in her consciousness, the revelation of the golden shower flying about without a gleam of gold for herself. It remained prodigious to the end, the money her fine friends were able to spend to get still more, or even to complain to fine friends of their own that they were in want. The pleasures they proposed were equalled only by those they declined, and they made their appointments often so expensively that she was left wondering at the nature of the delights to which the mere approaches were so paved with shillings. She quivered on occasion into the perception of this and that one whom she would, at all events, have just simply liked to *be*. Her conceit, her baffled vanity were possibly monstrous; she certainly often threw herself into a defiant conviction that she would have done the whole thing much better. But her greatest comfort, on the whole, was her comparative vision of the men; by whom I mean the unmistakable gentlemen, for she had no interest in the spurious or the shabby, and no mercy at all for the poor. She could have found a sixpence, outside, for an appearance of want; but her fancy, in some directions so alert, had never a throb of response for any sign of the sordid. The men she did follow, moreover, she followed mainly in one relation, the relation as to which the cage convinced her, she believed, more than anything else could have done, that it was quite the most diffused.

She found her ladies, in short, almost always in communication with her gentlemen, and her gentlemen with her ladies, and she read into the immensity of their intercourse stories and meanings without end. Incontestably she grew to think that the men cut the best figure; and in this particular, as in many others, she arrived at a philosophy of her own, all made up of her private notations and cynicisms. It was a striking part of the business, for example, that it was much more the women, on the whole, who were after the men than the men who were after the women: it was literally visible that the general attitude of the one sex was that of the object pursued and defensive, apologetic and attenuating, while the light of her own nature helped her more or less to conclude as to the attitude of the other. Perhaps she herself a little even fell into the custom of pursuit in occasionally deviating only for gentlemen from her high rigour about the stamps. She had early in the day made up her mind, in fine, that they had the best manners; and if there were none of them she noticed when Captain Everard was there, there were plenty she could place and trace and name at other times, plenty who, with their way of being "nice" to her, and of handling, as if their pockets were private tills, loose, mixed masses of silver and gold, were such pleasant appearances that she could envy them without dislike. *They* never had to give change—they only had to get it. They ranged through every suggestion, every shade of fortune, which evidently included indeed lots of bad luck as well as of good, declining even toward Mr. Mudge and his bland, firm thrift, and ascending, in wild signals and rocket-flights, almost to within hail of her highest standard. So, from month to month, she went on with them all, through a thousand ups and downs and a thousand pangs and indifferences. What virtually happened was that in the shuffling herd that passed before her by far the greater part only passed—a proportion but just appreciable stayed. Most of the elements swam straight away, lost themselves in the bottomless common, and by so doing really kept the page clear. On the clearness, therefore, what she did retain stood sharply out; she nipped and caught it, turned it over and interwove it.

VI

She met Mrs. Jordan whenever she could, and learned from her more and more how the great people, under her gentle shake, and after going through everything with the mere shops, were waking up to the gain of putting into the hands of a person of real refinement the question that the shop-people spoke of so vulgarly as that of the floral decorations. The regular dealers in these decorations were all very well; but there was a peculiar magic in the play of

taste of a lady who had only to remember, through whatever inter-
vening dusk, all her own little tables, little bowls and little jars and
little other arrangements, and the wonderful thing she had made of
the garden of the vicarage. This small domain, which her young
friend had never seen, bloomed in Mrs. Jordan's discourse like a
new Eden, and she converted the past into a bank of violets by the
tone in which she said, "Of course you always knew my one passion!" She obviously met now, at any rate, a big contemporary need,
measured what it was rapidly becoming for people to feel they
could trust her without a tremor. It brought them a peace that—
during the quarter of an hour before dinner in especial—was worth
more to them than mere payment could express. Mere payment,
none the less, was tolerably prompt; she engaged by the month, taking over the whole thing; and there was an evening on which, in respect to our heroine, she at last returned to the charge. "It's growing
and growing, and I see that I must really divide the work. One
wants an associate—of one's own kind, don't you know? You know
the look they want it all to have?—of having come, not from a
florist, but from one of themselves. Well, I'm sure *you* could give
it—because you *are* one. Then we *should* win. Therefore just come
in with me."

"And leave the P.O.?"

"Let the P.O. simply bring you your letters. It would bring you
lots, you'd see: orders, after a bit, by the dozen." It was on this, in
due course, that the great advantage again came up: "One seems to
live again with one's own people." It had taken some little time
(after their having parted company in the tempest of their troubles
and then, in the glimmering dawn, finally sighted each other again)
for each to admit that the other was, in her private circle, her only
equal; but the admission came, when it did come, with an honest
groan; and since equality *was* named, each found much personal
profit in exaggerating the other's original grandeur. Mrs. Jordan was
ten years the older, but her young friend was struck with the
smaller difference this now made: it had counted otherwise at the
time when, much more as a friend of her mother's, the bereaved

lady, without a penny of provision, and with stop-gaps, like their own, all gone, had, across the sordid landing on which the opposite doors of the pair of scared miseries opened and to which they were bewilderedly bolted, borrowed coals and umbrellas that were re-paid in potatoes and postage-stamps. It had been a questionable help, at that time, to ladies submerged, floundering, panting, swim-ming for their lives, that they *were* ladies; but such an advantage could come up again in proportion as others vanished, and it had grown very great by the time it was the only ghost of one they possessed. They had literally watched it take to itself a portion of the substance of each that had departed; and it became prodigious now, when they could talk of it together, when they could look back at it across a desert of accepted derogation, and when, above all, they could draw from each other a credulity about it that they could draw from no one else. Nothing was really so marked as that they felt the need to cultivate this legend much more after having found their feet and stayed their stomachs in the ultimate obscure than they had done in the upper air of mere frequent shocks. The thing they could now oftenest say to each other was that they knew what they meant; and the sentiment with which, all round, they knew it was known had been a kind of promise to stick well together again.

Mrs. Jordan was at present fairly dazzling on the subject of the way that, in the practice of her beautiful art, she more than peeped in—she penetrated. There was not a house of the great kind—and it was, of course, only a question of those, real homes of luxury—in which she was not, at the rate such people now had things, all over the place. The girl felt before the picture the cold breath of dis-inheritance as much as she had ever felt it in the cage; she knew, moreover, how much she betrayed this, for the experience of poverty had begun, in her life, too early, and her ignorance of the requirements of homes of luxury had grown, with other active knowledge, a depth of simplification. She had accordingly at first often found that in these colloquies she could only pretend she understood. Educated as she had rapidly been by her chances at Cocker's, there were still strange gaps in her learning—she could never, like Mrs. Jordan, have found her way about one of the "homes." Little by little, however, she had caught on, above all in the light of what Mrs. Jordan's redemption had materially made of that lady, giving her, though the years and the struggles had naturally not straightened a feature, an almost super-eminent air. There were women in and out of Cocker's who were quite nice and who yet didn't look well; whereas Mrs. Jordan looked well and yet, with her extraordinarily protrusive teeth, was by no means quite nice. It would seem, mystifyingly, that it might really come from all the greatness she could live with. It was fine to hear her talk so often of dinners of twenty and of her doing, as she said, exactly as she liked with them. She spoke as if, for that matter, she invited the company. "They simply *give* me the table—all the rest, all the other effects, come afterwards."

VII

"Then you *do* see them?" the girl again asked.

Mrs. Jordan hesitated, and indeed the point had been ambiguous before. "Do you mean the guests?"

Her young friend, cautious about an undue exposure of innocence, was not quite sure. "Well—the people who live there."

"Lady Ventnor? Mrs. Bubb? Lord Rye? Dear, yes. Why, they *like* one."

"But does one personally *know* them?" our young lady went on, since that was the way to speak. "I mean socially, don't you know?—as you know *me*."

"They're not so nice as you!" Mrs. Jordan charmingly cried. "But I *shall* see more and more of them."

Ah, this was the old story. "But how soon?"

"Why, almost any day. Of course," Mrs. Jordan honestly added, "they're nearly always out."

"Then why do they want flowers all over?"

"Oh, that doesn't make any difference." Mrs. Jordan was not

philosophic; she was only evidently determined it shouldn't make any. "They're awfully interested in my ideas, and it's inevitable they should meet me over them."

Her interlocutress was sturdy enough. "What do you call your ideas?"

Mrs. Jordan's reply was fine. "If you were to see me some day with a thousand tulips, you'd soon discover."

"A thousand?"—the girl gaped at such a revelation of the scale of it; she felt, for the instant, fairly planted out. "Well, but if in fact they never do meet you?" she none the less pessimistically insisted.

"Never? They *often* do—and evidently quite on purpose. We have grand long talks."

There was something in our young lady that could still stay her from asking for a personal description of these apparitions; that showed too starved a state. But while she considered, she took in afresh the whole of the clergyman's widow. Mrs. Jordan couldn't help her teeth, and her sleeves were a distinct rise in the world. A thousand tulips at a shilling clearly took one further than a thousand words at a penny; and the betrothed of Mr. Mudge, in whom the sense of the race for life was always acute, found herself wondering, with a twinge of her easy jealousy, if it mightn't after all then, for *her* also, be better—better than where she was—to follow some such scent. Where she was was where Mr. Buckton's elbow could freely enter her right side and the counter-clerk's breathing—he had something the matter with his nose—pervade her left ear. It was something to fill an office under Government, and she knew but too well there were places commoner still than Cocker's; but it never required much of a chance to bring back to her the picture of servitude and promiscuity that she must present to the eye of comparative freedom. She was so boxed up with her young men, and anything like a margin so absent, that it needed more art than she should ever possess to pretend in the least to compass, with any one in the nature of an acquaintance—say with Mrs. Jordan herself, flying in, as it might happen, to wire sympathetically to Mrs. Bubb—an approach to a relation of elegant privacy. She remembered the day when Mrs. Jordan *had,* in fact, by the greatest chance, come in with fifty-three words for Lord Rye and a five-pound note to change. This had been the dramatic manner of their reunion—their mutual recognition was so great an event. The girl could at first only see her from the waist up, besides making but little of her long telegram to his lordship. It was a strange whirligig that had converted the clergyman's widow into such a specimen of the class that went beyond the sixpence.

Nothing of the occasion, all the more, had ever become dim; least of all the way that, as her recovered friend looked up from counting, Mrs. Jordan had just blown, in explanation, through her teeth and through the bars of the cage: "I *do* flowers, you know." Our young woman had always, with her little finger crooked out, a pretty movement for counting; and she had not forgotten the small secret advantage, a sharpness of triumph it might even have been called, that fell upon her at this moment and avenged her for the incoherence of the message, an unintelligible enumeration of numbers, colours, days, hours. The correspondence of people she didn't know was one thing; but the correspondence of people she did had an aspect of its own for her, even when she couldn't understand it. The speech in which Mrs. Jordan had defined a position and announced a profession was like a tinkle of bluebells; but, for herself, her one idea about flowers was that people had them at funerals, and her present sole gleam of light was that lords probably had them most. When she watched, a minute later, through the cage, the swing of her visitor's departing petticoats, she saw the sight from the waist down; and when the counter-clerk, after a mere male glance, remarked, with an intention unmistakably low, "Handsome woman!" she had for him the finest of her chills: "She's the widow of a bishop." She always felt, with the counter-clerk, that it was impossible sufficiently to put it on; for what she wished to express to him was the maximum of her contempt, and that element in her nature was confusedly stored. "A bishop" *was* putting it on, but the counter-clerk's approaches were vile. The night, after this, when, in the fulness of time, Mrs. Jordan mentioned the grand long talks, the girl at last brought out: "Should *I* see them?—I mean if I *were* to give up everything for you."

Mrs. Jordan at this became most arch. "I'd send you to all the bachelors!"

Our young lady could be reminded by such a remark that she usually struck her friend as pretty. "Do *they* have their flowers?"

"Oceans. And they're the most particular." Oh, it was a wonderful world. "You should see Lord Rye's."

"His flowers?"

"Yes, and his letters. He writes me pages on pages—with the most adorable little drawings and plans. You should see his diagrams!"

VIII

The girl had in course of time every opportunity to inspect these documents, and they a little disappointed her; but in the meanwhile there had been more talk, and it had led to her saying, as if her friend's guarantee of a life of elegance were not quite definite: "Well, I see every one at *my* place."

"Every one?"

"Lots of swells. They flock. They live, you know, all round, and the place is filled with all the smart people, all the fast people, those whose names are in the papers—mamma has still the *Morning Post*—and who come up for the season."

Mrs. Jordan took this in with complete intelligence. "Yes, and I daresay it's some of your people that *I* do."

Her companion assented, but discriminated. "I doubt if you 'do' them as much as I! Their affairs, their appointments and arrangements, their little games and secrets and vices—those things all pass before me."

This was a picture that could impose on a clergyman's widow a certain strain; it was in intention, moreover, something of a retort to the thousand tulips. "Their vices? Have they got vices?"

Our young critic even more remarkably stared; then with a touch of contempt in her amusement: "Haven't you found *that* out?"

The homes of luxury, then, hadn't so much to give. "*I* find out everything," she continued.

Mrs. Jordan, at bottom a very meek person, was visibly struck. "I see. You do 'have' them."

"Oh, I don't care! Much good does it do me!"

Mrs. Jordan, after an instant, recovered her superiority. "No—it doesn't lead to much." Her own initiations so clearly did. Still—after all; and she was not jealous: "There must be a charm."

"In seeing them?" At this the girl suddenly let herself go. "I hate them; there's that charm!"

Mrs. Jordan gaped again. "The *real* 'smarts'?"

"Is that what you call Mrs. Bubb? Yes—it comes to me; I've had Mrs. Bubb. I don't think she has been in herself, but there are things her maid has brought. Well, my dear!"—and the young person from Cocker's, recalling these things and summing them up, seemed suddenly to have much to say. But she didn't say it; she checked it; she only brought out: "Her maid, who's horrid—*she* must have her!" Then she went on with indifference: "They're *too* real! They're selfish brutes."

Mrs. Jordan, turning it over, adopted at last the plan of treating it with a smile. She wished to be liberal. "Well, of course, they do lay it out."

"They bore me to death," her companion pursued with slightly more temperance.

But this was going too far. "Ah, that's because you've no sympathy!"

The girl gave an ironic laugh, only retorting that she wouldn't have any either if she had to count all day all the words in the dictionary; a contention Mrs. Jordan quite granted, the more that she shuddered at the notion of ever failing of the very gift to which she owed the vogue—the rage she might call it—that had caught her up. Without sympathy—or without imagination, for it came back again to that—how should she get, for big dinners, down the middle and toward the far corners at all? It wasn't the combinations, which were easily managed: the strain was over the ineffable simplicities, those that the bachelors above all, and Lord Rye perhaps most of any, threw off—just blew off, like cigarette-puffs—such sketches of. The betrothed of Mr. Mudge at all events accepted the explanation, which had the effect, as almost any turn of their talk was now apt to have, of bringing her round to the terrific question of that gentleman. She was tormented with the desire to get out of Mrs. Jordan, on this subject, what she was sure was at the back of Mrs. Jordan's head; and to get it out of her, queerly enough, if only to vent a certain irritation at it. She knew that what her friend would already have risked if she had not been timid and tortuous was: "Give him up—yes, give him up: you'll see that with your sure chances you'll be able to do much better."

Our young woman had a sense that if that view could only be put before her with a particular sniff for poor Mr. Mudge she should hate it as much as she morally ought. She was conscious of not, as yet, hating it quite so much as that. But she saw that Mrs. Jordan was conscious of something too, and that there was a sort of assurance she was waiting little by little to gather. The day came when the girl caught a glimpse of what was still wanting to make her friend feel strong; which was nothing less than the prospect of being able to announce the climax of sundry private dreams. The associate of the aristocracy had personal calculations—she pored over them in her lonely lodgings. If she did the flowers for the bachelors, in short, didn't she expect that to have consequences very different from the outlook, at Cocker's, that she had described as leading to nothing? There seemed in very truth something auspicious in the mixture of bachelors and flowers, though, when looked hard in the eye, Mrs. Jordan was not quite prepared to say she had expected a positive proposal from Lord Rye to pop out of it. Our young woman arrived at last, none the less, at a definite vision of what was in her mind. This was a vivid foreknowledge that the betrothed of Mr. Mudge would, unless conciliated in advance by a successful rescue, almost hate her on the day she should break a particular piece of news. How could that unfortunate otherwise endure to hear of what, under the protection of Lady Ventnor, was after all so possible?

I X

Meanwhile, since irritation sometimes relieved her, the betrothed of Mr. Mudge drew straight from that admirer an amount of it that was proportioned to her fidelity. She always walked with him on Sundays, usually in the Regent's Park,[9] and quite often, once or twice a month, he took her, in the Strand[10] or thereabouts, to see a piece that was having a run. The productions he always preferred were the really good ones—Shakespeare, Thompson,[11] or some funny American thing; which, as it also happened that she hated vulgar plays, gave him ground for what was almost the fondest of his approaches, the theory that their tastes were, blissfully, just the same. He was for ever reminding her of that, rejoicing over it, and being affectionate and wise about it. There were times when she wondered how in the world she could bear him, how she could bear any man so smugly unconscious of the immensity of her difference. It was just for this difference that, if she was to be liked at all, she wanted to be liked, and if that was not the source of Mr. Mudge's admiration, she asked herself, what on earth *could* be? She was not different only at one point, she was different all round; unless perhaps indeed in being practically human, which her mind just barely recognised that he also was. She would have made tremendous concessions in other quarters: there was no limit, for instance, to those she would have made to Captain Everard; but what I have named was the most she was prepared to do for Mr. Mudge. It was because *he* was different that, in the oddest way, she liked as well as deplored him; which was after all a proof that the disparity, should they frankly recognise it, wouldn't necessarily be fatal. She felt that, oleaginous—too oleaginous—as he was, he was somehow comparatively primitive: she had once, during the portion of his time at Cocker's that had overlapped her own, seen him collar a drunken soldier, a big, violent man, who, having come in with a mate to get a postal-order cashed, had made a grab at the money before his friend could reach it and had so produced, among the hams and cheeses and the lodgers from Thrupp's, reprisals instantly ensuing, a scene of scandal and consternation. Mr. Buckton and the counter-clerk had crouched within the cage, but Mr. Mudge had, with a very quiet but very quick step round the counter, triumphantly interposed in the scrimmage, parted the combatants, and shaken the delinquent in his skin. She had been proud of him at that moment, and had felt that if their affair had not already been settled the neatness of his execution would have left her without resistance.

Their affair had been settled by other things: by the evident sincerity of his passion and by the sense that his high white apron resembled a front of many floors. It had gone a great way with her that he would build up a business to his chin, which he carried quite in the air. This could only be a question of time; he would have all Piccadilly[12] in the pen behind his ear. That was a merit in itself for a girl who had known what she had known. There were hours at which she even found him good-looking, though, frankly, there could be no crown for her effort to imagine, on the part of the tailor or the barber, some such treatment of his appearance as would make him resemble even remotely a gentleman. His very beauty was the beauty of a grocer, and the finest future would offer it none too much room to expand. She had engaged herself, in short, to the perfection of a type, and perfection of anything was much for a person who, out of early troubles, had just escaped with her life. But it contributed hugely at present to carry on the two parallel lines of her contacts in the cage and her contacts out of it. After keeping quiet for some time about this opposition, she suddenly—one Sunday afternoon on a penny chair[13] in the Regent's Park—broke, for him, capriciously, bewilderingly, into an intimation of what it came to. He naturally pressed more and more on the subject of her again placing herself where he could see her hourly, and for her to recognise that she had as yet given him no sane reason for delay he had small need to describe himself as unable to make out what she was up to. As if, with her absurd bad reasons, she could have begun to tell him! Sometimes she thought it would be amusing to let him have them full in the face, for she felt she should die of him unless she once in a while stupefied him; and sometimes she thought it would be disgusting and perhaps even fatal. She liked him, how-ever, to think her silly, for that gave her the margin which, at the best, she would always require; and the only difficulty about this was that he hadn't enough imagination to oblige her. It produced, none the less, something of the desired effect—to leave him simply wondering why, over the matter of their reunion, she didn't yield to his arguments. Then at last, simply as if by accident and out of mere boredom on a day that was rather flat, she preposterously produced her own. "Well, wait a bit. Where I am I still see things." And she talked to him even worse, if possible, than she had talked to Mrs. Jordan.

Little by little, to her own stupefaction, she caught that he was trying to take it as she meant it, and that he was neither astonished nor angry. Oh, the British tradesman—this gave her an idea of his resources! Mr. Mudge would be angry only with a person who, like the drunken soldier in the shop, should have an unfavourable effect upon business. He seemed positively to enter, for the time and without the faintest flash of irony or ripple of laughter, into the whimsical grounds of her enjoyment of Cocker's custom, and in-stantly to be casting up whatever it might, as Mrs. Jordan had said, lead to. What he had in mind was not, of course, what Mrs. Jordan had had: it was obviously not a source of speculation with him that his sweetheart might pick up a husband. She could see perfectly that this was not, for a moment, even what he supposed she herself dreamed of. What she had done was simply to give his fancy an-other push into the dim vast of trade. In that direction it was all alert, and she had whisked before it the mild fragrance of a "con-nection." That was the most he could see in any picture of her keeping in with the gentry; and when, getting to the bottom of this, she quickly proceeded to show him the kind of eye she turned on such people and to give him a sketch of what that eye discovered, she reduced him to the particular confusion in which he could still be amusing to her.

X

"They're the most awful wretches, I assure you—the lot all about there."

"Then why do you want to stay among them?"

"My dear man, just because they *are*. It makes me hate them so."

"Hate them? I thought you liked them."

"Don't be stupid. What I 'like' is just to loathe them. You wouldn't believe what passes before my eyes."

"Then why have you never told me? You didn't mention anything before I left."

"Oh, I hadn't got into it then. It's the sort of thing you don't believe at first; you have to look round you a bit and then you understand. You work into it more and more. Besides," the girl went on, "this is the time of the year when the worst lot come up. They're simply packed together in those smart streets. Talk of the numbers of the poor! What *I* can vouch for is the numbers of the rich! There are new ones every day, and they seem to get richer and richer. Oh, they do come up!" she cried, imitating, for her private recreation— she was sure it wouldn't reach Mr. Mudge—the low intonation of the counter-clerk.

"And where do they come from?" her companion candidly inquired.

She had to think a moment; then she found something. "From the 'spring meetings.' They bet tremendously."

"Well, they bet enough at Chalk Farm, if that's all."

"It *isn't* all. It isn't a millionth part!" she replied with some sharpness. "It's immense fun"—she would tantalise him. Then, as she had heard Mrs. Jordan say, and as the ladies at Cocker's even sometimes wired, "It's quite too dreadful!" She could fully feel how it was Mr. Mudge's propriety, which was extreme—he had a horror of coarseness and attended a Wesleyan chapel[14]—that prevented his asking for details. But she gave him some of the more innocuous in spite of himself, especially putting before him how, at Simpkin's and Ladle's, they all made the money fly. That was indeed what he liked to hear: the connection was not direct, but one was somehow more in the right place where the money was flying than where it was simply and meagrely nesting. It enlivened the air, he had to acknowledge, much less at Chalk Farm than in the district in which his beloved so oddly enjoyed her footing. She gave him, she could see, a restless sense that these might be familiarities not to be sacrificed; germs, possibilities, faint foreshowings—heaven knew what—of the initiation it would prove profitable to have arrived at when, in the fulness of time, he should have his own shop in some such paradise. What really touched him—that was discernible— was that she could feed him with so much mere vividness of reminder, keep before him, as by the play of a fan, the very wind of the swift bank-notes and the charm of the existence of a class that Providence had raised up to be the blessing of grocers. He liked to think that the class was there, that it was always there, and that she contributed in her slight but appreciable degree to keep it up to the mark. He couldn't have formulated his theory of the matter, but the exuberance of the aristocracy was the advantage of trade, and everything was knit together in a richness of pattern that it was good to follow with one's finger-tips. It was a comfort to him to be thus assured that there were no symptoms of a drop. What did the sounder, as she called it, nimbly worked, do but keep the ball going?

What it came to, therefore, for Mr. Mudge, was that all enjoyments were, in short, interrelated, and that the more people had the more they wanted to have. The more flirtations, as he might roughly express it, the more cheese and pickles. He had even in his own small way been dimly struck with the concatenation between the tender passion and cheap champagne. What he would have liked to say had he been able to work out his thought to the end was: "I see, I see. Lash them up then, lead them on, keep them going: some of it can't help, some time, coming *our* way." Yet he was troubled by the suspicion of subtleties on his companion's part that spoiled the straight view. He couldn't understand people's hating what they liked or liking what they hated; above all it hurt him somewhere—for he had his private delicacies—to see anything *but* money made out of his betters. To be curious at the expense of the gentry was vaguely wrong; the only thing that was distinctly right was to be prosperous. Wasn't it just because they were up there aloft that they were lucrative? He concluded, at any rate, by saying to his young friend: "If it's improper for you to remain at Cocker's, then that falls in exactly with the other reasons that I have put before you for your removal."

"Improper?"—her smile became a long, wide look at him. "My dear boy, there's no one like you!"

"I daresay," he laughed; "but that doesn't help the question."

"Well," she returned, "I can't give up my friends. I'm making even more than Mrs. Jordan."

Mr. Mudge considered. "How much is *she* making?"

"Oh, you dear donkey!"—and, regardless of all the Regent's Park, she patted his cheek. This was the sort of moment at which she was absolutely tempted to tell him that she liked to be near Park Chambers. There was a fascination in the idea of seeing if, on a mention of Captain Everard, he wouldn't do what she thought he might; wouldn't weigh against the obvious objection the still more obvious advantage. The advantage, of course, could only strike him at the best as rather fantastic; but it was always to the good to keep hold when you *had* hold, and such an attitude would also after all involve a high tribute to her fidelity. Of one thing she absolutely never doubted: Mr. Mudge believed in her with a belief——! She believed in herself too, for that matter: if there was a thing in the world no one could charge her with, it was being the kind of low barmaid person who rinsed tumblers and bandied slang. But she forbore as yet to speak; she had not spoken even to Mrs. Jordan; and the hush that on her lips surrounded the Captain's name maintained itself as a kind of symbol of the success that, up to this time, had attended something or other—she couldn't have said what— that she humoured herself with calling, without words, her relation with him.

XI

She would have admitted indeed that it consisted of little more than the fact that his absences, however frequent and however long, always ended with his turning up again. It was nobody's business in the world but her own if that fact continued to be enough for her. It was of course not enough just in itself; what it had taken on to make it so was the extraordinary possession of the elements of his life that memory and attention had at last given her. There came a day when this possession, on the girl's part, actually seemed to enjoy, between them, while their eyes met, a tacit recognition that was half a joke and half a deep solemnity. He bade her good morning always now; he often quite raised his hat to her. He passed a remark when there was time or room, and once she went so far as to say to him that she had not seen him for "ages." "Ages" was the word she consciously and carefully, though a trifle tremulously, used; "ages" was exactly what she meant. To this he replied in terms doubtless less anxiously selected, but perhaps on that account not the less remarkable, "Oh yes, hasn't it been awfully wet?" That was a specimen of their give and take; it fed her fancy that no form of intercourse so transcendent and distilled had ever been established on earth. Everything, so far as they chose to consider it so, might mean almost anything. The want of margin in the cage, when he peeped through the bars, wholly ceased to be appreciable. It was a drawback only in superficial commerce. With Captain Everard she had simply the margin of the universe. It may be imagined, therefore, how their unuttered reference to all she knew about him could, in this immensity, play at its ease. Every time he handed in a telegram it was an addition to her knowledge: what did his constant smile mean to mark if it didn't mean to mark that? He never came into the place without saying to her in this manner: "Oh yes, you have me by this time so completely at your mercy that it doesn't in the least matter what I give you now. You've become a comfort, I assure you!"

She had only two torments; the greatest of which was that she couldn't, not even once or twice, touch with him on some individual fact. She would have given anything to have been able to allude to one of his friends by name, to one of his engagements by date, to one of his difficulties by the solution. She would have given almost as much for just the right chance—it would have to be tremendously right—to show him in some sharp, sweet way that she had perfectly penetrated the greatest of these last and now lived with it in a kind of heroism of sympathy. He was in love with a woman to whom, and to any view of whom, a lady-telegraphist, and especially one who passed a life among hams and cheeses, was as the sand on the floor; and what her dreams desired was the possibility of its somehow coming to him that her own interest in him could take a pure and noble account of such an infatuation and even of such an impropriety. As yet, however, she could only rub along with the hope that an accident, sooner or later, might give her a lift toward popping out with something that would surprise and perhaps even, some fine day, assist him. What could people mean, moreover—cheaply sarcastic people—by not feeling all that could be got out of the weather? *She* felt it all, and seemed literally to feel it most when she went quite wrong, speaking of the stuffy days as cold, of the cold ones as stuffy, and betraying how little she knew, in her cage, of whether it was foul or fair. It was, for that matter, always stuffy at Cocker's, and she finally settled down to the safe proposition that the outside element was "changeable." Anything seemed true that made him so radiantly assent.

This indeed is a small specimen of her cultivation of insidious ways of making things easy for him—ways to which of course she couldn't be at all sure that he did real justice. Real justice was not of this world: she had had too often to come back to that; yet, strangely, happiness was, and her traps had to be set for it in a manner to keep them unperceived by Mr. Buckton and the counter-clerk. The most she could hope for apart from the question, which constantly flickered up and died down, of the divine chance of his consciously liking her, would be that, without analysing it, he should arrive at a vague sense that Cocker's was—well, attractive; easier, smoother, sociably brighter, slightly more picturesque, in short more propitious in general to his little affairs, than any other establishment just thereabouts. She was quite aware that they couldn't be, in so huddled a hole, particularly quick; but she found her account in the slowness—she certainly could bear it if *he* could. The great pang was that, just thereabouts, post-offices were so awfully thick. She was always seeing him, in imagination, in other places and with other girls. But she would defy any other girl to follow him as she followed. And though they weren't, for so many reasons, quick at Cocker's, she could hurry for him when, through an intimation light as air, she gathered that he was pressed.

When hurry was, better still, impossible, it was because of the pleasantest thing of all, the particular element of their contact—she would have called it their friendship—that consisted of an almost humorous treatment of the look of some of his words. They would never perhaps have grown half so intimate if he had not, by the blessing of heaven, formed some of his letters with a queerness——! It was positive that the queerness could scarce have been greater if he had practised it for the very purpose of bringing their heads together over it as far as was possible to heads on different sides of a cage. It had taken her in reality but once or twice to master these tricks, but, at the cost of striking him perhaps as stupid, she could still challenge them when circumstances favoured. The great circumstance that favoured was that she sometimes actually believed he knew she only feigned perplexity. If he knew it, therefore, he tolerated it; if he tolerated it he came back; and if he came back he liked her. This was her seventh heaven; and she didn't ask much of his liking—she only asked of it to reach the point of his not going away because of her own. He had at times to be away for weeks; he had to lead his life; he had to travel—there were places to which he was constantly wiring for "rooms": all this she granted him, forgave him; in fact, in the long-run, literally blessed and thanked him for. If he had to lead his life, that precisely fostered his leading it so much by telegraph: therefore the benediction was to come in when he could. That was all she asked—that he shouldn't wholly deprive her.

Sometimes she almost felt that he couldn't have done so even had he been minded, on account of the web of revelation that was woven between them. She quite thrilled herself with thinking what, with such a lot of material, a bad girl would do. It would be a scene better than many in her ha'penny novels, this going to him in the dusk of evening at Park Chambers and letting him at last have it. "I know too much about a certain person now not to put it to you—excuse my being so lurid—that it's quite worth your while to buy me off. Come, therefore; buy me!" There was a point indeed at which such flights had to drop again—the point of an unreadiness to name, when it came to that, the purchasing medium. It wouldn't, certainly, be anything so gross as money, and the matter accordingly remained rather vague, all the more that *she* was not a bad girl. It was not for any such reason as might have aggravated a mere minx that she often hoped he would again bring Cissy. The difficulty of this, however, was constantly present to her, for the kind of communion to which Cocker's so richly ministered rested on the fact that Cissy and he were so often in different places. She knew by this time all the places—Suchbury, Monkhouse, Whiteroy, Finches,—and even how the parties, on these occasions, were composed; but her subtlety found ways to make her knowledge fairly protect and promote their keeping, as she had heard Mrs. Jordan say, in touch. So, when he actually sometimes smiled as if he really felt the awkwardness of giving her again one of the same old addresses, all her being went out in the desire—which her face must have expressed—that he should recognise her forbearance to criticise as one of the finest, tenderest sacrifices a woman had ever made for love.

XII

She was occasionally worried, all the same, by the impression that these sacrifices, great as they were, were nothing to those that his own passion had imposed; if indeed it was not rather the passion of his confederate, which had caught him up and was whirling him round like a great steam-wheel. He was at any rate in the strong grip of a dizzy, splendid fate; the wild wind of his life blew him straight before it. Didn't she catch in his face, at times, even through

his smile and his happy habit, the gleam of that pale glare with
which a bewildered victim appeals, as he passes, to some pair of
pitying eyes? He perhaps didn't even himself know how scared he
was; but *she* knew. They were in danger, they were in danger, Captain Everard and Lady Bradeen: it beat every novel in the shop. She
thought of Mr. Mudge and his safe sentiment; she thought of herself and blushed even more for her tepid response to it. It was a
comfort to her at such moments to feel that in another relation—a
relation supplying that affinity with her nature that Mr. Mudge, de-
luded creature, would never supply—she should have been no
more tepid than her ladyship. Her deepest soundings were on two
or three occasions of finding herself almost sure that, if she dared,
her ladyship's lover would have gathered relief from "speaking" to
her. She literally fancied once or twice that, projected as he was
toward his doom, her own eyes struck him, while the air roared in
his ears, as the one pitying pair in the crowd. But how could he
speak to her while she sat sandwiched there between the counter-
clerk and the sounder?

She had long ago, in her comings and goings, made acquaintance
with Park Chambers, and reflected, as she looked up at their luxu-
rious front, that *they,* of course, would supply the ideal setting for
the ideal speech. There was not a picture in London that, before the
season was over, was more stamped upon her brain. She went round
about to pass it, for it was not on the short way; she passed on the
opposite side of the street and always looked up, though it had
taken her a long time to be sure of the particular set of windows.
She had made that out at last by an act of audacity that, at the time,
had almost stopped her heart-beats and that, in retrospect, greatly
quickened her blushes. One evening, late, she had lingered and
watched—watched for some moment when the porter, who was in
uniform and often on the steps, had gone in with a visitor. Then she
followed boldly, on the calculation that he would have taken the
visitor up and that the hall would be free. The hall *was* free, and
the electric light played over the gilded and lettered board that
showed the names and numbers of the occupants of the different
floors. What she wanted looked straight at her—Captain Everard

was on the third. It was as if, in the immense intimacy of this, they were, for the instant and the first time, face to face outside the cage. Alas! they were face to face but a second or two: she was whirled out on the wings of a panic fear that he might just then be entering or issuing. This fear was indeed, in her shameless deflections, never very far from her, and was mixed in the oddest way with depressions and disappointments. It was dreadful, as she trembled by, to run the risk of looking to him as if she basely hung about; and yet it was dreadful to be obliged to pass only at such moments as put an encounter out of the question.

At the horrible hour of her first coming to Cocker's he was always—it was to be hoped—snug in bed; and at the hour of her final departure he was of course—she had such things all on her fingers'-ends—dressing for dinner. We may let it pass that if she could not bring herself to hover till he was dressed, this was simply because such a process for such a person could only be terribly prolonged. When she went in the middle of the day to her own dinner she had too little time to do anything but go straight, though it must be added that for a real certainty she would joyously have omitted the repast. She had made up her mind as to there being on the whole no decent pretext to justify her flitting casually past at three o'clock in the morning. That was the hour at which, if the ha'penny novels were not all wrong, he probably came home for the night. She was therefore reduced to merely picturing that miraculous meeting toward which a hundred impossibilities would have to conspire. But if nothing was more impossible than the fact, nothing was more intense than the vision. What may not, we can only moralise, take place in the quickened, muffled perception of a girl of a certain kind of soul? All our young friend's native distinction, her refinement of personal grain, of heredity, of pride, took refuge in this small throbbing spot; for when she was most conscious of the abjection of her vanity and the pitifulness of her little flutters and manœuvres, then the consolation and the redemption were most sure to shine before her in some just discernible sign. He did like her!

XIII

He never brought Cissy back, but Cissy came one day without him, as fresh as before from the hands of Marguerite, or only, at the season's end, a trifle less fresh. She was, however, distinctly less serene. She had brought nothing with her, and looked about with some impatience for the forms and the place to write. The latter convenience, at Cocker's, was obscure and barely adequate, and her clear voice had the light note of disgust which her lover's never showed as she responded with a "There?" of surprise to the gesture made by the counter-clerk in answer to her sharp inquiry. Our young friend was busy with half a dozen people, but she had despatched them in her most business-like manner by the time her ladyship flung through the bars the light of re-appearance. Then the directness with which the girl managed to receive this missive was the result of the concentration that had caused her to make the stamps fly during the few minutes occupied by the production of it. This concentration, in turn, may be described as the effect of the apprehension of imminent relief. It was nineteen days, counted and checked off, since she had seen the object of her homage; and as, had he been in London, she should, with his habits, have been sure to see him often, she was now about to learn what other spot his presence might just then happen to sanctify. For she thought of them, the other spots, as ecstatically conscious of it, expressively happy in it.

But, gracious, how handsome *was* her ladyship, and what an added price it gave him that the air of intimacy he threw out should have flowed originally from such a source! The girl looked straight through the cage at the eyes and lips that must so often have been so near his own—looked at them with a strange passion that, for an instant, had the result of filling out some of the gaps, supplying the missing answers, in his correspondence. Then, as she made out that the features she thus scanned and associated were totally unaware of it, that they glowed only with the colour of quite other and not at all guessable thoughts, this directly added to their splendour, gave the girl the sharpest impression she had yet received of the uplifted, the unattainable plains of heaven, and yet at the same time

caused her to thrill with a sense of the high company she did somehow keep. She was with the absent through her ladyship and with
her ladyship through the absent. The only pang—but it didn't
matter—was the proof in the admirable face, in the sightless pre-
occupation of its possessor, that the latter hadn't a notion of her.
Her folly had gone to the point of half believing that the other
party to the affair must sometimes mention in Eaton Square the extraordinary little person at the place from which he so often wired.
Yet the perception of her visitor's blankness actually helped this extraordinary little person, the next instant, to take refuge in a reflection that could be as proud as it liked. "How little she knows, how
little she knows!" the girl cried to herself; for what did that show
after all but that Captain Everard's telegraphic confidant was Captain Everard's charming secret? Our young friend's perusal of her
ladyship's telegram was literally prolonged by a momentary daze:
what swam between her and the words, making her see them as
through rippled, shallow, sunshot water, was the great, the perpetual flood of "How much *I* know—how much *I* know!" This produced a delay in her catching that, on the face, these words didn't
give her what she wanted, though she was prompt enough with her
remembrance that her grasp was, half the time, just of what was *not*
on the face. "Miss Dolman, Parade Lodge, Parade Terrace, Dover.[15]
Let him instantly know right one, Hôtel de France, Ostend. Make it
seven nine four nine six one. Wire me alternative Burfield's."

The girl slowly counted. Then he was at Ostend. This hooked on
with so sharp a click that, not to feel she was as quickly letting it all
slip from her, she had absolutely to hold it a minute longer and to
do something to that end. Thus it was that she did on this occasion
what she never did—threw off an "Answer paid?" that sounded of-
ficious, but that she partly made up for by deliberately affixing the
stamps and by waiting till she had done so to give change. She had,
for so much coolness, the strength that she considered she knew all
about Miss Dolman.

"Yes—paid." She saw all sorts of things in this reply, even to a
small, suppressed start of surprise at so correct an assumption; even

to an attempt, the next minute, at a fresh air of detachment. "How much, with the answer?" The calculation was not abstruse, but our intense observer required a moment more to make it, and this gave her ladyship time for a second thought. "Oh, just wait!" The white, begemmed hand bared to write rose in sudden nervousness to the side of the wonderful face which, with eyes of anxiety for the paper on the counter, she brought closer to the bars of the cage. "I think I must alter a word!" On this she recovered her telegram and looked over it again; but she had a new, obvious trouble, and studied it without deciding and with much of the effect of making our young woman watch her.

This personage, meanwhile, at the sight of her expression, had decided on the spot. If she had always been sure they were in danger, her ladyship's expression was the best possible sign of it. There was a word wrong, but she had lost the right one, and much, clearly, depended on her finding it again. The girl, therefore, sufficiently estimating the affluence of customers and the distraction of Mr. Buckton and the counter-clerk, took the jump and gave it. "Isn't it Cooper's?"

It was as if she had bodily leaped—cleared the top of the cage and alighted on her interlocutress. "Cooper's?"—the stare was heightened by a blush. Yes, she had made Juno blush.

This was all the more reason for going on. "I mean instead of Burfield's."

Our young friend fairly pitied her; she had made her in an instant so helpless, and yet not a bit haughty nor outraged. She was only mystified and scared. "Oh, you know——?"

"Yes, I know!" Our young friend smiled, meeting the other's eyes, and, having made Juno blush, proceeded to patronise her. "*I'll* do it"—she put out a competent hand. Her ladyship only submitted, confused and bewildered, all presence of mind quite gone; and the next moment the telegram was in the cage again and its author out of the shop. Then quickly, boldly, under all the eyes that might have witnessed her tampering, the extraordinary little person at Cocker's made the proper change. People were really too giddy, and if they *were*, in a certain case, to be caught, it shouldn't be the fault of her own grand memory. Hadn't it been settled weeks before?—for Miss Dolman it was always to be "Cooper's."

XIV

But the summer "holidays" brought a marked difference; they were holidays for almost everyone but the animals in the cage. The August days were flat and dry, and, with so little to feed it, she was conscious of the ebb of her interest in the secrets of the refined. She was in a position to follow the refined to the extent of knowing— they had made so many of their arrangements with her aid— exactly where they were; yet she felt quite as if the panorama had ceased unrolling and the band stopped playing. A stray member of the latter occasionally turned up, but the communications that passed before her bore now largely on rooms at hotels, prices of furnished houses, hours of trains, dates of sailings and arrangements for being "met": she found them for the most part prosaic and coarse. The only thing was that they brought into her stuffy corner as straight a whiff of Alpine meadows and Scotch moors as she might hope ever to inhale; there were moreover, in especial, fat, hot, dull ladies who had out with her, to exasperation, the terms for seaside lodgings, which struck her as huge, and the matter of the number of beds required, which was not less portentous: this in reference to places of which the names—Eastbourne, Folkestone, Cromer, Scarborough, Whitby—tormented her with something of the sound of the plash of water that haunts the traveller in the desert. She had not been out of London for a dozen years, and the only thing to give a taste to the present dead weeks was the spice of a chronic resentment. The sparse customers, the people she did see, were the people who were "just off"—off on the decks of fluttered yachts, off to the uttermost point of rocky headlands where the very breeze was then playing for the want of which she said to herself that she sickened.

There was accordingly a sense in which, at such a period, the great differences of the human condition could press upon her more than ever; a circumstance drawing fresh force, in truth, from the very fact of the chance that at last, for a change, did squarely meet her—the chance to be "off," for a bit, almost as far as anybody. They took their turns in the cage as they took them both in the shop and at Chalk Farm, and she had known these two months that time was to be allowed in September—no less than eleven days— for her personal, private holiday. Much of her recent intercourse with Mr. Mudge had consisted of the hopes and fears, expressed mainly by himself, involved in the question of their getting the same dates—a question that, in proportion as the delight seemed assured, spread into a sea of speculation over the choice of where and how. All through July, on the Sunday evenings and at such other odd times as he could seize, he had flooded their talk with wild waves of calculation. It was practically settled that, with her mother, somewhere "on the south coast" (a phrase of which she liked the sound) they should put in their allowance together; but she already felt the prospect quite weary and worn with the way he went round and round on it. It had become his sole topic, the theme alike of his most solemn prudences and most placid jests, to which every opening led for return and revision and in which every little flower of a foretaste was pulled up as soon as planted. He had announced at the earliest day—characterising the whole busi- ness, from that moment, as their "plans," under which name he han- dled it as a syndicate handles a Chinese, or other, Loan—he had promptly declared that the question must be thoroughly studied, and he produced, on the whole subject, from day to day, an amount of information that excited her wonder and even, not a little, as she frankly let him know, her disdain. When she thought of the danger in which another pair of lovers rapturously lived, she inquired of him anew why he could leave nothing to chance. Then she got for answer that this profundity was just his pride, and he pitted Rams- gate against Bournemouth and even Boulogne against Jersey—for he had great ideas—with all the mastery of detail that was some day, professionally, to carry him far.

The longer the time since she had seen Captain Everard, the

more she was booked, as she called it, to pass Park Chambers; and this was the sole amusement that, in the lingering August days and the long, sad twilights, it was left her to cultivate. She had long since learned to know it for a feeble one, though its feebleness was perhaps scarce the reason for her saying to herself each evening as her time for departure approached: "No, no—not to-night." She never failed of that silent remark, any more than she failed of feeling, in some deeper place than she had even yet fully sounded, that one's remarks were as weak as straws, and that, however one might indulge in them at eight o'clock, one's fate infallibly declared itself in absolute indifference to them at about eight-fifteen. Remarks were remarks, and very well for that; but fate was fate, and this young lady's was to pass Park Chambers every night in the working week. Out of the immensity of her knowledge of the life of the world there bloomed on these occasions a specific remembrance that it was regarded in that region, in August and September, as rather pleasant just to be caught for something or other in passing through town. Somebody was always passing and somebody might catch somebody else. It was in full cognisance of this subtle law that she adhered to the most ridiculous circuit she could have made to get home. One warm, dull, featureless Friday, when an accident had made her start from Cocker's a little later than usual, she became aware that something of which the infinite possibilities had for so long peopled her dreams was at last prodigiously upon her, though the perfection in which the conditions happened to present it was almost rich enough to be but the positive creation of a dream. She saw, straight before her, like a vista painted in a picture, the empty street and the lamps that burned pale in the dusk not yet established. It was into the convenience of this quiet twilight that a gentleman on the door-step of the Chambers gazed with a vagueness that our young lady's little figure violently trembled, in the approach, with the measure of its power to dissipate. Everything indeed grew in a flash terrific and distinct; her old uncertainties fell away from her, and, since she was so familiar with fate, she felt as if the very nail that fixed it were driven in by the hard look with which, for a moment, Captain Everard awaited her.

The vestibule was open behind him and the porter as absent as on the day she had peeped in; he had just come out—was in town, in a tweed suit and a pot hat, but between two journeys—duly bored over his evening and at a loss what to do with it. Then it was that she was glad she had never met him in that way before: she reaped with such ecstasy the benefit of his not being able to think she passed often. She jumped in two seconds to the determination that he should even suppose it to be the first time and the queerest chance: this was while she still wondered if he would identify or notice her. His original attention had not, she instinctively knew, been for the young woman at Cocker's; it had only been for any young woman who might advance with an air of not upholding ugliness. Ah, but then, and just as she had reached the door, came his second observation, a long, light reach with which, visibly and quite amusedly, he recalled and placed her. They were on different sides, but the street, narrow and still, had only made more of a stage for the small momentary drama. It was not over, besides, it was far from over, even on his sending across the way, with the pleasantest laugh she had ever heard, a little lift of his hat and an "Oh, good evening!" It was still less over on their meeting, the next minute, though rather indirectly and awkwardly, in the middle of the road—a situation to which three or four steps of her own had unmistakably contributed,—and then passing not again to the side on which she had arrived, but back toward the portal of Park Chambers.

"I didn't know you at first. Are you taking a walk?"

"Oh, I don't take walks at night! I'm going home after my work."

"Oh!"

That was practically what they had meanwhile smiled out, and his exclamation, to which, for a minute, he appeared to have nothing to add, left them face to face and in just such an attitude as, for his part, he might have worn had he been wondering if he could properly ask her to come in. During this interval, in fact, she really felt his question to be just "*How* properly——?" It was simply a question of the degree of properness.

XV

She never knew afterwards quite what she had done to settle it, and at the time she only knew that they presently moved, with vagueness, but with continuity, away from the picture of the lighted vestibule and the quiet stairs and well up the street together. This also must have been in the absence of a definite permission, of anything vulgarly articulate, for that matter, on the part of either; and it was to be, later on, a thing of remembrance and reflection for her that the limit of what, just here, for a longish minute, passed between them was his taking in her thoroughly successful deprecation, though conveyed without pride or sound or touch, of the idea that she might be, out of the cage, the very shopgirl at large that she hugged the theory she was not. Yes, it was strange, she afterwards thought, that so much could have come and gone and yet not troubled the air either with impertinence or with resentment, with any of the horrid notes of that kind of acquaintance. He had taken no liberty, as she would have called it; and, through not having to betray the sense of one, she herself had, still more charmingly, taken none. Yet on the spot, nevertheless, she could speculate as to what it meant that, if his relation with Lady Bradeen continued to be what her mind had built it up to, he should feel free to proceed in any private direction. This was one of the questions he was to leave her to deal with—the question whether people of his sort still asked girls up to their rooms when they were so awfully in love with other women. Could people of his sort do that without what people of *her* sort would call being "false to their love"? She had already a vision of how the true answer was that people of her sort didn't, in such cases, matter—didn't count as infidelity, counted only as something else: she might have been curious, since it came to that, to see exactly what.

Strolling together slowly in their summer twilight and their empty corner of Mayfair, they found themselves emerge at last opposite to one of the smaller gates of the Park; upon which, without any particular word about it—they were talking so of other things—they crossed the street and went in and sat down on a bench. She had gathered by this time one magnificent hope about him—the hope that he would say nothing vulgar. She knew what she meant by that; she meant something quite apart from any matter of his being "false." Their bench was not far within; it was near the Park Lane[16] paling and the patchy lamplight and the rumbling cabs and 'buses. A strange emotion had come to her, and she felt indeed excitement within excitement; above all a conscious joy in testing him with chances he didn't take. She had an intense desire he should know the type she really was without her doing anything so low as tell him, and he had surely begun to know it from the moment he didn't seize the opportunities into which a common man would promptly have blundered. These were on the mere surface, and *their* relation was behind and below them. She had questioned so little on the way what they were doing, that as soon as they were seated she took straight hold of it. Her hours, her confinement, the many conditions of service in the post-office, had—with a glance at his own postal resources and alternatives—formed, up to this stage, the subject of their talk. "Well, here we are, and it may be right enough; but this isn't the least, you know, where I was going."

"You were going home?"

"Yes, and I was already rather late. I was going to my supper."

"You haven't had it?"

"No, indeed!"

"Then you haven't eaten——?"

He looked, of a sudden, so extravagantly concerned that she laughed out. "All day? Yes, we do feed once. But that was long ago. So I must presently say good-bye."

"Oh, deary *me*!" he exclaimed, with an intonation so droll and yet a touch so light and a distress so marked—a confession of helplessness for such a case, in short, so unrelieved—that she felt sure, on the spot, she had made the great difference plain. He looked at her with the kindest eyes and still without saying what she had known he wouldn't. She had known he wouldn't say, "Then sup with *me*!" but the proof of it made her feel as if she had feasted.

"I'm not a bit hungry," she went on.

"Ah, you *must* be, awfully!" he made answer, but settling himself on the bench as if, after all, that needn't interfere with his spending his evening. "I've always quite wanted the chance to thank you for the trouble you so often take for me."

"Yes, I know," she replied; uttering the words with a sense of the situation far deeper than any pretence of not fitting his allusion. She immediately saw that he was surprised and even a little puzzled at her frank assent; but, for herself, the trouble she had taken could only, in these fleeting minutes—they would probably never come back—be all there like a little hoard of gold in her lap. Certainly he might look at it, handle it, take up the pieces. Yet if he understood anything he must understand all. "I consider you've already immensely thanked me." The horror was back upon her of having seemed to hang about for some reward. "It's awfully odd that you should have been there just the one time——!"

"The one time you've passed my place?"

"Yes; you can fancy I haven't many minutes to waste. There was a place to-night I had to stop at."

"I see, I see"—he knew already so much about her work. "It must be an awful grind—for a lady."

"It is; but I don't think I groan over it any more than my companions—and you've seen *they're* not ladies!" She mildly jested, but with an intention. "One gets used to things, and there are employments I should have hated much more." She had the finest conception of the beauty of not, at least, boring him. To whine, to count up her wrongs, was what a barmaid or a shopgirl would do, and it was quite enough to sit there like one of these.

"If you had had another employment," he remarked after a moment, "we might never have become acquainted."

"It's highly probable—and certainly not in the same way." Then, still with her heap of gold in her lap and something of the pride of it in her manner of holding her head, she continued not to move— she only smiled at him. The evening had thickened now; the scattered lamps were red; the Park, all before them, was full of obscure and ambiguous life; there were other couples on other benches, whom it was impossible not to see, yet at whom it was impossible to look. "But I've walked so much out of my way with you only just to show you that—that"—with this she paused; it was not, after all, so easy to express—"that anything you may have thought is perfectly true."

"Oh, I've thought a tremendous lot!" her companion laughed. "Do you mind my smoking?"

"Why should I? You always smoke *there*."

"At your place? Oh yes, but here it's different."

"No," she said, as he lighted a cigarette, "that's just what it isn't. It's quite the same."

"Well, then, that's because 'there' it's so wonderful!"

"Then you're conscious of how wonderful it is?" she returned.

He jerked his handsome head in literal protest at a doubt. "Why, that's exactly what I mean by my gratitude for all your trouble. It has been just as if you took a particular interest." She only looked at him in answer to this, in such sudden, immediate embarrassment, as she was quite aware, that, while she remained silent, he showed he was at a loss to interpret her expression. "You *have*—haven't you?—taken a particular interest?"

"Oh, a particular interest!" she quavered out, feeling the whole thing—her immediate embarrassment—get terribly the better of her, and wishing, with a sudden scare, all the more to keep her emotion down. She maintained her fixed smile a moment and turned her eyes over the peopled darkness, unconfused now, because there was something much more confusing. This, with a fatal great rush, was simply the fact that they were thus together. They were near, near, and all that she had imagined of that had only become more true, more dreadful and overwhelming. She stared straight away in silence till she felt that she looked like an idiot; then, to say something, to say nothing, she attempted a sound which ended in a flood of tears.

XVI

Her tears helped her really to dissimulate, for she had instantly, in so public a situation, to recover herself. They had come and gone in half a minute, and she immediately explained them. "It's only because I'm tired. It's that—it's that!" Then she added a trifle incoherently: "I shall never see you again."

"Ah, but why not?" The mere tone in which her companion asked this satisfied her once for all as to the amount of imagination for which she could count on him. It was naturally not large: it had exhausted itself in having arrived at what he had already touched upon—the sense of an intention in her poor zeal at Cocker's. But any deficiency of this kind was no fault in him: *he* wasn't obliged to have an inferior cleverness—to have second-rate resources and virtues. It had been as if he almost really believed she had simply cried for fatigue, and he had accordingly put in some kind, confused plea—"You ought really to take something: won't you have something or other *somewhere?*"—to which she had made no response but a headshake of a sharpness that settled it. "Why shan't we all the more keep meeting?"

"I mean meeting this way—only this way. At my place there— *that* I've nothing to do with, and I hope of course you'll turn up, with your correspondence, when it suits you. Whether I stay or not, I mean; for I shall probably not stay."

"You're going somewhere else?"—he put it with positive anxiety.

"Yes; ever so far away—to the other end of London. There are all sorts of reasons I can't tell you; and it's practically settled. It's better for me, much; and I've only kept on at Cocker's for you."

"For me?"

Making out in the dusk that he fairly blushed, she now measured how far he had been from knowing too much. Too much, she called it at present; and that was easy, since it proved so abundantly enough for her that he should simply be where he was. "As we shall never talk this way but tonight—never, never again!—here it all is; I'll say it; I don't care what you think; it doesn't matter; I only want to help you. Besides, you're kind—you're kind. I've been thinking, then, of leaving for ever so long. But you've come so often—at times,—and you've had so much to do, and it has been so pleasant and interesting, that I've remained, I've kept putting off any change.

More than once, when I had nearly decided, you've turned up again and I've thought, 'Oh no!' That's the simple fact!" She had by this time got her confusion down so completely that she could laugh. "This is what I meant when I said to you just now that I 'knew.' I've known perfectly that you knew I took trouble for you; and that knowledge has been for me, and I seemed to see it was for you, as if there were something—I don't know what to call it!—between us. I mean something unusual and good—something not a bit horrid or vulgar."

She had by this time, she could see, produced a great effect upon him; but she would have spoken the truth to herself if she had at the same moment declared that she didn't in the least care: all the more that the effect must be one of extreme perplexity. What, in it all, was visibly clear for him, none the less, was that he was tremendously glad he had met her. She held him, and he was astonished at the force of it; he was intent, immensely considerate. His elbow was on the back of the seat, and his head, with the pot-hat pushed quite back, in a boyish way, so that she really saw almost for the first time his forehead and hair, rested on the hand into which he had crumpled his gloves. "Yes," he assented, "it's not a bit horrid or vulgar."

She just hung fire a moment; then she brought out the whole truth. "I'd do anything for you. I'd do anything for you." Never in her life had she known anything so high and fine as this, just letting him have it and bravely and magnificently leaving it. Didn't the place, the associations and circumstances, perfectly make it sound what it was not? and wasn't that exactly the beauty?

So she bravely and magnificently left it, and little by little she felt him take it up, take it down, as if they had been on a satin sofa in a boudoir. She had never seen a boudoir, but there had been lots of boudoirs in the telegrams. What she had said, at all events, sank into him, so that after a minute he simply made a movement that had the result of placing his hand on her own—presently indeed that of her feeling herself firmly enough grasped. There was no pressure she need return, there was none she need decline; she just sat admirably still, satisfied, for the time, with the surprise and bewilderment of the impression she made on him. His agitation was even greater, on the whole, than she had at first allowed for. "I say, you know, you mustn't think of leaving!" he at last broke out.

"Of leaving Cocker's, you mean?"

"Yes, you must stay on there, whatever happens, and help a fellow."

She was silent a little, partly because it was so strange and exquisite to feel him watch her as if it really mattered to him and he were almost in suspense. "Then you *have* quite recognised what I've tried to do?" she asked.

"Why, wasn't that exactly what I dashed over from my door just now to thank you for?"

"Yes; so you said."

"And don't you believe it?"

She looked down a moment at his hand, which continued to cover her own; whereupon he presently drew it back, rather restlessly folding his arms. Without answering his question she went on: "Have you ever spoken of me?"

"Spoken of you?"

"Of my being there—of my knowing, and that sort of thing."

"Oh, never to a human creature!" he eagerly declared.

She had a small drop at this, which was expressed in another pause; after which she returned to what he had just asked her. "Oh yes, I quite believe you like it—my always being there and our taking things up so familiarly and successfully: if not exactly where we left them," she laughed, "almost always, at least, in an interesting place!" He was about to say something in reply to this, but her friendly gaiety was quicker. "You want a great many things in life, a great many comforts and helps and luxuries—you want everything as pleasant as possible. Therefore, so far as it's in the power of any particular person to contribute to all that——" She had turned her face to him smiling, just thinking.

"Oh, see here!" But he was highly amused. "Well, what then?" he inquired, as if to humour her.

"Why, the particular person must never fail. We must manage it for you somehow."

He threw back his head, laughing out; he was really exhilarated. "Oh yes, somehow!"

"Well, I think we each do—don't we?—in one little way and another and according to our limited lights. I'm pleased, at any rate, for myself, that you are; for I assure you I've done my best."

"You do better than any one!" He had struck a match for another cigarette, and the flame lighted an instant his responsive, finished face, magnifying into a pleasant grimace the kindness with which he paid her this tribute. "You're awfully clever, you know; cleverer, cleverer, cleverer——!" He had appeared on the point of making some tremendous statement; then suddenly, puffing his cigarette and shifting almost with violence on his seat, let it altogether fall.

XVII

In spite of this drop, if not just by reason of it, she felt as if Lady Bradeen, all but named out, had popped straight up; and she practically betrayed her consciousness by waiting a little before she rejoined: "Cleverer than who?"

"Well, if I wasn't afraid you'd think I swagger, I should say—than anybody! If you leave your place there, where shall you go?" he more gravely demanded.

"Oh, too far for you ever to find me!"

"I'd find you anywhere."

The tone of this was so still more serious that she had but her one acknowledgement. "I'd do anything for you—I'd do anything for you," she repeated. She had already, she felt, said it all; so what did anything more, anything less, matter? That was the very reason indeed why she could, with a lighter note, ease him generously of any awkwardness produced by solemnity, either his own or hers. "Of course it must be nice for you to be able to think there are people all about who feel in such a way."

In immediate appreciation of this, however, he only smoked without looking at her. "But you don't want to give up your present work?" he at last inquired. "I mean you *will* stay in the post-office?"

"Oh yes; I think I've a genius for that."

"Rather! No one can touch you." With this he turned more to her again. "But you can get, with a move, greater advantages?"

"I can get, in the suburbs, cheaper lodgings. I live with my mother. We need some space; and there's a particular place that has other inducements."

He just hesitated. "Where is it?"

"Oh, quite out of *your* way. You'd never have time."

"But I tell you I'd go anywhere. Don't you believe it?"

"Yes, for once or twice. But you'd soon see it wouldn't do for you."

He smoked and considered; seemed to stretch himself a little and, with his legs out, surrender himself comfortably. "Well, well, well—I believe everything you say. I take it from you—anything you like—in the most extraordinary way." It struck her certainly—and almost without bitterness—that the way in which she was already, as if she had been an old friend, arranging for him and preparing the only magnificence she could muster, was quite the most extraordinary. "Don't, *don't* go!" he presently went on. "I shall miss you too horribly!"

"So that you just put it to me as a definite request?"—oh, how she tried to divest this of all sound of the hardness of bargaining! That ought to have been easy enough, for what was she arranging to get? Before he could answer she had continued: "To be perfectly fair, I should tell you I recognise at Cocker's certain strong attractions. All you people come. I like all the horrors."

"The horrors?"

"Those you all—you know the set I mean, *your* set—show me with as good a conscience as if I had no more feeling than a letter-box."

He looked quite excited at the way she put it. "Oh, they don't know!"

"Don't know I'm not stupid? No, how should they?"

"Yes, how should they?" said the Captain sympathetically. "But isn't 'horrors' rather strong?"

"What you *do* is rather strong!" the girl promptly returned.

"What *I* do?"

"Your extravagance, your selfishness, your immorality, your crimes," she pursued, without heeding his expression.

"I *say!*"—her companion showed the queerest stare.

"I like them, as I tell you—I revel in them. But we needn't go into that," she quietly went on; "for all I get out of it is the harmless pleasure of knowing. I know, I know, I know!"—she breathed it ever so gently.

"Yes; that's what has been between us," he answered much more simply.

She could enjoy his simplicity in silence, and for a moment she did so. "If I do stay because you want it—and I'm rather capable of that—there are two or three things I think you ought to remember. One is, you know, that I'm there sometimes for days and weeks together without your ever coming."

"Oh, I'll come every day!" he exclaimed.

She was on the point, at this, of imitating with her hand his movement of shortly before; but she checked herself, and there was no want of effect in the tranquillising way in which she said: "How can you? How can you?" He had, too manifestly, only to look at it there, in the vulgarly animated gloom, to see that he couldn't; and at this point, by the mere action of his silence, everything they had so definitely not named, the whole presence round which they had been circling became a part of their reference, settled solidly between them. It was as if then, for a minute, they sat and saw it all in each other's eyes, saw so much that there was no need of a transition for sounding it at last. "Your danger, your danger——!" Her voice indeed trembled with it, and she could only, for the moment, again leave it so.

During this moment he leaned back on the bench, meeting her in silence and with a face that grew more strange. It grew so strange that, after a further instant, she got straight up. She stood there as if their talk were now over, and he just sat and watched her. It was as if now—owing to the third person they had brought in—they must be more careful; so that the most he could finally say was: "That's where it is!"

"That's where it is!" the girl as guardedly replied. He sat still, and she added: "I won't abandon you. Good-bye."

"Good-bye?"—he appealed, but without moving.

"I don't quite see my way, but I won't abandon you," she repeated. "There. Good-bye."

It brought him with a jerk to his feet, tossing away his cigarette. His poor face was flushed. "See here—see here!"

"No, I won't; but I must leave you now," she went on as if not hearing him.

"See here—see here!" He tried, from the bench, to take her hand again.

But that definitely settled it for her: this would, after all, be as bad as his asking her to supper. "You mustn't come with me—no, no!"

He sank back, quite blank, as if she had pushed him. "I mayn't see you home?"

"No, no; let me go." He looked almost as if she had struck him, but she didn't care; and the manner in which she spoke—it was literally as if she were angry—had the force of a command. "Stay where you are!"

"See here—see here!" he nevertheless pleaded.

"I won't abandon you!" she cried once more—this time quite with passion; on which she got away from him as fast as she could and left him staring after her.

XVIII

Mr. Mudge had lately been so occupied with their famous "plans" that he had neglected, for a while, the question of her transfer; but down at Bournemouth, which had found itself selected as the field of their recreation by a process consisting, it seemed, exclusively of innumerable pages of the neatest arithmetic in a very greasy but most orderly little pocket-book, the distracting possible melted away—the fleeting irremediable ruled the scene. The plans, hour by hour, were simply superseded, and it was much of a rest to the girl, as she sat on the pier and overlooked the sea and the company, to see them evaporate in rosy fumes and to feel that from moment to moment there was less left to cipher about. The week proved blissfully fine, and her mother, at their lodgings—partly to her embarrassment and partly to her relief—struck up with the landlady an alliance that left the younger couple a great deal of freedom. This relative took her pleasure of a week at Bournemouth in a stuffy back-kitchen and endless talks; to that degree even that Mr. Mudge himself—habitually inclined indeed to a scrutiny of all mysteries and to seeing, as he sometimes admitted, too much in things—made remarks on it as he sat on the cliff with his betrothed, or on the decks of steamers that conveyed them, close-packed items in terrific totals of enjoyment, to the Isle of Wight[17] and the Dorset coast.

He had a lodging in another house, where he had speedily learned the importance of keeping his eyes open, and he made no secret of his suspecting that sinister mutual connivances might spring, under the roof of his companions, from unnatural sociabilities. At the same time he fully recognised that, as a source of anxiety, not to say of expense, his future mother-in-law would have weighted them more in accompanying their steps than in giving her hostess, in the interest of the tendency they considered that they never mentioned, equivalent pledges as to the tea-caddy and the jam-pot. These were the questions—these indeed the familiar commodities—that he had now to put into the scales; and his betrothed had, in consequence, during her holiday, the odd, and yet pleasant and almost languid, sense of an anticlimax. She had become conscious of an extraordinary collapse, a surrender to stillness and to retrospect. She cared neither to walk nor to sail; it was enough for her to sit on benches and wonder at the sea and taste the air and not be at Cocker's and not see the counter-clerk. She still seemed to wait for something—something in the key of the immense discussions that had mapped out their little week of idleness on the scale of a world-atlas. Something came at last, but without perhaps appearing quite adequately to crown the monument.

Preparation and precaution were, however, the natural flowers of Mr. Mudge's mind, and in proportion as these things declined in one quarter they inevitably bloomed elsewhere. He could always, at the worst, have on Tuesday the project of their taking the Swanage boat on Thursday, and on Thursday that of their ordering minced kidneys on Saturday. He had, moreover, a constant gift of inexorable inquiry as to where and what they should have gone and have done if they had not been exactly as they were. He had in short his resources, and his mistress had never been so conscious of them; on the other hand they had never interfered so little with her own. She liked to be as she was—if it could only have lasted. She could accept even without bitterness a rigour of economy so great that the little fee they paid for admission to the pier had to be balanced against other delights. The people at Ladle's and at Thrupp's had *their* ways of amusing themselves, whereas she had to sit and hear Mr. Mudge talk of what he might do if he didn't take a bath, or of the bath he might take if he only hadn't taken something else. He was always with her now, of course, always beside her; she saw him more than "hourly," more than ever yet, more even than he had planned she should do at Chalk Farm. She preferred to sit at the far end, away from the band and the crowd; as to which she had frequent differences with her friend, who reminded her often that they could have only in the thick of it the sense of the money they were getting back. That had little effect on her, for she got back her money by seeing many things, the things of the past year, fall together and connect themselves, undergo the happy relegation that transforms melancholy and misery, passion and effort, into experience and knowledge.

She liked having done with them, as she assured herself she had practically done, and the strange thing was that she neither missed the procession now nor wished to keep her place for it. It had become there, in the sun and the breeze and the sea-smell, a far-away story, a picture of another life. If Mr. Mudge himself liked processions, liked them at Bournemouth and on the pier quite as much as at Chalk Farm or anywhere, she learned after a little not to be worried by his perpetual counting of the figures that made them up. There were dreadful women in particular, usually fat and in men's caps and white shoes, whom he could never let alone—not that *she* cared; it was not the great world, the world of Cocker's and Ladle's and Thrupp's, but it offered an endless field to his faculties of memory, philosophy, and frolic. She had never accepted him so much, never arranged so successfully for making him chatter while she carried on secret conversations. Her talks were with herself; and if they both practised a great thrift, she had quite mastered that of merely spending words enough to keep him imperturbably and continuously going.

He was charmed with the panorama, not knowing—or at any rate not at all showing that he knew—what far other images peopled her mind than the women in the navy caps and the shopboys in the blazers. His observations on these types, his general interpretation of the show, brought home to her the prospect of Chalk Farm. She wondered sometimes that he should have derived so little illumination, during his period, from the society at Cocker's. But one evening, as their holiday cloudlessly waned, he gave her such a proof of his quality as might have made her ashamed of her small reserves. He brought out something that, in all his overflow, he had been able to keep back till other matters were disposed of. It was the announcement that he was at last ready to marry—that he saw his way. A rise at Chalk Farm had been offered him; he was to be taken into the business, bringing with him a capital the estimation of which by other parties constituted the handsomest recognition yet made of the head on his shoulders. Therefore their waiting was over—it could be a question of a near date. They would settle this date before going back, and he meanwhile had his eye on a sweet little home. He would take her to see it on their first Sunday.

XIX

His having kept this great news for the last, having had such a card up his sleeve and not floated it out in the current of his chatter and the luxury of their leisure, was one of those incalculable strokes by which he could still affect her; the kind of thing that reminded her of the latent force that had ejected the drunken soldier—an example of the profundity of which his promotion was the proof. She listened a while in silence, on this occasion, to the wafted strains of the music; she took it in as she had not quite done before that her future was now constituted. Mr. Mudge was distinctly her fate; yet at this moment she turned her face quite away from him, showing him so long a mere quarter of her cheek that she at last again heard his voice. He couldn't see a pair of tears that were partly the reason of her delay to give him the assurance he required; but he expressed at a venture the hope that she had had her fill of Cocker's.

She was finally able to turn back. "Oh, quite. There's nothing going on. No one comes but the Americans at Thrupp's, and *they* don't do much. They don't seem to have a secret in the world."

"Then the extraordinary reason you've been giving me for holding on there has ceased to work?"

She thought a moment. "Yes, that one. I've seen the thing through—I've got them all in my pocket."

"So you're ready to come?"

For a little, again, she made no answer. "No, not yet, all the same. I've still got a reason—a different one."

He looked her all over as if it might have been something she kept in her mouth or her glove or under her jacket—something she was even sitting upon. "Well, I'll have it, please."

"I went out the other night and sat in the Park with a gentleman," she said at last.

Nothing was ever seen like his confidence in her; and she wondered a little now why it didn't irritate her. It only gave her ease and space, as she felt, for telling him the whole truth that no one knew. It had arrived at present at her really wanting to do that, and yet to do it not in the least for Mr. Mudge, but altogether and only for herself. This truth filled out for her there the whole experience she was about to relinquish, suffused and coloured it as a picture that she should keep and that, describe it as she might, no one but herself would ever really see. Moreover she had no desire whatever to make Mr. Mudge jealous; there would be no amusement in it, for the amusement she had lately known had spoiled her for lower pleasures. There were even no materials for it. The odd thing was that she never doubted that, properly handled, his passion was poisonable; what had happened was that he had cannily selected a partner with no poison to distil. She read then and there that she should never interest herself in anybody as to whom some other sentiment, some superior view, wouldn't be sure to interfere, for him, with jealousy. "And what did you get out of that?" he asked with a concern that was not in the least for his honour.

"Nothing but a good chance to promise him I wouldn't forsake him. He's one of my customers."

"Then it's for him not to forsake *you*."

"Well, he won't. It's all right. But I must just keep on as long as he may want me."

"Want you to sit with him in the Park?"

"He may want me for that—but I shan't. I rather liked it, but once, under the circumstances, is enough. I can do better for him in another manner."

"And what manner, pray?"

"Well, elsewhere."

"Elsewhere?—I *say*!"

This was an ejaculation used also by Captain Everard, but, oh, with what a different sound! "You needn't 'say'—there's nothing to be said. And yet you ought perhaps to know."

"Certainly I ought. But *what*—up to now?"

"Why, exactly what I told him. That I would do anything for him."

"What do you mean by 'anything'?"

"Everything."

Mr. Mudge's immediate comment on this statement was to draw from his pocket a crumpled paper containing the remains of half a pound of "sundries." These sundries had figured conspicuously in his prospective sketch of their tour, but it was only at the end of three days that they had defined themselves unmistakably as chocolate-creams. "Have another?—*that* one," he said. She had another, but not the one he indicated, and then he continued: "What took place afterwards?"

"Afterwards?"

"What did you do when you had told him you would do everything?"

"I simply came away."

"Out of the Park?"

"Yes, leaving him there. I didn't let him follow me."

"Then what did you let him do?"

"I didn't let him do anything."

Mr. Mudge considered an instant. "Then what did you go there for?" His tone was even slightly critical.

"I didn't quite know at the time. It was simply to be with him, I suppose—just once. He's in danger, and I wanted him to know I know it. It makes meeting him—at Cocker's, for it's that I want to stay on for—more interesting."

"It makes it mighty interesting for *me!*" Mr. Mudge freely declared. "Yet he didn't follow you?" he asked. "*I* would!"

"Yes, of course. That was the way you began, you know. You're awfully inferior to him."

"Well, my dear, you're not inferior to anybody. You've got a cheek! What is he in danger of?"

"Of being found out. He's in love with a lady—and it isn't right—and *I've* found him out."

"That'll be a look-out for *me!*" Mr. Mudge joked. "You mean she has a husband?"

"Never mind what she has! They're in awful danger, but his is the worst, because he's in danger from her too."

"Like me from you—the woman *I* love? If he's in the same funk as me——"

"He's in a worse one. He's not only afraid of the lady—he's afraid of other things."

Mr. Mudge selected another chocolate-cream. "Well, I'm only afraid of one! But how in the world can you help this party?"

"I don't know—perhaps not at all. But so long as there's a chance——"

"You won't come away?"

"No, you've got to wait for me."

Mr. Mudge enjoyed what was in his mouth. "And what will he give you?"

"Give me?"

"If you do help him."

"Nothing. Nothing in all the wide world."

"Then what will he give *me*?" Mr. Mudge inquired. "I mean for waiting."

The girl thought a moment; then she got up to walk. "He never heard of you," she replied.

"You haven't mentioned me?"

"We never mention anything. What I've told you is just what I've found out."

Mr. Mudge, who had remained on the bench, looked up at her; she often preferred to be quiet when he proposed to walk, but now that he seemed to wish to sit she had a desire to move. "But you haven't told me what *he* has found out."

She considered her lover. "He'd never find *you*, my dear!"

Her lover, still on his seat, appealed to her in something of the attitude in which she had last left Captain Everard, but the impression was not the same. "Then where do I come in?"

"You don't come in at all. That's just the beauty of it!"—and with this she turned to mingle with the multitude collected round the band. Mr. Mudge presently overtook her and drew her arm into his own with a quiet force that expressed the serenity of possession; in consonance with which it was only when they parted for the night at her door that he referred again to what she had told him.

"Have you seen him since?"

"Since the night in the Park? No, not once."

"Oh, what a cad!" said Mr. Mudge.

XX

It was not till the end of October that she saw Captain Everard again, and on that occasion—the only one of all the series on which hindrance had been so utter—no communication with him proved possible. She had made out, even from the cage, that it was a charming golden day: a patch of hazy autumn sunlight lay across the sanded floor and also, higher up, quickened into brightness a row of ruddy bottled syrups. Work was slack and the place in general empty; the town, as they said in the cage, had not waked up, and the feeling of the day likened itself to something that in happier conditions she would have thought of romantically as St. Martin's summer. The counter-clerk had gone to his dinner; she herself was busy with arrears of postal jobs, in the midst of which she became aware that Captain Everard had apparently been in the shop a minute and that Mr. Buckton had already seized him.

He had, as usual, half a dozen telegrams; and when he saw that she saw him and their eyes met, he gave, on bowing to her, an exaggerated laugh in which she read a new consciousness. It was a confession of awkwardness; it seemed to tell her that of course he knew he ought better to have kept his head, ought to have been clever enough to wait, on some pretext, till he should have found her free. Mr. Buckton was a long time with him, and her attention was soon demanded by other visitors; so that nothing passed between them but the fulness of their silence. The look she took from him was his greeting, and the other one a simple sign of the eyes sent her before going out. The only token they exchanged, therefore, was his tacit assent to her wish that, since they couldn't attempt a certain frankness, they should attempt nothing at all. This was her intense preference; she could be as still and cold as any one when that was the sole solution.

Yet, more than any contact hitherto achieved, these counted instants struck her as marking a step: they were built so—just in the mere flash—on the recognition of his now definitely knowing what it was she would do for him. The "anything, anything" she had uttered in the Park went to and fro between them and under the poked-out chins that interposed. It had all at last even put on the air of their not needing now clumsily to manoeuvre to converse: their former little postal make-believes, the intense implications of questions and answers and change, had become in the light of the personal fact, of their having had their moment, a possibility comparatively poor. It was as if they had met for all time—it exerted on their being in presence again an influence so prodigious. When she watched herself, in the memory of that night, walk away from him as if she were making an end, she found something too pitiful in the primness of such a gait. Hadn't she precisely established on the part of each a consciousness that could end only with death?

It must be admitted that, in spite of this brave margin, an irritation, after he had gone, remained with her; a sense that presently became one with a still sharper hatred of Mr. Buckton, who, on her friend's withdrawal, had retired with the telegrams to the sounder and left her the other work. She knew indeed she should have a chance to see them, when she would, on file; and she was divided, as the day went on, between the two impressions of all that was lost and all that was re-asserted. What beset her above all, and as she had almost never known it before, was the desire to bound straight out, to overtake the autumn afternoon before it passed away for ever and hurry off to the Park and perhaps be with him there again on a bench. It became, for an hour, a fantastic vision with her that he might just have gone to sit and wait for her. She could almost hear him, through the tick of the sounder, scatter with his stick, in his impatience, the fallen leaves of October. Why should such a vision seize her at this particular moment with such a shake? There was a time—from four to five—when she could have cried with happiness and rage.

Business quickened, it seemed, toward five, as if the town did wake up; she had therefore more to do, and she went through it with little sharp stampings and jerkings: she made the crisp postal-orders fairly snap while she breathed to herself: "It's the last day— the last day!" The last day of what? She couldn't have told. All she knew now was that if she *were* out of the cage she wouldn't in the least have minded, this time, its not yet being dark. She would have gone straight toward Park Chambers and have hung about there till no matter when. She would have waited, stayed, rung, asked, have gone in, sat on the stairs. What the day was the last of was probably, to her strained inner sense, the group of golden ones, of any occasion for seeing the hazy sunshine slant at that angle into the smelly

shop, of any range of chances for his wishing still to repeat to her
the two words that, in the Park, she had scarcely let him bring out.
"See here—see here!"—the sound of these two words had been
with her perpetually; but it was in her ears to-day without mercy,
with a loudness that grew and grew. What was it they then expressed? what was it he had wanted her to see? She seemed, whatever it was, perfectly to see it now—to see that if she should just
chuck the whole thing, should have a great and beautiful courage,
he would somehow make everything up to her. When the clock
struck five she was on the very point of saying to Mr. Buckton that
she was deadly ill and rapidly getting worse. This announcement
was on her lips, and she had quite composed the pale, hard face she
would offer him: "I can't stop—I must go home. If I feel better, later
on, I'll come back. I'm very sorry, but I *must* go." At that instant
Captain Everard once more stood there, producing in her agitated
spirit, by his real presence, the strangest, quickest revolution. He
stopped her off without knowing it, and by the time he had been a
minute in the shop she felt that she was saved.

That was from the first minute what she called it to herself.
There were again other persons with whom she was occupied, and
again the situation could only be expressed by their silence. It was
expressed, in fact, in a larger phrase than ever yet, for her eyes now
spoke to him with a kind of supplication. "Be quiet, be quiet!" they
pleaded; and they saw his own reply: "I'll do whatever you say; I
won't even look at you—see, see!" They kept conveying thus, with
the friendliest liberality, that they wouldn't look, quite positively
wouldn't. What she was to see was that he hovered at the other end
of the counter, Mr. Buckton's end, surrendered himself again to that
frustration. It quickly proved so great indeed that what she was to
see further was how he turned away before he was attended to, and
hung off, waiting, smoking, looking about the shop; how he went
over to Mr. Cocker's own counter and appeared to price things,
gave in fact presently two or three orders and put down money,
stood there a long time with his back to her, considerately abstain-
ing from any glance round to see if she were free. It at last came to

pass in this way that he had remained in the shop longer than she had ever yet known him to do, and that, nevertheless, when he did turn about she could see him time himself—she was freshly taken up—and cross straight to her postal subordinate, whom some one else had released. He had in his hand all this while neither letters nor telegrams, and now that he was close to her—for she was close to the counter-clerk—it brought her heart into her mouth merely to see him look at her neighbour and open his lips. She was too nervous to bear it. He asked for a Post-Office Guide, and the young man whipped out a new one; whereupon he said that he wished not to purchase, but only to consult one a moment; with which, the copy kept on loan being produced, he once more wandered off.

What was he doing to her? What did he want of her? Well, it was just the aggravation of his "See here!" She felt at this moment strangely and portentously afraid of him—had in her ears the hum of a sense that, should it come to that kind of tension, she must fly on the spot to Chalk Farm. Mixed with her dread and with her reflection was the idea that, if he wanted her so much as he seemed to show, it might be after all simply to do for him the "anything" she had promised, the "everything" she had thought it so fine to bring out to Mr. Mudge. He might want her to help him, might have some particular appeal; though, of a truth, his manner didn't denote that—denoted, on the contrary, an embarrassment, an indecision, something of a desire not so much to be helped as to be treated rather more nicely than she had treated him the other time. Yes, he considered quite probably that he had help rather to offer than to ask for. Still, none the less, when he again saw her free he continued to keep away from her; when he came back with his *Guide* it was Mr. Buckton he caught—it was from Mr. Buckton he obtained half-a-crown's-worth of stamps.

After asking for the stamps he asked, quite as a second thought, for a postal-order for ten shillings. What did he want with so many stamps when he wrote so few letters? How could he enclose a postal-order in a telegram? She expected him, the next thing, to go into the corner and make up one of his telegrams—half a dozen of them—on purpose to prolong his presence. She had so completely stopped looking at him that she could only guess his movements—guess even where his eyes rested. Finally she saw him make a dash that might have been towards the nook where the forms were hung; and at this she suddenly felt that she couldn't keep it up. The counter-clerk had just taken a telegram from a slavey,[18] and, to give herself something to cover her, she snatched it out of his hand. The gesture was so violent that he gave her an odd look, and she also perceived that Mr. Buckton noticed it. The latter personage, with a quick stare at her, appeared for an instant to wonder whether his snatching it in *his* turn mightn't be the thing she would least like, and she anticipated this practical criticism by the frankest glare she had ever given him. It sufficed: this time it paralysed him; and she sought with her trophy the refuge of the sounder.

XXI

It was repeated the next day; it went on for three days; and at the end of that time she knew what to think. When, at the beginning, she had emerged from her temporary shelter Captain Everard had quitted the shop; and he had not come again that evening, as it had struck her he possibly might—might all the more easily that there were numberless persons who came, morning and afternoon, numberless times, so that he wouldn't necessarily have attracted attention. The second day it was different and yet on the whole worse. His access to her had become possible—she felt herself even reaping the fruit of her yesterday's glare at Mr. Buckton; but transacting his business with him didn't simplify—it could, in spite of the rigour of circumstance, feed so her new conviction. The rigour was tremendous, and his telegrams—not, now, mere pretexts for getting at her—were apparently genuine; yet the conviction had taken but a night to develop. It could be simply enough expressed; she had had the glimmer of it the day before in her idea that he needed no more help than she had already given; that it was help he himself was prepared to render. He had come up to town but for three or four days; he had been absolutely obliged to be absent after the other time; yet he would, now that he was face to face with her, stay on as much longer as she liked. Little by little it was thus clarified, though from the first flash of his reappearance she had read into it the real essence.

That was what the night before, at eight o'clock, her hour to go, had made her hang back and dawdle. She did last things or pretended to do them; to be in the cage had suddenly become her safety, and she was literally afraid of the alternate self who might be waiting outside. *He* might be waiting; it was he who was her alternate self, and of him she was afraid. The most extraordinary change had taken place in her from the moment of her catching the impression he seemed to have returned on purpose to give her. Just before she had done so, on that bewitched afternoon, she had seen herself approach, without a scruple, the porter at Park Chambers; then, as the effect of the rush of a consciousness quite altered, she had, on at last quitting Cocker's, gone straight home for the first time since her return from Bournemouth. She had passed his door every night for weeks, but nothing would have induced her to pass it now. This change was the tribute of her fear—the result of a change in himself as to which she needed no more explanation than his mere face vividly gave her; strange though it was to find an element of deterrence in the object that she regarded as the most beautiful in the world. He had taken it from her in the Park that night that she wanted him not to propose to her to sup; but he had put away the lesson by this time—he practically proposed supper every time he looked at her. This was what, for that matter, mainly filled the three days. He came in twice on each of these, and it was as if he came in to give her a chance to relent. That was, after all, she said to herself in the intervals, the most that he did. There were ways, she fully recognised, in which he spared her, and other particular ways as to which she meant that her silence should be full, to him, of exquisite pleading. The most particular of all was his not being outside, at the corner, when she quitted the place for the night. This he might so easily have been—so easily if he hadn't been so nice. She continued to recognise in his forbearance the fruit of her dumb supplication, and the only compensation he found for it was the harmless freedom of being able to appear to say: "Yes, I'm in town only for three or four days, but, you know, I *would* stay on." He struck her as calling attention each day, each hour, to the rapid ebb of time; he exaggerated to the point of putting it that there were only two days more, that there was at last, dreadfully, only one.

There were other things still that he struck her as doing with a special intention; as to the most marked of which—unless indeed it were the most obscure—she might well have marvelled that it didn't seem to her more horrid. It was either the frenzy of her imagination or the disorder of his baffled passion that gave her once or twice the vision of his putting down redundant money— sovereigns not concerned with the little payments he was perpetually making—so that she might give him some sign of helping him to slip them over to her. What was most extraordinary in this impression was the amount of excuse that, with some incoherence, she found for him. He wanted to pay her because there was nothing to pay her for. He wanted to offer her things that he knew she wouldn't take. He wanted to show her how much he respected her by giving her the supreme chance to show *him* she was respectable. Over the driest transactions, at any rate, their eyes had out these questions. On the third day he put in a telegram that had evidently something of the same point as the stray sovereigns—a message that was, in the first place, concocted, and that, on a second thought, he took back from her before she had stamped it. He had given her time to read it, and had only then bethought himself that he had better not send it. If it was not to Lady Bradeen at Twindle—where she knew her ladyship then to be—this was because an address to Doctor Buzzard at Brickwood was just as good, with the added merit of its not giving away quite so much a person whom he had still, after all, in a manner to consider. It was of course most complicated, only half lighted; but there was, discernibly enough, a scheme of communication in which Lady Bradeen at Twindle and Dr. Buzzard at Brickwood were, within limits, one and the same person. The words he had shown her and then taken back consisted, at all events, of the brief but vivid phrase: "Absolutely impossible." The point was not that she should transmit it; the point was just that she should see it. What was absolutely impossible was that before he had settled something at Cocker's he should go either to Twindle or to Brickwood.

The logic of this, in turn, for herself, was that she could lend herself to no settlement so long as she so intensely knew. What she knew was that he was, almost under peril of life, clenched in a situation: therefore how could she also know where a poor girl in the P.O. might really stand? It was more and more between them that if he might convey to her that he was free, that everything she had seen so deep into was a closed chapter, her own case might become different for her, she might understand and meet him and listen. But he could convey nothing of the sort, and he only fidgeted and floundered in his want of power. The chapter wasn't in the least closed, not for the other party; and the other party had a pull, somehow and somewhere: this his whole attitude and expression confessed, at the same time that they entreated her not to remember and not to mind. So long as she did remember and did mind he could only circle about and go and come, doing futile things of which he was ashamed. He was ashamed of his two words to Dr. Buzzard, and went out of the shop as soon as he had crumpled up the paper again and thrust it into his pocket. It had been an abject little exposure of dreadful, impossible passion. He appeared in fact to be too ashamed to come back. He had left town again, and a first week elapsed, and a second. He had had naturally to return to the real mistress of his fate; she had insisted—she knew how, and he couldn't put in another hour. There was always a day when she called time. It was known to our young friend moreover that he had now been despatching telegrams from other offices. She knew at last so much, that she had quite lost her earlier sense of merely guessing. There were no shades of distinctness—it all bounced out.

XXII

Eighteen days elapsed, and she had begun to think it probable she should never see him again. He too then understood now: he had made out that she had secrets and reasons and impediments, that even a poor girl at the P.O. might have her complications. With the charm she had cast on him lightened by distance he had suffered a final delicacy to speak to him, had made up his mind that it would be only decent to let her alone. Never so much as during these latter days had she felt the precariousness of their relation—the happy, beautiful, untroubled original one, if it could only have been restored,—in which the public servant and the casual public only were concerned. It hung at the best by the merest silken thread, which was at the mercy of any accident and might snap at any minute. She arrived by the end of the fortnight at the highest sense of actual fitness, never doubting that her decision was now complete. She would just give him a few days more to come back to her on a proper impersonal basis—for even to an embarrassing representative of the casual public a public servant with a conscience did owe something,—and then would signify to Mr. Mudge that she was ready for the little home. It had been visited, in the further talk she had had with him at Bournemouth, from garret to cellar, and they had especially lingered, with their respectively darkened brows, before the niche into which it was to be broached to her mother that she was to find means to fit.

He had put it to her more definitely than before that his calculations had allowed for that dingy presence, and he had thereby marked the greatest impression he had ever made on her. It was a stroke superior even again to his handling of the drunken soldier. What she considered that, in the face of it, she hung on at Cocker's for, was something that she could only have described as the common fairness of a last word. Her actual last word had been, till it should be superseded, that she wouldn't abandon her other friend, and it stuck to her, through thick and thin, that she was still at her post and on her honour. This other friend had shown so much beauty of conduct already that he would surely, after all, just reappear long enough to relieve her, to give her something she could take away. She saw it, caught it, at times, his parting present; and there were moments when she felt herself sitting like a beggar with a hand held out to an almsgiver who only fumbled. She hadn't taken the sovereigns, but she *would* take the penny. She heard, in imagination, on the counter, the ring of the copper. "Don't put yourself out any longer," he would say, "for so bad a case. You've done all there is to be done. I thank and acquit and release you. Our lives take us. I don't know much—though I have really been interested—about yours; but I suppose you've got one. Mine, at any rate, will take *me*—and where it will. Heigh-ho! Good-bye." And then once more, for the sweetest, faintest flower of all: "Only, I say—see here!" She had framed the whole picture with a squareness that included also the image of how again she would decline to "see there," decline, as she might say, to see anywhere or anything. Yet it befell that just in the fury of this escape she saw more than ever.

He came back one night with a rush, near the moment of their closing, and showed her a face so different and new, so upset and anxious, that almost anything seemed to look out of it but clear recognition. He poked in a telegram very much as if the simple sense of pressure, the distress of extreme haste, had blurred the remembrance of where in particular he was. But as she met his eyes a light came; it broke indeed on the spot into a positive, conscious glare. That made up for everything, for it was an instant proclamation of the celebrated "danger"; it seemed to pour things out in a flood. "Oh yes, here it is—it's upon me at last! Forget, for God's sake, my having worried or bored you, and just help me, just *save* me, by getting this off without the loss of a second!" Something grave had clearly occurred, a crisis declared itself. She recognised immediately the person to whom the telegram was addressed—the Miss Dolman, of Parade Lodge, to whom Lady Bradeen had wired, at Dover, on the last occasion, and whom she had then, with her recollection of previous arrangements, fitted into a particular setting. Miss Dolman had figured before and not figured since, but she was now the subject of an imperative appeal. "Absolutely necessary to see you. Take last train Victoria if you can catch it. If not, earliest morning, and answer me direct either way."

"Reply paid?" said the girl. Mr. Buckton had just departed, and the counter-clerk was at the sounder. There was no other representative of the public, and she had never yet, as it seemed to her, not even in the street or in the Park, been so alone with him.

"Oh yes, reply paid, and as sharp as possible, please."

She affixed the stamps in a flash. "She'll catch the train!" she then declared to him breathlessly, as if she could absolutely guarantee it.

"I don't know—I hope so. It's awfully important. So kind of you. Awfully sharp, please." It was wonderfully innocent now, his oblivion of all but his danger. Anything else that had ever passed between them was utterly out of it. Well, she had wanted him to be impersonal!

There was less of the same need therefore, happily, for herself; yet she only took time, before she flew to the sounder, to gasp at him: "You're in trouble?"

"Horrid, horrid—there's a row!" But they parted, on it, in the next breath; and as she dashed at the sounder, almost pushing, in her violence, the counter-clerk off the stool, she caught the bang with which, at Cocker's door, in his further precipitation, he closed the apron of the cab into which he had leaped. As he rushed off to some other precaution suggested by his alarm, his appeal to Miss Dolman flashed straight away.

But she had not, on the morrow, been in the place five minutes before he was with her again, still more discomposed and quite, now, as she said to herself, like a frightened child coming to its mother. Her companions were there, and she felt it to be remarkable how, in the presence of his agitation, his mere scared, exposed nature, she suddenly ceased to mind. It came to her as it had never come to her before that with absolute directness and assurance they might carry almost anything off. He had nothing to send—she was sure he had been wiring all over,—and yet his business was evidently huge. There was nothing but that in his eyes—not a glimmer of reference or memory. He was almost haggard with anxiety, and had clearly not slept a wink. Her pity for him would have given her any courage, and she seemed to know at last why she had been such a fool. "She didn't come?" she panted.

"Oh yes, she came; but there has been some mistake. We want a telegram."

"A telegram?"

"One that was sent from here ever so long ago. There was something in it that has to be recovered. Something very, *very* important, please—we want it immediately."

He really spoke to her as if she had been some strange young woman at Knightsbridge or Paddington; but it had no other effect on her than to give her the measure of his tremendous flurry. Then it was that, above all, she felt how much she had missed in the gaps and blanks and absent answers—how much she had had to dispense with: it was black darkness now, save for this little wild red flare. So much as that she saw and possessed. One of the lovers was quaking somewhere out of town, and the other was quaking just where he stood. This was vivid enough, and after an instant she knew it was all she wanted. She wanted no detail, no fact—she wanted no nearer vision of discovery or shame. "When was your telegram? Do you mean you sent it from here?" She tried to do the young woman at Knightsbridge.

"Oh yes, from here—several weeks ago. Five, six, seven"—he was confused and impatient,—"don't you remember?"

"Remember?" she could scarcely keep out of her face, at the word, the strangest of smiles.

But the way he didn't catch what it meant was perhaps even stranger still. "I mean, don't you keep the old ones?"

"For a certain time."

"But how long?"

She thought; she *must* do the young woman, and she knew exactly what the young woman would say and, still more, wouldn't. "Can you give me the date?"

"Oh God, no! It was some time or other in August—toward the end. It was to the same address as the one I gave you last night."

"Oh!" said the girl, knowing at this the deepest thrill she had ever felt. It came to her there, with her eyes on his face, that she held the whole thing in her hand, held it as she held her pencil, which might have broken at that instant in her tightened grip. This made her feel like the very fountain of fate, but the emotion was such a flood that she had to press it back with all her force. That was positively the reason, again, of her flute-like Paddington tone. "You can't give us anything a little nearer?" Her "little" and her "us" came straight from Paddington. These things were no false note for him—his difficulty absorbed them all. The eyes with which he pressed her, and in the depths of which she read terror and rage and literal tears, were just the same he would have shown any other prim person.

"I don't know the date. I only know the thing went from here, and just about the time I speak of. It wasn't delivered, you see. We've got to recover it."

XXIII

She was as struck with the beauty of his plural pronoun as she had judged he might be with that of her own; but she knew now so well what she was about that she could almost play with him and with her new-born joy. "You say 'about the time you speak of.' But I don't think you speak of an exact time—*do* you?"

He looked splendidly helpless. "That's just what I want to find out. Don't you keep the old ones?—can't you look it up?"

Our young lady—still at Paddington—turned the question over. "It wasn't delivered?"

"Yes, it *was;* yet, at the same time, don't you know? it wasn't." He just hung back, but he brought it out. "I mean it was intercepted, don't you know? and there was something in it." He paused again and, as if to further his quest and woo and supplicate success and recovery, even smiled with an effort at the agreeable that was almost ghastly and that turned the knife in her tenderness. What must be the pain of it all, of the open gulf and the throbbing fever, when this was the mere hot breath? "We want to get what was in it—to know what it was."

"I see—I see." She managed just the accent they had at Paddington when they stared like dead fish. "And you have no clue?"

"Not at all—I've the clue I've just given you."

"Oh, the last of August?" If she kept it up long enough she would make him really angry.

"Yes, and the address, as I've said."

"Oh, the same as last night?"

He visibly quivered, as if with a gleam of hope; but it only poured oil on her quietude, and she was still deliberate. She ranged some papers. "Won't you look?" he went on.

"I remember your coming," she replied.

He blinked with a new uneasiness; it might have begun to come to him, through her difference, that he was somehow different himself. "You were much quicker then, you know!"

"So were you—you must do me that justice," she answered with a smile. "But let me see. Wasn't it Dover?"

"Yes, Miss Dolman—"

"Parade Lodge, Parade Terrace?"

"Exactly—thank you so awfully much!" He began to hope again. "Then you *have* it—the other one?"

She hesitated afresh; she quite dangled him. "It was brought by a lady?"

"Yes; and she put in by mistake something wrong. That's what we've got to get hold of!"

Heavens! what was he going to say?—flooding poor Paddington with wild betrayals! She couldn't too much, for her joy, dangle him, yet she couldn't either, for his dignity, warn or control or check him. What she found herself doing was just to treat herself to the middle way. "It was intercepted?"

"It fell into the wrong hands. But there's something in it," he continued to blurt out, "that *may* be all right. That is, if it's wrong, don't you know? It's all right if it's wrong," he remarkably explained.

What *was* he, on earth, going to say? Mr. Buckton and the counter-clerk were already interested; no one *would* have the decency to come in; and she was divided between her particular terror for him and her general curiosity. Yet she already saw with what brilliancy she could add, to carry the thing off, a little false knowledge to all her real. "I quite understand," she said with benevolent, with almost patronising quickness. "The lady has forgotten what she did put."

"Forgotten most wretchedly, and it's an immense inconvenience. It has only just been found that it didn't get there; so that if we could immediately have it—"

"Immediately?"

"Every minute counts. You *have*," he pleaded, "surely got them on file?"

"So that you can see it on the spot?"

"Yes, please—this very minute." The counter rang with his knuckles, with the knob of his stick, with his panic of alarm. "Do, *do* hunt it up!" he repeated.

"I daresay we could get it for you," the girl sweetly returned.

"Get it?"—he looked aghast. "When?"

"Probably by to-morrow."

"Then it isn't here?"—his face was pitiful.

She caught only the uncovered gleams that peeped out of the blackness, and she wondered what complication, even among the most supposable, the very worst, could be bad enough to account for the degree of his terror. There were twists and turns, there were places where the screw drew blood, that she couldn't guess. She was more and more glad she didn't want to. "It has been sent on."

"But how do you know if you don't look?"

She gave him a smile that was meant to be, in the absolute irony of its propriety, quite divine. "It was August 23rd, and we have nothing later here than August 27th."

Something leaped into his face. "27th—23rd? Then you're sure? You know?"

She felt she scarce knew what—as if she might soon be pounced upon for some lurid connection with a scandal. It was the queerest of all sensations, for she had heard, she had read, of these things, and the wealth of her intimacy with them at Cocker's might be supposed to have schooled and seasoned her. This particular one that she had really quite lived with was, after all, an old story; yet what it had been before was dim and distant beside the touch under which she now winced. Scandal?—it had never been but a silly word. Now it was a great palpable surface, and the surface was, somehow, Captain Everard's wonderful face. Deep down in his eyes was a picture, the vision of a great place like a chamber of justice, where, before a watching crowd, a poor girl, exposed but heroic, swore with a quavering voice to a document, proved an *alibi*, supplied a link. In this picture she bravely took her place. "It was the 23rd."

"Then can't you get it this morning—or some time to-day?"

She considered, still holding him with her look, which she then turned on her two companions, who were by this time unreservedly enlisted. She didn't care—not a scrap, and she glanced about for a piece of paper. With this she had to recognise the rigour of official thrift—a morsel of blackened blotter was the only loose paper to be seen. "Have you got a card?" she said to her visitor. He was quite away from Paddington now, and the next instant, with a pocket-book in his hand, he had whipped a card out. She gave no glance at the name on it—only turned it to the other side. She continued to hold him, she felt at present, as she had never held him; and her command of her colleagues was, for the moment, not less marked. She wrote something on the back of the card and pushed it across to him.

He fairly glared at it. "Seven, nine, four—"

"Nine, six, one"—she obligingly completed the number. "Is it right?" she smiled.

He took the whole thing in with a flushed intensity; then there broke out in him a visibility of relief that was simply a tremendous exposure. He shone at them all like a tall light-house, embracing even, for sympathy, the blinking young men. "By all the powers—it's wrong!" And without another look, without a word of thanks, without time for anything or anybody, he turned on them the broad back of his great stature, straightened his triumphant shoulders, and strode out of the place.

She was left confronted with her habitual critics. " 'If it's wrong it's all right!' " she extravagantly quoted to them.

The counter-clerk was really awe-stricken. "But how did you know, dear?"

"I remembered, love!"

Mr. Buckton, on the contrary, was rude. "And what game is that, miss?"

No happiness she had ever known came within miles of it, and some minutes elapsed before she could recall herself sufficiently to reply that it was none of his business.

XXIV

If life at Cocker's, with the dreadful drop of August, had lost something of its savour, she had not been slow to infer that a heavier blight had fallen on the graceful industry of Mrs. Jordan. With Lord Rye and Lady Ventnor and Mrs. Bubb all out of town, with the blinds down on all the homes of luxury, this ingenious woman might well have found her wonderful taste left quite on her hands. She bore up, however, in a way that began by exciting much of her young friend's esteem; they perhaps even more frequently met as the wine of life flowed less free from other sources, and each, in the lack of better diversion, carried on with more mystification for the other an intercourse that consisted not a little of peeping out and drawing back. Each waited for the other to commit herself, each profusely curtained for the other the limits of low horizons. Mrs. Jordan was indeed probably the more reckless skirmisher; nothing could exceed her frequent incoherence unless it was indeed her occasional bursts of confidence. Her account of her private affairs rose and fell like a flame in the wind—sometimes the bravest bonfire and sometimes a handful of ashes. This our young woman took to be an effect of the position, at one moment and another, of the famous door of the great world. She had been struck in one of her ha'penny volumes with the translation of a French proverb according to which a door had to be either open or shut; and it seemed a part of the precariousness of Mrs. Jordan's life that hers mostly managed to be neither. There had been occasions when it appeared to gape wide—fairly to woo her across its threshold; there had been others, of an order distinctly disconcerting, when it was all but banged in her face. On the whole, however, she had evidently not lost heart; these still belonged to the class of things in spite of which she looked well. She intimated that the profits of her trade had swollen so as to float her through any state of the tide, and she had, besides this, a hundred profundities and explanations.

She rose superior, above all, on the happy fact that there were always gentlemen in town and that gentlemen were her greatest admirers; gentlemen from the City in especial—as to whom she was full of information about the passion and pride excited in such breasts by the objects of her charming commerce. The City men *did*, in short, go in for flowers. There was a certain type of awfully smart stockbroker—Lord Rye called them Jews and "bounders," but she didn't care—whose extravagance, she more than once threw out, had really, if one had any conscience, to be forcibly restrained. It was not perhaps a pure love of beauty: it was a matter of vanity and a sign of business; they wished to crush their rivals, and that was one of their weapons. Mrs. Jordan's shrewdness was extreme; she knew, in any case, her customer—she dealt, as she said, with all sorts; and it was, at the worst, a race for her—a race even in the dull months—from one set of chambers to another. And then, after all, there were also still the ladies; the ladies of stockbroking circles were perpetually up and down. They were not quite perhaps Mrs. Bubb or Lady Ventnor; but you couldn't tell the difference unless you quarrelled with them, and then you knew it only by their making-up sooner. These ladies formed the branch of her subject on which she most swayed in the breeze; to that degree that her confidant had ended with an inference or two tending to banish regret for opportunities not embraced. There were indeed tea-gowns[19] that Mrs. Jordan described—but tea-gowns were not the whole of respectability, and it was odd that a clergyman's widow should sometimes speak as if she almost thought so. She came back, it was true, unfailingly, to Lord Rye, never, evidently, quite losing sight of him even on the longest excursions. That he was kindness itself had become in fact the very moral it all pointed—pointed in strange flashes of the poor woman's nearsighted eyes. She launched at her young friend many portentous looks, solemn heralds of some extraordinary communication. The communication itself, from week to week, hung fire; but it was to the facts over which it hovered that she owed her power of going on. "They *are,* in one way *and* another," she often emphasised, "a tower of strength"; and as the allusion was to the aristocracy, the girl could quite wonder why, if they were so in "one" way, they should require to be so in two. She thoroughly knew, however, how many ways Mrs. Jordan counted in. It all meant simply that her fate was pressing her close. If that fate was to be sealed at the matrimonial altar it was perhaps not remarkable that she shouldn't come all at once to the scratch of overwhelming a mere telegraphist. It would necessarily present to such a person a prospect of regretful sacrifice. Lord Rye—if it *was* Lord Rye— wouldn't be "kind" to a nonentity of that sort, even though people quite as good had been.

One Sunday afternoon in November they went, by arrangement, to church together; after which—on the inspiration of the moment; the arrangement had not included it—they proceeded to Mrs. Jordan's lodging in the region of Maida Vale.[20] She had raved to her friend about her service of predilection; she was excessively "high," and had more than once wished to introduce the girl to the same comfort and privilege. There was a thick brown fog, and Maida Vale tasted of acrid smoke; but they had been sitting among chants and incense and wonderful music, during which, though the effect of such things on her mind was great, our young lady had indulged in a series of reflections but indirectly related to them. One of these was the result of Mrs. Jordan's having said to her on the way, and with a certain fine significance, that Lord Rye had been for some time in town. She had spoken as if it were a circumstance to which little required to be added—as if the bearing of such an item on her life might easily be grasped. Perhaps it was the wonder of whether

Lord Rye wished to marry her that made her guest, with thoughts straying to that quarter, quite determine that some other nuptials also should take place at St. Julian's. Mr. Mudge was still an attendant at his Wesleyan chapel, but this was the least of her worries—it had never even vexed her enough for her to so much as name it to Mrs. Jordan. Mr. Mudge's form of worship was one of several things—they made up in superiority and beauty for what they wanted in number—that she had long ago settled he should take from her, and she had now moreover for the first time definitely established her own. Its principal feature was that it was to be the same as that of Mrs. Jordan and Lord Rye; which was indeed very much what she said to her hostess as they sat together later on. The brown fog was in this hostess's little parlour, where it acted as a postponement of the question of there being, besides, anything else than the teacups and a pewter pot, and a very black little fire, and a paraffin lamp without a shade. There was at any rate no sign of a flower; it was not for herself Mrs. Jordan gathered sweets. The girl waited till they had had a cup of tea—waited for the announcement that she fairly believed her friend had, this time, possessed herself of her formally at last to make; but nothing came, after the interval, save a little poke at the fire, which was like the clearing of a throat for a speech.

XXV

"I think you must have heard me speak of Mr. Drake?" Mrs. Jordan had never looked so queer, nor her smile so suggestive of a large benevolent bite.

"Mr. Drake? Oh yes; isn't he a friend of Lord Rye?"

"A great and trusted friend. Almost—I may say—a loved friend."

Mrs. Jordan's "almost" had such an oddity that her companion was moved, rather flippantly perhaps, to take it up. "Don't people as good as love their friends when they 'trust' them?"

It pulled up a little the eulogist of Mr. Drake. "Well, my dear, I love *you*——"

"But you don't trust me?" the girl unmercifully asked.

Again Mrs. Jordan paused—still she looked queer. "Yes," she replied with a certain austerity; "that's exactly what I'm about to give you rather a remarkable proof of." The sense of its being remarkable was already so strong that, while she bridled a little, this held her auditor in a momentary muteness of submission. "Mr. Drake has rendered his lordship, for several years, services that his lordship has highly appreciated and that make it all the more—a—unexpected that they should, perhaps a little suddenly, separate."

"Separate?" Our young lady was mystified, but she tried to be interested; and she already saw that she had put the saddle on the wrong horse. She had heard something of Mr. Drake, who was a member of his lordship's circle—the member with whom, apparently, Mrs. Jordan's avocations had most happened to throw her. She was only a little puzzled at the "separation." "Well, at any rate," she smiled, "if they separate as friends——!"

"Oh, his lordship takes the greatest interest in Mr. Drake's future. He'll do anything for him; he has in fact just done a great deal. There *must,* you know, be changes——!"

"No one knows it better than I," the girl said. She wished to draw her interlocutress out. "There will be changes enough for me."

"You're leaving Cocker's?"

The ornament of that establishment waited a moment to answer, and then it was indirect. "Tell me what *you're* doing."

"Well, what will you think of it?"

"Why, that you've found the opening you were always so sure of."

Mrs. Jordan, on this, appeared to muse with embarrassed intensity. "I was always sure, yes—and yet I often wasn't!"

"Well, I hope you're sure now. Sure, I mean, of Mr. Drake."

"Yes, my dear, I think I may say I *am.* I kept him going till I was."

"Then he's yours?"

"My very own."

"How nice! And awfully rich?" our young woman went on.

Mrs. Jordan showed promptly enough that she loved for higher things. "Awfully handsome—six foot two. And he *has* put by."

"Quite like Mr. Mudge, then!" that gentleman's friend rather desperately exclaimed.

"Oh, not *quite!*" Mr. Drake's was ambiguous about it, but the name of Mr. Mudge had evidently given her some sort of stimulus. "He'll have more opportunity now, at any rate. He's going to Lady Bradeen."

"To Lady Bradeen?" This was bewilderment. " 'Going—'?"

The girl had seen, from the way Mrs. Jordan looked at her, that the effect of the name had been to make her let something out. "Do you know her?"

She hesitated; then she found her feet. "Well, you'll remember I've often told you that if you have grand clients, I have them too."

"Yes," said Mrs. Jordan; "but the great difference is that you hate yours, whereas I really love mine. *Do* you know Lady Bradeen?" she pursued.

"Down to the ground! She's always in and out."

Mrs. Jordan's foolish eyes confessed, in fixing themselves on this sketch, to a degree of wonder and even of envy. But she bore up and, with a certain gaiety, "Do you hate *her?*" she demanded.

Her visitor's reply was prompt. "Dear no!—not nearly so much as some of them. She's too outrageously beautiful."

Mrs. Jordan continued to gaze. "Outrageously?"

"Well, yes; deliciously." What was really delicious was Mrs. Jordan's vagueness. "You don't know her—you've not seen her?" her guest lightly continued.

"No, but I've heard a great deal about her."

"So have I!" our young lady exclaimed.

Mrs. Jordan looked an instant as if she suspected her good faith, or at least her seriousness. "You know some friend—?"

"Of Lady Bradeen's? Oh yes—I know one."

"Only one?"

The girl laughed out. "Only one—but he's so intimate."

Mrs. Jordan just hesitated. "He's a gentleman?"

"Yes, he's not a lady."

Her interlocutress appeared to muse. "She's immensely surrounded."

"She *will* be—with Mr. Drake!"

Mrs. Jordan's gaze became strangely fixed. "Is she *very* good-looking?"

"The handsomest person I know."

Mrs. Jordan continued to contemplate. "Well, *I* know some beauties." Then, with her odd jerkiness, "Do you think she looks *good?*" she inquired.

"Because that's not always the case with the good-looking?"—the other took it up. "No, indeed, it isn't: that's one thing Cocker's has taught me. Still, there are some people who have everything. Lady Bradeen, at any rate, has enough: eyes and a nose and a mouth, a complexion, a figure—"

"A figure?" Mrs. Jordan almost broke in.

"A figure, a head of hair!" The girl made a little conscious motion that seemed to let the hair all down, and her companion watched the wonderful show. "But Mr. Drake *is* another—?"

"Another?"—Mrs. Jordan's thoughts had to come back from a distance.

"Of her ladyship's admirers. He's 'going,' you say, to her?"

At this Mrs. Jordan really faltered. "She has engaged him."

"Engaged him?"—our young woman was quite at sea.

"In the same capacity as Lord Rye."

"And was Lord Rye engaged?"

XXVI

Mrs. Jordan looked away from her now—looked, she thought, rather injured and, as if trifled with, even a little angry. The mention of Lady Bradeen had frustrated for a while the convergence of our heroine's thoughts; but with this impression of her old friend's combined impatience and diffidence they began again to whirl round her, and continued it till one of them appeared to dart at her, out of the dance, as if with a sharp peck. It came to her with a lively shock, with a positive sting, that Mr. Drake was—could it be possible? With the idea she found herself afresh on the edge of laughter, of a sudden and strange perversity of mirth. Mr. Drake loomed, in a swift image, before her; such a figure as she had seen in open door-ways of houses in Cocker's quarter—majestic, middle-aged, erect, flanked on either side by a footman and taking the name of a visitor. Mr. Drake then verily *was* a person who opened the door! Before she had time, however, to recover from the effect of her evocation, she was offered a vision which quite engulfed it. It was communicated to her somehow that the face with which she had seen it rise prompted Mrs. Jordan to dash, at a venture, at something that might attenuate criticism. "Lady Bradeen is re-arranging—she's going to be married."

"Married?" The girl echoed it ever so softly, but there it was at last.

"Didn't you know it?"

She summoned all her sturdiness. "No, she hasn't told me."

"And her friends—haven't they?"

"I haven't seen any of them lately. I'm not so fortunate as *you*."

Mrs. Jordan gathered herself. "Then you haven't even heard of Lord Bradeen's death?"

Her comrade, unable for a moment to speak, gave a slow head-shake. "You know it from Mr. Drake?" It was better surely not to learn things at all than to learn them by the butler.

"She tells him everything."

"And he tells *you*—I see." Our young lady got up; recovering her muff and her gloves, she smiled. "Well, I haven't, unfortunately, any Mr. Drake. I congratulate you with all my heart. Even without your sort of assistance, however, there's a trifle here and there that I do pick up. I gather that if she's to marry any one, it must quite necessarily be my friend."

Mrs. Jordan was now also on her feet. "Is Captain Everard your friend?"

The girl considered, drawing on a glove. "I saw, at one time, an immense deal of him."

Mrs. Jordan looked hard at the glove, but she had not, after all, waited for that to be sorry it was not cleaner. "What time was that?"

"It must have been the time you were seeing so much of Mr.

Drake." She had now fairly taken it in: the distinguished person Mrs. Jordan was to marry would answer bells and put on coals and superintend, at least, the cleaning of boots for the other distinguished person whom *she* might—well, whom she might have had, if she had wished, so much more to say to. "Good-bye," she added; "good-bye."

Mrs. Jordan, however, again taking her muff from her, turned it over, brushed it off, and thoughtfully peeped into it. "Tell me this before you go. You spoke just now of your own changes. Do you mean that Mr. Mudge——?"

"Mr. Mudge has had great patience with me—he has brought me at last to the point. We're to be married next month and have a nice little home. But he's only a grocer, you know"—the girl met her friend's intent eyes—"so that I'm afraid that, with the set you've got into, you won't see your way to keep up our friendship."

Mrs. Jordan for a moment made no answer to this; she only held the muff up to her face, after which she gave it back. "You don't like it. I see, I see."

To her guest's astonishment there were tears now in her eyes. "I don't like what?" the girl asked.

"Why, my engagement. Only, with your great cleverness," the poor lady quavered out, "you put it in your own way. I mean that you'll cool off. You already *have*——!" And on this, the next instant, her tears began to flow. She succumbed to them and collapsed; she sank down again, burying her face and trying to smother her sobs.

Her young friend stood there, still in some rigour, but taken much by surprise even if not yet fully moved to pity. "I don't put anything in any 'way,' and I'm very glad you're suited. Only, you know, you did put to *me* so splendidly what, even for me, if I had listened to you, it might lead to."

Mrs. Jordan kept up a mild, thin, weak wail; then, drying her eyes, as feebly considered this reminder. "It has led to my not starving!" she faintly gasped.

Our young lady, at this, dropped into the place beside her, and now, in a rush, the small, silly misery was clear. She took her hand as a sign of pitying it, then, after another instant, confirmed this expression with a consoling kiss. They sat there together; they looked out, hand in hand, into the damp, dusky, shabby little room and into the future, of no such very different suggestion, at last accepted by each. There was no definite utterance, on either side, of Mr. Drake's position in the great world, but the temporary collapse of his prospective bride threw all further necessary light; and what our heroine saw and felt for in the whole business was the vivid reflection of her own dreams and delusions and her own return to reality. Reality, for the poor things they both were, could only be ugliness and obscurity, could never be the escape, the rise. She pressed her friend—she had tact enough for that—with no other personal question, brought on no need of further revelations, only just continued to hold and comfort her and to acknowledge by stiff little forbearances the common element in their fate. She felt indeed magnanimous in such matters; for if it was very well, for condolence or re-assurance, to suppress just then invidious shrinkings, she yet by no means saw herself sitting down, as she might say, to the same table with Mr. Drake. There would luckily, to all appearance, be little question of tables; and the circumstance that, on their peculiar lines, her friend's interests would still attach themselves to Mayfair flung over Chalk Farm the first radiance it had shown. Where was one's pride and one's passion when the real way to judge of one's luck was by making not the wrong, but the right, comparison? Before she had again gathered herself to go she felt very small and cautious and thankful. "We shall have our own house," she said, "and you must come very soon and let me show it you."

"*We* shall have our own too," Mrs. Jordan replied: "for, don't you know, he makes it a condition that he sleeps out?"

"A condition?"—the girl felt out of it.

"For any new position. It was on that he parted with Lord Rye. His lordship can't meet it; so Mr. Drake has given him up."

"And all for you?"—our young woman put it as cheerfully as possible.

"For me and Lady Bradeen. Her ladyship's too glad to get him at any price. Lord Rye, out of interest in us, has in fact quite *made* her take him. So, as I tell you, he will have his own establishment."

Mrs. Jordan, in the elation of it, had begun to revive; but there was nevertheless between them rather a conscious pause—a pause in which neither visitor nor hostess brought out a hope or an invitation. It expressed in the last resort that, in spite of submission and sympathy, they could now, after all, only look at each other across the social gulf. They remained together as if it would be indeed their last chance, still sitting, though awkwardly, quite close, and feeling also—and this most unmistakably—that there was one thing more to go into. By the time it came to the surface, moreover, our young friend had recognised the whole of the main truth, from which she even drew again a slight irritation. It was not the main truth perhaps that most signified; but after her momentary effort, her embarrassment and her tears, Mrs. Jordan had begun to sound afresh—and even without speaking—the note of a social connection. She hadn't really let go of it that she was marrying into society. Well, it was a harmless compensation, and it was all that the prospective bride of Mr. Mudge had to leave with her.

XXVII

This young lady at last rose again, but she lingered before going. "And has Captain Everard nothing to say to it?"

"To what, dear?"

"Why, to such questions—the domestic arrangements, things in the house."

"How *can* he, with any authority, when nothing in the house is his?"

"Not his?" The girl wondered, perfectly conscious of the appearance she thus conferred on Mrs. Jordan of knowing, in comparison with herself, so tremendously much about it. Well, there were things she wanted so to get at that she was willing at last, though it hurt her, to pay for them with humiliation. "Why are they not his?"

"Don't you know, dear, that he has nothing?"

"Nothing?" It was hard to see him in such a light, but Mrs. Jordan's power to answer for it had a superiority that began, on the spot, to grow. "Isn't he rich?"

Mrs. Jordan looked immensely, looked both generally and particularly, informed. "It depends upon what you call—! Not, at any rate, in the least as *she* is. What does he bring? Think what she has. And then, my love, his debts."

"His debts?" His young friend was fairly betrayed into helpless innocence. She could struggle a little, but she had to let herself go; and if she had spoken frankly she would have said: "Do tell me, for I don't know so much about him as *that*!" As she didn't speak frankly she only said: "His debts are nothing—when she so adores him."

Mrs. Jordan began to fix her again, and now she saw that she could only take it all. That was what it had come to: his having sat with her there, on the bench and under the trees, in the summer darkness, and put his hand on her, making her know what he would have said if permitted; his having returned to her afterwards, repeatedly, with supplicating eyes and a fever in his blood; and her having, on her side, hard and pedantic, helped by some miracle and with her impossible condition, only answered him, yet supplicating back, through the bars of the cage,—all simply that she might hear of him, now for ever lost, only through Mrs. Jordan, who touched him through Mr. Drake, who reached him through Lady Bradeen. "She adores him—but of course that wasn't all there was about it."

The girl met her eyes a minute, then quite surrendered. "What was there else about it?"

"Why, don't you know?"—Mrs. Jordan was almost compassionate.

Her interlocutress had, in the cage, sounded depths, but there was a suggestion here somehow of an abyss quite measureless. "Of course I know that she would never let him alone."

"How *could* she—fancy!—when he had so compromised her?"

The most artless cry they had ever uttered broke, at this, from the younger pair of lips. "*Had* he so—?"

"Why, don't you know the scandal?"

Our heroine thought, recollected; there was something, whatever it was, that she knew, after all, much more of than Mrs. Jordan. She saw him again as she had seen him come that morning to recover the telegram—she saw him as she had seen him leave the shop. She perched herself a moment on this. "Oh, there was nothing public."

"Not exactly public—no. But there was an awful scare and an awful row. It was all on the very point of coming out. Something was lost—something was found."

"Ah yes," the girl replied, smiling as if with the revival of a blurred memory; "something was found."

"It all got about—and there was a point at which Lord Bradeen had to act."

"Had to—yes. But he didn't."

Mrs. Jordan was obliged to admit it. "No, he didn't. And then, luckily for them, he died."

"I didn't know about his death," her companion said.

"It was nine weeks ago, and most sudden. It has given them a prompt chance."

"To get married"—this was a wonder—"within nine weeks?"

"Oh, not immediately, but—in all the circumstances—very quietly and, I assure you, very soon. Every preparation's made. Above all, she holds him."

"Oh yes, she holds him!" our young friend threw off. She had this before her again a minute; then she continued: "You mean through his having made her talked about?"

"Yes, but not only that. She has still another pull."

"Another?"

Mrs. Jordan hesitated. "Why, he was *in* something."

Her comrade wondered. "In what?"

"I don't know. Something bad. As I tell you, something was found."

The girl stared. "Well?"

"It would have been very bad for him. But she helped him some way—she recovered it, got hold of it. It's even said she stole it!"

Our young woman considered afresh. "Why, it was what was found that precisely saved him."

Mrs. Jordan, however, was positive. "I beg your pardon. I happen to know."

Her disciple faltered but an instant. "Do you mean through Mr. Drake? Do they tell *him* these things?"

"A good servant," said Mrs. Jordan, now thoroughly superior and proportionately sententious, "doesn't need to be told! Her ladyship saved—as a woman so often saves!—the man she loves."

This time our heroine took longer to recover herself, but she found a voice at last. "Ah well—of course I don't know! The great thing was that he got off. They seem then, in a manner," she added, "to have done a great deal for each other."

"Well, it's she that has done most. She has him tight."

"I see, I see. Good-bye." The women had already embraced, and this was not repeated; but Mrs. Jordan went down with her guest to the door of the house. Here again the younger lingered, reverting, though three or four other remarks had on the way passed between them, to Captain Everard and Lady Bradeen. "Did you mean just now that if she hadn't saved him, as you call it, she wouldn't hold him so tight?"

"Well, I daresay." Mrs. Jordan, on the door-step, smiled with a reflection that had come to her; she took one of her big bites of the brown gloom. "Men always dislike one when they have done one an injury."

"But what injury had he done her?"

"The one I've mentioned. He *must* marry her, you know."

"And didn't he want to?"

"Not before."

"Not before she recovered the telegram?"

Mrs. Jordan was pulled up a little. "Was it a telegram?"

The girl hesitated. "I thought you said so. I mean whatever it was."

"Yes, whatever it was, I don't think she saw *that*."

"So she just nailed him?"

"She just nailed him." The departing friend was now at the

bottom of the little flight of steps; the other was at the top, with a certain thickness of fog. "And when am I to think of you in your little home?—next month?" asked the voice from the top.

"At the very latest. And when am I to think of you in yours?"

"Oh, even sooner. I feel, after so much talk with you about it, as if I were already there!" Then "*Good*-bye!" came out of the fog.

"Good-*bye*!" went into it. Our young lady went into it also, in the opposed quarter, and presently, after a few sightless turns, came out on the Paddington canal. Distinguishing vaguely what the low parapet enclosed, she stopped close to it and stood a while, very intently, but perhaps still sightlessly, looking down on it. A policeman, while she remained, strolled past her; then, going his way a little further and half lost in the atmosphere, paused and watched her. But she was quite unaware—she was full of her thoughts. They were too numerous to find a place just here, but two of the number may at least be mentioned. One of these was that, decidedly, her little home must be not for next month, but for next week; the other, which came indeed as she resumed her walk and went her way, was that it was strange such a matter should be at last settled for her by Mr. Drake.

NOTES

The Turn of the Screw

1. *Christmas Eve:* The group is telling ghost stories, the traditional Christmas Eve pastime.

2. *another turn of the screw:* What Douglas refers to by "turn of the screw" is the heightening, by the inclusion of a young child as a character, of the intensity and terror of the ghost story Griffin had told earlier that evening. The friends agree that having two such children would make the tale that much more terrifying.

3. *town:* London. The group is spending Christmas at a house in the country, and Douglas offers to send his key back to London.

4. *hung fire:* hesitated, paused dramatically. The phrase derives from an expression used to describe a delay in the discharge of firearms.

5. *Trinity:* Trinity College is one of the many colleges at Cambridge University.

6. Raison de plus: French for "all the more reason."

7. *candlestuck:* As the friends prepare to go to bed, they shake hands for the night and stick candles into holders to light the way to their bedrooms.

8. *Harley Street:* The inclusion of Harley Street is significant only in that it is a fashionable location in central London. It had not, by the time of James's writing, been associated with the practice of medicine.

9. *Hampshire:* A county in England to the northwest of London.

10. *Essex:* a county in England to the northeast of London.

11. *commodious fly:* a large, comfortable carriage.

12. *Raphael's holy infants:* The infants referred to are the frequently depicted cherubs in the paintings of the Italian Renaissance artist Raphael (1483–1520).

13. *machicolated:* The tower is made in an antique design with a balustrade and crenellations like those of a medieval castle. Machicolations are jutting parapets from which soldiers can fire arrows at attacking forces while being protected by the battlements.

14. *mystery ... confinement:* James makes reference to two works in this sentence. The first is another story of the supernatural, Ann Radcliffe's *The Mysteries of Udolpho* (1749). The second is Charlotte Brontë's *Jane Eyre,* in which a governess moves to a house in which her master's insane wife is imprisoned in the attic.

15. *muff:* slang for sissy.

16. *cherubs ... whack:* The "anecdote" is variously attributed by scholars, but the essence of the passage is clear: Cherubs would never do anything that would deserve punishment by spanking; moreover, such a punishment would be impossible anyway since they are noncorporeal and have nothing to be spanked.

17. *Quint:* The name Peter Quint has been of consistent controversy among James scholars. One of the more believable attributions has been to Peter Quince, in Shakespeare's *A Midsummer Night's Dream.* There is also *queynte,* the Middle English world for "quaint," as well as the Latin root for "five." None of these bear significantly on the text, however, and there is no kind of agreement as to the actual significance, if any, of Quint's name.

18. *Sea of Azof:* an inlet on the northern coast of the Black Sea.

19. *Miss Jessel:* The name is strongly reminiscent of the name Jezebel, from II Kings 9:30: "And when Jehu was come to Jezreel, Jezebel heard of it; and she painted her face." Again, in II Kings 9:36–37: "In the portion of Jezreel shall dogs eat the flesh of Jezebel: and the carcass of Jezebel shall be as dung upon the face of the field in the portion of Jezreel; so that they shall not say, This is Jezebel." While the name connotes the wickedness of Jezebel in parallel to the immorality of Miss Jessel, it is also important to note the implication that the fate of such a woman is not to be laid to rest, but to be scattered across the earth and forgotten.

20. *natural man:* that part of human nature which, when unchecked by morals or civilization, will lend itself to evil acts.
21. *Fielding's* Amelia: One of the last novels of Henry Fielding (1707–54), concerning the life and romantic trials of a virtuous woman.
22. *Mrs. Marcet:* Jane Marcet (1769–1858) was a prolific children's textbook writer whose books appeared in classrooms throughout England.
23. mot: French, meaning "word" or "saying." It is unclear exactly what is meant by this phrase. This could refer to one of the stories of the "old women of our village" mentioned earlier, or perhaps it is a nursery rhyme of which the children were particularly fond.
24. *gaoler:* British variant of the American "jailer."
25. *David ... Saul:* This refers to the passage in I Samuel 16:23, "And it came to pass, when the evil spirit from God was upon Saul, that David took an harp, and played with his hand: so Saul was refreshed, and was well, and the evil spirit departed from him."

IN THE CAGE
1. *sounder:* This is the girl's name for the telegraph equipment.
2. *Court Guide:* A periodically published listing of the names of members of the nobility.
3. *Mayfair, Chalk Farm:* Mayfair was the most affluent area in London at the time James was writing. Chalk Farm was a suburb in the northern part of London, significantly less expensive than the central part of London in which most of the story's place-names are located.
4. *work:* needlework.
5. Picciola: A whimsical romance by the French writer Joseph Xavier Boniface (also known as Saintine), written in 1837 and subsequently translated into English. The story is of a count held captive in prison who falls in love with a weed growing outside his cell.
6. *Regent Street, Hyde Park Place:* Both these addresses were among the most exclusive in London at the time. All the addresses given in the telegrams, within London and without, are meant to conjure up images of great wealth and privilege.
7. *Juno:* mother of the pantheon of Roman gods and the sister and wife of Jupiter, the king of the gods. She was the patron goddess of the hearth and of childbearing and is known for her power, beauty, and vengefulness.
8. *Buttonses:* a colloquial expression meaning domestic servant, so called because their uniforms had rows of buttons on the front.

9. *Regent's Park:* One of the Royal Parks of London in the northern part of the city.

10. *the Strand:* A street in central London, just north of the Thames, with a large number of theatres and shops.

11. *Thompson:* possibly a misspelled reference to James Thomson (1700–48), Scottish poet and dramatist known for his tragedies in the classical mode.

12. *Piccadilly:* a street in central London featuring shopping arcades.

13. *penny chair:* Chairs could be rented for the day to sit in the grassy fields of the park for a small sum of money.

14. *Wesleyan chapel:* The Wesleyan church was a branch of the Methodist church, widely considered a faith common to the middle class.

15. *Dover:* a city on the southeast coast of England and a common vacation spot.

16. *Park Lane:* the street that borders Hyde Park on the East and divides Hyde Park from Mayfair.

17. *Isle of Wight, Dorset coast:* vacation destinations for the middle class, mentioned here to contrast with the more expensive locations mentioned in the telegrams of the girl's clients.

18. *slavey:* a slang term for any lower-level male servant.

19. *tea-gowns:* special dresses worn by ladies at tea-time.

20. *Maida Vale:* an inexpensive suburb to the north of London.

COMMENTARY

HENRY JAMES

VIRGINIA WOOLF

MORTON DAUWEN ZABEL

STUART HUTCHINSON

HENRY JAMES

… That particular challenge at least *The Turn of the Screw* doesn't incur; and this perfectly independent and irresponsible little fiction rejoices, beyond any rival on a like ground, in a conscious provision of prompt retort to the sharpest question that may be addressed to it. For it has the small strength—if I shouldn't say rather the unattackable ease—of a perfect homogeneity, of being, to the very last grain of its virtue, all of a kind; the very kind, as happens, least apt to be baited by earnest criticism, the only sort of criticism of which account need be taken. To have handled again this so full-blown flower of high fancy is to be led back by it to easy and happy recognitions. Let the first of these be that of the starting-point itself—the sense, all charming again, of the circle, one winter afternoon, round the hall-fire of a grave old country-house where (for all the world as if to resolve itself promptly and obligingly into convertible, into "literary" stuff) the talk turned, on I forget what homely pretext, to apparitions and night-fears, to the marked and sad drop in the general supply, and still more in the general quality, of such commodities. The good, the really effective and heart-shaking ghost-stories (roughly so to term them) appeared all to have been told, and neither new crop nor new type in any quarter awaited us. The new type indeed, the mere modern "psychical" case, washed clean of all queerness as by exposure to a flowing laboratory tap, and equipped with credentials vouching for this—the new type clearly promised little, for the more it was respectably certified the less it seemed of a nature to rouse the dear old sacred terror. Thus it was, I remember, that amid our lament for a beautiful lost form, our distinguished host expressed the wish that he might but have recovered for us one of the scantest of fragments of this form at its best. He had never forgotten the impression made on him as a young man by the withheld glimpse, as it were, of a dreadful matter that had been reported years before, and with as few particulars, to a lady with whom he had youthfully talked. The story would have been thrilling could she but have found herself in better possession of it, dealing as it did with a couple of small children in an out-of-the-way place, to whom the spirits of certain "bad" servants, dead in the employ of the house, were believed to have appeared with the design of "getting hold" of them. This was all, but there had been more, which my friend's old converser had lost the thread of: she could only assure him of the wonder of the allegations as she had anciently heard them made. He himself could give us but this shadow of a shadow—my own appreciation of which, I need scarcely say, was exactly wrapped up in that thinness. On the surface there wasn't much, but another grain, none the less, would have spoiled the precious pinch addressed to its end as neatly as some modicum extracted from an old silver snuff-box and held between finger and thumb. I was to remember the haunted children and the prowling servile spirits as a "value," of the disquieting sort, in all conscience sufficient; so that when, after an interval, I was asked for something seasonable by the promoters of a periodical dealing in the time-honoured Christmastide toy, I bethought myself at once of the vividest little note for sinister romance that I had ever jotted down.

Such was the private source of *The Turn of the Screw;* and I wondered, I confess, why so fine a germ, gleaming there in the wayside dust of life, had never been deftly picked up. The thing had for me the immense merit of allowing the imagination absolute freedom of hand, of inviting it to act on a perfectly clear field, with no "outside" control involved, no pattern of the usual or the true or the terrible "pleasant" (save always, of course, the high pleasantry of one's very form) to consort with. This makes, in fact, the charm of my second reference, that I find here a perfect example of an exercise of the imagination unassisted, unassociated—playing the game, making the score, in the phrase of our sporting day, off its own bat. To what degree the game was worth playing I needn't attempt to say: the exercise I have noted strikes me now, I confess, as the interesting thing, the imaginative faculty acting with the *whole* of the case on its hands. The exhibition involved is, in other words, a fairy-tale pure and simple—save indeed as to its springing not from an artless and measureless, but from a conscious and cultivated credulity. Yet the fairy-tale belongs mainly to either of two classes, the short and sharp and single, charged more or less with the compactness of anecdote (as to which let the familiars of our childhood, *Cinderella* and *Blue-Beard* and *Hop o' my Thumb* and *Little Red Riding-Hood* and many of the gems of the Brothers Grimm directly testify), or else the long and loose, the copious, the various, the endless, where, dramatically speaking, roundness is quite sacrificed—sacrificed to fulness, sacrificed to exuberance, if one will: witness at hazard almost any one of the *Arabian Nights.* The charm of all these things for the distracted modern mind is in the clear field of experience, as I call it, over which we are thus led to roam; an annexed but independent world in which nothing is right save as we rightly imagine it. We have to do *that*, and we do it happily for the short spurt and in the smaller piece, achieving so perhaps beauty and lucidity; we flounder, we lose breath, on the other hand—that is, we fail, not of continuity, but of an agreeable unity, of the "roundness" in which beauty and lucidity largely reside—when we go in, as they say, for great lengths and breadths. And this, oddly enough, not because "keeping it up" isn't abundantly within the compass of the imagination appealed to in certain conditions, but because the finer interest depends just on *how* it is kept up.

Nothing is so easy as improvisation, the running on and on of invention; it is sadly compromised, however, from the moment its stream breaks bounds and gets into flood. Then the waters may spread indeed, gathering houses and herds and crops and cities into their arms and wrenching off, for our amusement, the whole face of the land—only violating by the same stroke our sense of the course and the channel, which is our sense of the uses of a stream and the virtue of a story. Improvisation, as in the *Arabian Nights*, may keep on terms with encountered objects by sweeping them in and floating them on its breast; but the great effect it so loses—that of keeping on terms with itself. This is ever, I intimate, the hard thing for the fairy-tale; but by just so much as it struck me as hard did it in *The Turn of the Screw* affect me as irresistibly prescribed. To improvise with extreme freedom and yet at the same time without the possibility of ravage, without the hint of a flood; to keep the stream, in a word, on something like ideal terms with itself: that was here my definite business. The thing was to aim at absolute singleness, clearness and roundness, and yet to depend on an imagination working freely, working (call it) with extravagance; by which law it wouldn't be thinkable except as free and wouldn't be amusing except as controlled. The merit of the tale, as it stands, is accordingly, I judge, that it has struggled successfully with its dangers. It is an excursion into chaos while remaining, like *Blue-Beard* and *Cinderella*, but an anecdote—though an anecdote amplified and highly emphasised and returning upon itself; as, for that matter, *Cinderella* and *Blue-Beard* return. I need scarcely add after this that it is a piece of ingenuity pure and simple, of cold artistic calculation, an *amusette* to catch those not easily caught (the "fun" of the capture of the merely witless being ever but small), the jaded, the disillusioned, the fastidious. Otherwise expressed, the study is of a conceived "tone," the tone of suspected and felt trouble, of an inordinate and incalculable sort—the tone of tragic, yet of exquisite, mystification. To knead the subject of my young friend's, the supposititious narrator's, mystification thick, and yet strain the expression of it so clear and fine that beauty would result: no side of the matter so revives for me as that endeavour. Indeed, if the artistic value of such an experiment be measured by the intellectual echoes it may again, long after, set in motion, the case would make in favour of this little firm fantasy—which I seem to see draw behind it to-day a train of associations. I ought doubtless to blush for thus confessing them so numerous that I can but pick among them for reference. I recall for instance a reproach made me by a reader capable evidently, for the time, of some attention, but not quite capable of enough, who complained that I hadn't sufficiently "characterised" my young woman engaged in her labyrinth; hadn't endowed her with signs and marks, features and humours, hadn't in a word invited her to deal with her own mystery as well as with that of Peter Quint, Miss Jessel and the hapless children. I remember well, whatever the absurdity of its now coming back to me, my reply to that criticism—under which one's artistic, one's ironic heart shook for the instant almost to breaking. "You indulge in that stricture at your ease, and I don't mind confiding to you that—strange as it may appear!—one has to choose ever so delicately among one's difficulties, attaching one's self to the greatest, bearing hard on those and intelligently neglecting the others. If one attempts to tackle them all one is certain to deal completely with none; whereas the effectual dealing with a few casts a blest golden haze under cover of which, like wanton mocking goddesses in clouds, the others find prudent to retire. It was 'déjà très-joli,' in *The Turn of the Screw*, please believe, the general proposition of our young woman's keeping crystalline her record of so many intense anomalies and obscurities—by which I don't of course mean her explanation of them, a different matter; and I saw no way, I feebly grant (fighting, at the best too, periodically, for every grudged inch of my space) to exhibit her in relations other than those; one of which, precisely, would have been her relation to her own nature. We have surely as much of her own nature as we can swallow in watching it reflect her anxieties and inductions. It constitutes no little of a character indeed, in such conditions, for a young person, as she says, 'privately bred,' that she is able to make her particular credible statement of such strange matters. She has 'authority,' which is a good deal to have given her, and I couldn't have arrived at so much had I clumsily tried for more."

For which truth I claim part of the charm latent on occasion in the extracted reasons of beautiful things—putting for the beautiful always, in a work of art, the close, the curious, the deep. Let me place above all, however, under the protection of that presence the side by which this fiction appeals most to consideration: its choice of its way of meeting its gravest difficulty. There were difficulties not so grave: I had for instance simply to renounce all attempt to keep the kind and degree of impression I wished to produce on terms with the to-day so copious psychical record of cases of apparitions. Different signs and circumstances, in the reports, mark these cases: different things are done—though on the whole very little appears to be—by the persons appearing; the point is, however, that some things are never done at all: this negative quantity is large—certain reserves and proprieties and immobilities consistently impose themselves. Recorded and attested "ghosts" are, in other words, as little expressive, as little dramatic, above all as little continuous and conscious and responsive, as is consistent with their taking the trouble—and an immense trouble they find it, we gather—to appear at all. Wonderful and interesting, therefore, at a given moment, they are inconceivable figures in an *action*—and *The Turn of the Screw* was an action, desperately, or it was nothing. I had to decide in fine between having my apparitions correct and having my story "good"—that is, producing my impression of the dreadful, my designed horror. Good ghosts, speaking by book, make poor subjects, and it was clear that from the first my hovering prowling blighting presences, my pair of abnormal agents, would have to depart altogether from the rules. They would be agents in fact; there would be laid on them the dire duty of causing the situation to reek with the air of Evil. Their desire and their ability to do so, visibly measuring meanwhile their effect, together with their observed and described success—this was exactly my central idea; so that, briefly, I cast my lot with pure romance, the appearances conforming to the true type being so little romantic.

This is to say, I recognise again, that Peter Quint and Miss Jessel are not "ghosts" at all, as we now know the ghost, but goblins, elves, imps, demons as loosely constructed as those of the old trials for witchcraft; if not, more pleasingly, fairies of the legendary order, wooing their victims forth to see them dance under the moon. Not indeed that I suggest their reducibility to any form of the pleasing pure and simple; they please at the best but through having helped me to express my subject all directly and intensely. Here it was—in the use made of them—that I felt a high degree of art really required; and here it is that, on reading the tale over, I find my precautions justified. The essence of the matter was the villainy of motive in the evoked predatory creatures; so that the result would be ignoble—by which I mean would be trivial—were this element of evil but feebly or inanely suggested. Thus arose on behalf of my idea the lively interest of a possible suggestion and process of *adumbration;* the question of how best to convey that sense of the depths of the sinister without which my fable would so woefully limp. Portentous evil—how was I to save that, as an intention on the part of my demon-spirits, from the drop, the comparative vulgarity, inevitably attending, throughout the whole range of possible brief illustration, the offered example, the imputed vice, the cited act, the limited deplorable presentable instance? To bring the bad dead back to life for a second round of badness is to warrant them as indeed prodigious, and to become hence as shy of specifications as of a waiting anti-climax. One had seen, in fiction, some grand form of wrong-doing, or better still of wrong-being, imputed, seen it promised and announced as by the hot breath of the Pit—and then, all lamentably, shrink to the compass of some particular brutality, some particular immorality, some particular infamy portrayed: with the result, alas, of the demonstration's falling sadly short. If *my* bad things, for *The Turn of the Screw,* I felt, should succumb to this danger, if they shouldn't seem sufficiently bad, there would be nothing for me but to hang my artistic head lower than I had ever known occasion to do.

The view of that discomfort and the fear of that dishonour, it accordingly must have been, that struck the proper light for my right, though by no means easy, short cut. What, in the last analysis, had I to give the sense of? Of their being, the haunting pair, capable, as the phrase is, of everything—that is of exerting, in respect to the children, the very worst action small victims so conditioned might be conceived as subject to. What would *be* then, on reflexion, this utmost conceivability?—a question to which the answer all admirably came. There is for such a case no eligible *absolute* of the wrong; it remains relative to fifty other elements, a matter of appreciation, speculation, imagination—these things, moreover, quite exactly in the light of the spectator's, the critic's, the reader's experience. Only make the reader's general vision of evil intense enough, I said to myself—and that already is a charming job—and his own experience, his own imagination, his own sympathy (with the children) and horror (of their false friends) will supply him quite sufficiently with all the particulars. Make him *think* the evil, make him think it for himself, and you are released from weak specifications. This ingenuity I took pains—as indeed great pains were required—to apply; and with a success apparently beyond my liveliest hope. Droll enough at the same time, I must add, some of the evidence—even when most convincing—of this success. How can I feel my calculation to have failed, my wrought suggestion not to have worked, that is, on my being assailed, as has befallen me, with the charge of a monstrous emphasis, the charge of all indecently expatiating? There is not only from beginning to end of the matter not an inch of expatiation, but my values are positively all blanks save so far as an excited horror, a promoted pity, a created expertness—on which punctual effects of strong causes no writer can ever fail to plume himself—proceed to read into them more or less fantastic figures. Of high interest to the author meanwhile—and by the same stroke a theme for the moralist—the artless resentful reaction of the entertained person who has bounded in the sense of the situation. He visits his abundance, morally, on the artist—who has but clung to an ideal of faultlessness. Such indeed, for this latter, are some of the observations by which the prolonged strain of that clinging may be enlivened!

From James's preface to the *New York Edition*
version of "The Turn of the Screw"

Lamb House, Rye.
Dec. 9th, 1898.

My dear H. G. Wells,

Your so liberal and graceful letter is to my head like coals of fire—so repeatedly for all these weeks have I had feebly to suffer frustrations in the matter of trundling over the marsh to ask for your news and wish for your continued amendment. The shortening days and the deepening mud have been at the bottom of this affair. I never get out of the house till 3 o'clock, when night is quickly at one's heels. I would have taken a regular day—I mean started in the a.m.—but have been so ridden, myself, by the black care of an unfinished and *running* (galloping, leaping and bounding,) serial that parting with a day has been like parting with a pound of flesh. I am still a neck ahead, however, and *this* week will see me through; I accordingly hope very much to be able to turn up on one of the ensuing days. I will sound a horn, so that you yourself be not absent on the chase. Then I will express more articulately my appreciation of your various signs of critical interest, as well as assure you of my sympathy in your own martyrdom. What will you have? It's all a grind and a bloody battle—as well as a considerable lark, and the difficulty itself is the refuge from the vulgarity. Bless your heart, I think I could easily say worse of the T. of the S., the young woman, the spooks, the style, the everything, than the worst any one else could manage. One knows the most damning things about one's self. Of course I had, about my young woman, to take a very sharp line. The grotesque business I had to make her picture and the childish psychology I had to make her trace and present, were, for me at least, a very difficult job, in which absolute lucidity and logic, a singleness of effect, were imperative. Therefore I had to rule out subjective complications of her own—play of tone etc.; and keep her impersonal save for the most obvious and indispensable little note of neatness, firmness and courage—without which she wouldn't have had her data. But the thing is essentially a pot-boiler and a *jeu d'esprit*....

Believe me yours ever,

Henry James

From *The Letters of Henry James,* vol. 4, ed. Leon Edel

Lamb House, Rye.
Dec. 19th, 1898.

My dear [F.W.H.] Myers,

I don't know what you will think of my unconscionable delay to acknowledge your letter of so many, so very many days ago, nor exactly how I can make vivid to you the nature of my hindrances and excuses. I have, in truth, been (until some few days since) intensely and anxiously busy, finishing, under pressure, a long job that had from almost the first—I mean from long before I had reached the end—begun to be (loathsome name and fact!) "serialized"—so that the printers were at my heels and I had to make a sacrifice of my correspondence *utterly*—to keep the sort of cerebral freshness required for not losing my head or otherwise collapsing. But I won't expatiate. Please believe my silence has been wholly involuntary. And yet, now that I *am* writing I scarce know what to say to you on the subject on which you wrote, especially as I'm afraid I don't quite *understand* the principal question you put to me about "The Turn of the Screw." However, that scantily matters; for in truth I am afraid I have on some former occasions rather awkwardly signified to you that I somehow can't pretend to give any coherent account of my small inventions "after the fact." There they are—the fruit, at best, of a very imperfect ingenuity and with all the imperfections thereof on their heads. The one thing and another that are questionable and ambiguous in them I mostly take to be conditions of their having got themselves pushed through at all. The *T. of the S.* is a very mechanical matter, I honestly think—an inferior, a merely *pictorial,* subject and rather a shameless pot-boiler. The thing that, as I recall it, I most wanted not to fail of doing, under penalty of extreme platitude, was to give the impression of the communication to the children of the most infernal imaginable evil and danger—the condition, on their part, of being as *exposed* as we can humanly conceive children to be. This was my artistic knot to untie, to put any sense of logic into the thing, and if I had known any way of producing *more* the image of their contact and condition I should assuredly have been proportionately eager to resort to it. I evoked the worst I could, and only feel tempted to say, as in French: "Excusez du peu!"

I am living so much down here that I fear I am losing hold of some of my few chances of occasionally seeing you. The charming old humble-minded "quaintness" and quietness of this little brown hilltop city lays a spell upon me. I send you and your wife and all your house all the greetings of the season and am, my dear Myers, yours very constantly,

Henry James

From *The Letters of Henry James,* vol. 4, ed. Leon Edel
(Myers, a minor poet, was a founder of the Society of
Psychical Research, of which William James was once the president)

VIRGINIA WOOLF

Henry James's ghosts have nothing in common with the violent old ghosts—the blood-stained sea captains, the white horses, the headless ladies of dark lanes and windy commons. They have their origin within us. They are present whenever the significant overflows our powers of expressing it; whenever the ordinary appears ringed by the strange. The baffling things that are left over, the frightening ones that persist—these are the emotions that he takes, embodies, makes consoling and companionable. But how can we be afraid? As the gentleman says when he has seen the ghost of Sir Edmund Orme for the first time: "I am ready to answer for it to all and sundry that ghosts are much less alarming and much more amusing than was commonly supposed." The beautiful urbane spirits are only not of this world because they are too fine for it. They have taken with them across the border their clothes, their manners, their breeding, their band-boxes, and valets and ladies' maids. They remain always a little worldly. We may feel clumsy in their presence, but we cannot feel afraid. What does it matter, then, if we do pick up "The Turn of the Screw" an hour or so before bedtime? After an exquisite entertainment we shall, if the other stories are to be trusted, end with this fine music in our ears, and sleep the sounder.

Perhaps it is the silence that first impresses us. Everything at Bly is so profoundly quiet. The twitter of birds at dawn, the far-away cries of children, faint footsteps in the distance stir it but leave it unbroken. It accumulates; it weighs us down; it makes us strangely apprehensive of noise. At last the house and garden die out beneath it. "I can hear again, as I write, the intense hush in which the sounds of evening dropped. The rooks stopped cawing in the golden sky, and the friendly hour lost for the unspeakable minute all its voice." It is unspeakable. We know that the man who stands on the tower staring down at the governess beneath is evil. Some unutterable obscenity has come to the surface. It tries to get in; it tries to get at something. The exquisite little beings who lie innocently asleep must at all costs be protected. But the horror grows. Is it possible that the little girl, as she turns back from the window, has seen the woman outside? Has she been with Miss Jessel? Has Quint visited the boy? It is Quint who hangs about us in the dark; who is there in that corner and again there in that. It is Quint who must be reasoned away, and for all our reasoning returns. Can it be that we are afraid? But it is not a man with red hair and a white face whom we fear. We are afraid of something unnamed, of something, perhaps, in ourselves. In short, we turn on the light. If by its beams we examine the story in safety, note how masterly the telling is, how each sentence is stretched, each image filled, how the inner world gains from the robustness of the outer, how beauty and obscenity twined together worm their way to the depths—still we must own that something remains unaccounted for. We must admit that Henry James has conquered. That courtly, worldly, sentimental old gentleman can still make us afraid of the dark.

From "Henry James's Ghost Stories," in *Granite and Rainbow* (1958);
the piece was originally published in the (London)
Times Literary Supplement, December 21, 1921

MORTON DAUWEN ZABEL

In the Cage, the short novel that lends its title to this collection of eight tales of Henry James's high maturity, has always been one of his most fascinating works among a large number of his devotees. Most of them would probably not hesitate to rank it with *Daisy Miller,* "The Aspern Papers," "The Lesson of the Master," "The Turn of the Screw," and "The Beast in the Jungle" as one of his masterpieces of the *nouvelle* kind—"the beautiful and blest *nouvelle*" which he cultivated with special enthusiasm and raised to its first point of mastery in English fiction....

Like Catherine Sloper at the end of *Washington Square* [the heroine of *In the Cage*] too must sit down to her fate "—for life, as it were." Like Isabel Archer at the end of *The Portrait of a Lady,* though she may look "all about her" and listen "a little," she now knows "where to turn": "there [is] a very straight path." Like Maggie Verver at the end of *The Golden Bowl* she stands "in the cool twilight and [takes] in, all about her, where it lurked, her reason for what she had done" and "how, to her soul, all the while, it had been for the sake of this end."

She stands, like these other heroines of James in their hours of defeat or secret triumph, face to face with a recognition. It is, true enough, a recognition of her obscurity and surrender, of what bleak disillusionment has overtaken her "dreams and delusions"; yet it is something more. Her cruel experience of reality, whatever it brings of sacrifice or a diminishment of her faith in life, also brings what the foredoomed *peripeteia* must always compel—what one of the perceptive students of this subject in James has called "the extension and refinement of consciousness, of that intelligence which, in Santayana's words, is 'the highest form of vitality.'" Of that illumination, the ultimate goal in James's moral faith, the little telegraphist can finally boast her share. She joins the other heroes and heroines of the Jamesian drama—Christopher Newman, Catherine Sloper, Isabel Archer, Hyacinth Robinson, Maisie, Fleda Vetch, Strether, Milly Theale, Maggie Verver—who, caught, caged, or pinioned in situations that bring them to defeat, tragedy, or a liberating disillusionment, snatch from the baffling odds or denials of experience the only reward which the life condemned to limitation and reality permits. It is to this final comfort—a strength or access of character—that the "sense of exclusion from experience" must come at last: to a capture of the trophy of the spirit's "vitality" and self-knowledge, the "qualities making for life."

In the Cage thus provides an essential key to the reading of James, even if it must at once be conceded that no single clue—whether it be the international theme, the American fate, the antagonisms of life and art, appearance and reality, privilege and privation, innocence and experience—suffices of itself in the full experience of his art, where ideas or conflicts so intricately intermesh and the moral debate is so complex and continuous. The story was written out of James's observation of the humble life of hardship and privation; it joins with *The Princess Casamassima* and "The Bench of Desolation" in showing his study of a realm of life he is usually charged with leaving unexplored.

From the introduction to Henry James,
Eight Tales from the Major Phase (1958)

STUART HUTCHINSON

In the Cage is centred in the consciousness of an unnamed London telegraphist who, on the verge of marriage to Mr. Mudge, a grocer, becomes involved first in imagination but then in reality with Captain Everard. He frequently uses her services at the post-office to arrange his clandestine affair with Lady Bradeen. It is a story whose comparative neglect several critics have felt the need to alleviate. Their responses fall into two categories: those which are sympathetic to the telegraphist's experiences, and those which she herself might describe as being "cheaply sarcastic" at her expense. Both sets of responses, however, have one thing in common, and that is their rather straightforward application of the story's title to the telegraphist's life. This literalness, which I would like to redress, is evident in Morton Dauwen Zabel's representative conclusion. According to Zabel, the telegraphist "joins the other heroes and heroines of the Jamesian drama," whose condemnation to "limitation and reality" and "sense of exclusion from experience" bring them to "defeat, tragedy, or [as in the telegraphist's case] a liberating disillusionment." For Zabel ... the telegraphist is another of James's "trapped spectators." Her only comfort derives from final acceptance of deprivation.

Admittedly, the story's first paragraph seems to offer support for this approach. There, the telegraphist conceives herself as a "young person spending, in framed and wired confinement, the life of a guinea-pig or a magpie." But there are other notes that soon reveal Zabel's polarisation of the story's themes (in the cage is "limitation and reality"; outside is the experience the telegraphist is denied) to be too simple. For though it is evident that like most of us the telegraphist intermittently sees her life in these stark terms, and has a sense of personal worth that reaches beyond Cocker's, it's equally clear she has a strong pride *in* her situation. Her job after all is the reward for her admirable resilience. At Cocker's too she is free from the oppressive claims of Mudge. From the beginning, therefore, the "caged" state is presented as a relative condition. Far from regarding themselves as less than human behind their wire-grill, her two male companions identify their customers as "animals." Who can say that these workers are any more caged than Everard, pursued and eventually "nailed" by Lady Bradeen; or than Lady Bradeen, "so compromised" by Captain Everard? When it comes to it, who isn't in some sort of cage?

James's story plays more variations on its title than Zabel allows. In an objective sense the telegraphist's lot *is* an example of social injustice: "the immense disparity." But James's interest draws its vitality from the individuality that transforms this state of affairs. The telegraphist lives as much in a cage of her own making (especially by her imagination) as in that her lot prescribes. When critics have seen this, however, they have not appreciated its true significance. As if few people but the telegraphist have the problem, E. Duncan Aswell announces that "the girl has trouble articulating the point at which imagination stops and reality begins." This is so, but not as Aswell and others see it: not with respect to Everard. It's just because she is *consciously* imaginative about Everard and his class that she becomes perceptive about him. With respect to Everard, she *does* distinguish the real and imagined and, though she wants the thrill of letting them touch, she wants to keep them apart. Ironically, it's Mr. Mudge whom the cage of her imagination can cause her to misapprehend—Mr. Mudge, whose reality she feels so sure of....

In this work, which at its close leaves us with a heroine who is abandoning her cage at Cocker's, but who has yet to relinquish virginity, the end undeniably is potential. It is sustained, as is the entire piece, by the liberating energy of its creator's imagination—an energy that frees *us* to understand fully the telegraphist's life "in the cage" as an analogue of our own.

From *"James's 'In the Cage': A New Interpretation"* (1982)

READING GROUP GUIDE

1. In *The Turn of the Screw*, the misbehavior of the children, Miles and Flora, as the story progresses makes us suspect that they are not as innocent as they seem. And yet the source of their misbehavior is left ambiguous: Is it natural mischievousness or has it been instigated by an evil, corrupting force in the form of the ghosts of Peter Quint and Miss Jessel? Trace through the story the changes in the way the governess views the children and their misbehaviors. How does the uncertainty about the children, and their possible awareness of the ghosts, intensify the governess's predicament?

2. In the beginning chapters of the story, the governess recounts several unsettling events: The children's uncle insists that he not be bothered with anything relating to the children's care; we learn of the death of the governess's predecessor, Miss Jessel; and we learn that sweet and charming Miles has been expelled from school. These are just some of the forebodings that set the stage for the supernatural events that soon follow, and so when the governess first relates the appearance of a ghost it doesn't seem entirely unexpected. To what degree is the governess a force of sense and reason in these unsettling surroundings, and to what degree does she become a destabilizing force herself as the story progresses? How does our answer to this question affect our understanding of the story's ending?

3. Any interpretation of *The Turn of the Screw* hinges on the question, debated vociferously by critics, of whether the ghosts of Peter Quint and Miss Jessel are real or whether they are figments of the governess's imagination. What are the implications of the governess's imagining them? If we read this not as an actual ghost story but as a story about the governess's perceptions of ghosts, what sort of psychological underpinnings are suggested? Could it be in *these* dimensions that the real horror of the story may lie?

4. The heroine of *In the Cage* works, literally, in a cage—behind bars in a telegraph office—but lives in a "caged" situation in more ways than just this one. How else is she caged in? She is a highly observant, intelligent woman. What are the effects on her perceptions of reality of her "caged" situation? What are the effects on her use of her imagination and its interplay with reality?

5. *In the Cage* is one of the few of Henry James's novels or novellas that center on the situation of a heroine of the lower or lower-middle class. Most often, James's heroines are members of the upper or upper-middle class—heroines caught in difficult, even "caged," situations, but situations that are the result of their own moral and emotional choices and these choices' far-reaching, sometimes unforeseen, impact. The heroine of *In the Cage* is in large part defined, from the very beginning, by her lack of any choices, a consequence of her low social position. In the heroine's climactic interaction with Captain Everard, when he comes to Cocker's to retrieve the lost telegram, how does the heroine make use of the choice open to her at this juncture—that is, the choice of how much to admit to remembering about the telegram? How does she make use of the power that the choice gives her in relation to Captain Everard? Why does she act as she does, and what do her actions say about her attitude toward the Captain?

6. On one of the occasions when the heroine and Mrs. Jordan are discussing their respective clients, Mrs. Jordan says, "Yes, but the great difference is that you hate yours, whereas I really love mine." In actuality, the lines aren't quite so clearly drawn. Why does Mrs. Jordan make this comment? What sort of complex mix of feelings do the heroine and Mrs. Jordan have for their clients? And for each other? How does James use his heroine's relationship with Mrs. Jordan to show the

complicity of both in upholding the hierarchical social structure within which they live? What are the advantages to them of their complicity?

7. If we make the assumption that the ghosts in *The Turn of the Screw* are a product of the governess's imagination, how might we think about the similarities in the imaginations of the governess and the heroine of *In the Cage?* Is there any sense in which, psychologically—like those of the heroine of *In the Cage*—the governess's perceptions create a "caged" situation for her? How do the heroine's perceptions of Captain Everard and the governess's perceptions of the children's uncle similarly contribute to the psychological traps these two characters may, in a sense, lay for themselves?

OTHER MODERN LIBRARY PAPERBACK CLASSICS
BY HENRY JAMES

The Bostonians
INTRODUCTION BY A. S. BYATT
Includes newly commissioned endnotes
0-8129-6996-0; trade paperback; 496 pp.

Daisy Miller
INTRODUCTION BY ELIZABETH HARDWICK
Includes newly commissioned endnotes
0-375-75966-2; trade paperback; 80 pp.

The Portrait of a Lady
INTRODUCTION BY ANITA BROOKNER
Includes newly commissioned endnotes
0-375-75919-0; trade paperback; 594 pp.

Washington Square
INTRODUCTION BY CYNTHIA OZICK
Includes newly commissioned endnotes
0-375-76122-5; trade paperback; 288 pp.

What Maisie Knew
INTRODUCTION BY DIANE JOHNSON
Includes newly commissioned endnotes
0-375-76008-3; trade paperback; 320 pp.

The Wings of the Dove
INTRODUCTION BY AMY BLOOM
Includes newly commissioned endnotes
0-8129-6719-4; trade paperback; 768 pp.

Available at bookstores everywhere
www.modernlibrary.com

Modern Library is online at
www.modernlibrary.com

MODERN LIBRARY ONLINE IS YOUR GUIDE
TO CLASSIC LITERATURE ON THE WEB

THE MODERN LIBRARY E-NEWSLETTER

Our free e-mail newsletter is sent to subscribers, and features sample chapters, interviews with and essays by our authors, upcoming books, special promotions, announcements, and news.

To subscribe to the Modern Library e-newsletter, send a blank e-mail to: **sub_modernlibrary@info.randomhouse.com** or visit **www.modernlibrary.com**

THE MODERN LIBRARY WEBSITE

Check out the Modern Library website at
www.modernlibrary.com for:

- The Modern Library e-newsletter
- A list of our current and upcoming titles and series
- Reading Group Guides and exclusive author spotlights
- Special features with information on the classics and other paperback series
- Excerpts from new releases and other titles
- A list of our e-books and information on where to buy them
- The Modern Library Editorial Board's 100 Best Novels and 100 Best Nonfiction Books of the Twentieth Century written in the English language
- News and announcements

Questions? E-mail us at **modernlibrary@randomhouse.com**.
For questions about examination or desk copies, please visit
the Random House Academic Resources site at
www.randomhouse.com/academic